The Siren's Call

By Stephanie Whitlock

Cover Art by
Lisa Buijteweg

This book is for my mother, Esther. She inspired me to write a historical romance simply by telling me it was her favorite genre and she should know this one is for her.

Love you, Momma!

Thank You

I want to say a heart-felt thank you to all of the people who supported and encouraged me to write, not only this book, but the two that came before and the multitude I hope will follow. I could not have found the time, courage, or determination to publish if not for you. First, I would like to say "I love you" to my husband who has been so understanding with me when I have chosen to write rather than play games or watch T.V. with him. My mother, aunts, cousins, and friends who volunteered to be "guinea pig" readers for me deserve more praise and appreciation than I can manage to fit here. My grandmother, Carolyn, needs to know that she has been an inspiration and rock to lean on through this process. I am not sure I would have finished if not for her voice in my head pushing me on. I would also like to thank Barb for her constructive criticism. I needed it and she did not let me down. I know the book is better for it and I can't wait to hear what she will tell me next time.

The pillow beneath his head had begun to reek with the foul odor of rot. The nurse, hired to care for him, had fled days before, unable to stand the sight of his body rotting away in front of her. Syphilitic death was almost always grotesque, but young Lord Alfred Terrance Everly's demise was becoming a scene taken right out of Shelley. His face, once pristine and well-formed, looked as if burned by acid, melting slowly into his sore-covered neck. His glossy, golden locks had all but fallen from his head and his teeth had long since slid from his jaws. Unable to do little more than mewl and writhe in pain, he had not spoken for days. His mother, despite the horrid stench, sat by his bed; wishing against hope his fate was different than the inevitable death looming before them.

It had taken him three months to reach the state to which one looking upon him now would find. His decline started with a fever. Then the sores had come. A decorated surgeon himself, Alfred had at first been unwilling to visit the family physician. But when, less than a month earlier, one of the atrocious marks appeared on his idyllic cheek, his mother had insisted. Their doctor, one of the most respected physicians in London, recognized the mark in an instant as Syphilis, much to the horror and dismay of his doting mother.

Alfred had taken the news of his illness with surprising acceptance, telling the doctor he had seen sores such as these periodically over the last two to three years, but they always vanished after a time and were never painful as this recent outbreak had become. While his mother sat lost in confusion and panic, he described how the sores had been preceded by headaches and fatigue in each case and now they were not a fleeting annoyance, but a constant companion, reluctantly conceding he had known the diagnosis prior to its delivery.

When the doctor regretfully informed him the illness had taken a serious turn and that it may indeed claim his life completely and very soon, his mother collapsed, cursing the name of his absent bride. She had ranted for days as her son's diagnosis shattered their family. Syphilis was a peasant's disease, reserved for philanderers and whores, of whom his wife must be the latter, not the sons of Lords. When he could no longer take her cold words for his spouse, Alfred confessed something to his mother that she found even more heart-crushing than his diagnosis; his bride was not the cause of his current deteriorating health, but his own philandering. Her rose-colored vision of her son's purity shattered, she began to fear for the wellbeing of the woman she had been condemning to hell moments earlier.

As fiercely as she wanted to warn the poor girl of her likely fate, young Lady Everly was far-flung across the ocean. They had sent several letters of his condition, but no return word from her, or even confirmation of delivery, had come back to them. For all they knew she was still horribly ignorant to his plight and would likely never see him again. Worse yet was the dread she had already succumbed to the same disease.

While Marie sat arguing with herself as to whether failing to return in time to see him in this terrifying state was a curse or a blessing, she allowed her tear-reddened gaze to drift over what was now barely recognizable as her baby. Resentment began to build in her chest. Vanessa should be here in her place, sparing her the sight of the decomposition happening before her eyes.

Her son had granted his wife the freedom to continue her education and worse yet, had allowed her to pursue a career that took her across the ocean to dig in foreign soil for rocks and old bowls. The purpose of which eluded Lady Marie Everly,

Baroness of Devonshire, entirely. There was some comfort in the daily visits from the missing girl's father. Her own husband had died shortly after the children were wed and, while her eldest son Stephen provided her with anything and everything she needed to continue her accustomed lifestyle, she appreciated the Earl's visits exceedingly.

They had been quite surprised when the Earl of Leicester, Winston Mansfield, had consented to their proposed betrothal, sure his wealth and title could have afforded his only child, Vanessa, a much grander marriage to a family more fitting his social station. He had readily accepted, citing a desire for his daughter to have happiness, which he feared her appearance would not afford her otherwise. Marie had never fully understood his position as she found Vanessa a lovely creature, a bit exotic perhaps, but winsome nonetheless.

Initially, Stephen, having ended his second childless marriage, vied for the right to wed her. It was Lord Mansfield who had requested Alfred instead. Nearer Vanessa's age, only two years her senior, he argued they would make a more sustainable match than Stephen and the nearly twenty years dividing him and her. He ventured their age difference would make them socially and intellectually divided; a fate not conducive to his goal. The arrangement was agreeable and the bargain was struck, much to Stephen's chagrin.

Distracted by garish thoughts, straining her eyes in the dying light of the candle on the table beside her, Marie heard the soft knock of the butler at the door. Clearing her throat, she made a slight noise, though not exactly words, and turned to see the Earl being allowed into the dank, foul-smelling room. For one brief second she saw the bunching of his nose as the rancid air hit him, but he soon washed away his apparent discomfort with his decorum.

"Lady Everly, are you well this day?" His greeting was constant, each visit beginning with the same good intentioned, and painfully depressing, query.

"As well as to be expected, considering the circumstances, Lord Mansfield." She made to remove the throw from her lap and stand to greet him, but he lifted a staying hand.

"Do not dislodge yourself on my account, and again, call me Winston. I came to share the news I have received from Vanessa." As he reached into his breast pocket, Marie stiffened in her seat.

"A letter? Is she returning to see Alfred? I hope she is already in crossing, he has precious few days left, I fear." Excitement and sadness coated her raspy voice, but the look that ghosted over the old gentleman's face was strangely unsettling.

"No, I am afraid she is not journeying to London. The letter is some three months written and contains no implication that she has any idea of poor Alfred's current state. It is likely this communique was written before he fell ill. She shares with me news from the dig site and her experiences in the Caribbean and how she wishes for me to share her thoughts and news with young Alfred, but no mention of a return. Nor any response to any communique we have ventured thus far, for that matter." Having removed the letter from his vest pocket, he pulled it from its envelope and handed the parchment, scribed by Vanessa's delicate hand, to Marie for her to read. She took the paper but did not even glance at it. Instead, her eyes cast over to her derelict son.

"Why has she not written directly to him? Not a single letter has she pinned to her husband. Even if she believes he is in fair health surely she would want to share her exploits with him just as much, if not more so, than with her father." She felt a pang of regret as the last of her words slipped from her lips, realizing a hint of bitterness was unmistakable within them.

"I think perhaps, Lady Everly, that it is safe to assume that she may have pinned several letters in the course of her time there. The crossing of the Atlantic is dangerous and long and something as innocuous and easily misplaced as a letter can be forgotten or destroyed without a thought. At least we can take comfort in the fact that she writes quite clearly her health is very well and there is no mention of any ill omens of this sickness in her." His face hovered between joy and tragedy as he tried and failed to hide his relief at his daughter's good health.

"Well that is a blessing at least, though strange. Your daughter must carry with her the grace of heaven to have avoided such a fate as befalls her husband." While she had not intended the comment to affect him, the gasp from Winston drew her eyes back to him. "Winston? Are you quite well?" His face had blanched and for a moment she feared the smell of rot from her son's body had proven too much even for his noble breeding. "Perhaps we should move to the parlor downstairs. The air here is rather disturbing, I'd imagine, to those unaccustomed to it."

"No Lady Marie, there is no need to adjourn. I was just contemplating your words and a fearful thought came to me. Forgive me. My idle thoughts have once again pulled me for the important events surrounding me. I must confess that Vanessa's flights of distraction are hereditary." A slight, forced smile creased his cheeks and then vanished as he moved farther into the death-filled room and took a seat in the chair near her.

Within a week Alfred's bed lay empty, the mattress removed and incinerated as soon as his lifeless body was lifted from it. For reasons of family pride, there was no wake or visitation to speak of, but that did not stop the young man's multitude of friends from stopping by to pay their respects. Well-mannered and well-dressed men of Alfred's age stopped by to offer their condolences to the family of their departed peer. The outpouring had become more than poor Marie, and her ever-weakening constitution could handle. After the internment, Marie found herself in the elegant parlor of the Mansfield estate, silently sipping a sweetly flavored liqueur to still her rattled nerves.

"I suppose I should compose the letter to Vanessa, informing her of this tragedy; however I feel the news is ill fit for a simple missive." Winston stood before the fire, staring at the flames licking over the logs within the hearth.

Stephen, standing beside him, spoke for the first time that day. "With all the letters we have sent, none of which appearing to have reached her, I fear even an eloquently written letter will fare no better. Not without special concern." His voice, normally cold and distant, held a certain lightness that did not seem to fit the sadness of the day. When Winston sighed, nodding his regretful agreement, Stephen continued. "Perhaps we should send the letter by way of a courier, door-to-door service, as it were."

Winston thought for a moment, and then asked, "Do such services exist? Outside of hiring an entire ship to sail out after her I fear there is little that could be done."

"Why not do just that? There is a ship anchored in the Thames at this very moment that is known for its efficiency. It is common knowledge in the trade markets that the Captain, a Clark by name, has never failed to make a crossing or lost even a single piece of cargo. When given a task, no matter the size, he has delivered and in record time, too. His last crossing was made in less than two months, round trip."

Winston's brow furrowed as he pondered Stephen's suggestion. "Perhaps you are right. Alas, I do not relish the writing, or the reading, of a letter filled only with tragedy." Winston shuddered at the thought of his daughter smiling as she was handed a letter from him only to tear it open and find horror and loss within.

"Then perhaps we could provide her with some happy news as well." Stephen failed to hide the excitement in his inflections this time and Marie, who had sat quietly through the exchange so far, spoke up.

"Your tone is unbecoming, Stephen. What joyous news could we possibly share in light of what has happened? The poor girl has lost her husband!"

Stephen's eyes twinkled as he turned to address his mother. "What of the news that, though Alfred is no longer with us, she was to remain an Everly. I expressed my interest in her hand three years ago and was cast aside for my younger brother. I revisit my earlier request now, though I know the day and circumstances are ill-fitted for it. I still wish greatly to marry your daughter, Lord Mansfield, and I truly believe the tragedy of my brother's departure might be lessened, at least slightly, by the knowledge I do not hold her widow status to her disadvantage. I swear to you that if I had her hand I would do all I could to make her happy. I desire an heir and she is a healthy, vibrant, young woman who is more than capable of providing this for me, just as I am wealthy and positioned and can easily provide for her."

"Stephen!" Marie's indignation was palpable, but Winston spoke next, taking the sting from Stephen's words.

"No, Marie, perhaps he is right. It is time Vanessa returns to London and I think her happiness might be found in the beginning of her own family. Stephen, have this Captain Clark sent to me. I will write the letter forth width and inform him that he is to take it directly to her in the Islands. Not only that, I will also place upon him responsibility of her safe and speedy return to my house. Will you do this?"

"As soon as I can venture down to the docks I will do as you request." Without even so much as a nod in his mother's direction, Stephen took his leave of the Mansfield house. Winston entertained Lady Everly for a while longer, but when her man came to take her home, he sat down to write the worst letter he had ever attempted to pin. He cared deeply for his daughter, but he had never felt comfortable communicating with her, especially when his conveyance contained foul news. In his writing he could not suppress his suspicions as to the reason for her good health and only moments after the letter was sealed his man, Casbolt, appeared at the door bearing news that a sea captain had arrived requesting to see him.

Chapter 1

"Lady Everly, the last of the empty crates have arrived from the settlement. We can begin packing them for transport whenever you give the word." The older gentleman waited for her to look up from the crate she was adding tomes to and nod before he made to leave. As he was just passing out of the door, she called after him, staying his departure.

"Thank you, Henry, but we are in no hurry. The cargo ship from the university is not set to arrive for almost a month yet. I simply cannot bring myself to believe that it has been a year. There is still so much left here to uncover. Seems a shame to leave things unfinished." When she sighed, he smiled warmly, nodded again, and disappeared. Her satiny olive brow furrowed as she glanced remorsefully over the disheveled command tent. She had worked long hours each and every day in this space since she arrived at the site, and in that time she had come to see it as home. The boarding house where she slept was little more than a place to lay her head, but this canvas structure had witnessed discoveries and revelations about a culture that, until the arrival of her team, had fallen from knowledge. She had spent untold hours deciphering their language and reading their messages. Found their remains and did the best she could to piece together who they were before time had stolen them away. To see her work scattered and boxed was heartbreaking.

"Tell me again, Andrew, why we decided to start the packing with the command tent? Would it not have made more sense to begin with the larger artifacts and leave this for last?" She propped her hands on her slender hips and glanced across the mess to her assistant. Andrew had been a student with her at Oxford and he had been one of a very few of her peers that had treated her with respect. When she had been offered the chance to lead this expedition she had recruited him first. He was smart and objective, if not a bit boorish. The son of a lesser nobleman, he was stout and round faced and had sought his future in school, as high society would likely find little room for him, just as it did for her.

"Because, Essie, if we had not you would never stray from it to see to the packing of any of the artifacts. You would remain here, as you have for the last eleven months, consumed by work that could just as easily be done in London. You remember London, don't you? A foggy, dark, place where it isn't 110 degrees in the shade and the insects are not the size of small house animals? We are starting here because, quite frankly, I, and the rest of the team, wish to leave as soon as the ship arrives. Not be stuck frantically packing long after it makes port." His hearty laughter was contagious and soon she was stifling her mirth as well.

"Point taken, Andrew. Shall we continue, then?" As she spoke, she hoisted a rather heavy crate of notebooks, filled with their thoughts and discoveries, into her shapely arms. Turning toward the open entry of the tent, bent on adding her container to the stack already waiting, she nearly dropped the heavy box on her toes. Gasping suddenly, she backed away from the hulking form of a man who had mysteriously appeared before her.

Andrew was instantly at her side. "My dear, are you all right?" Gripping her arm to support her, he faced their visitor and blurted, "Good lord man, where did you come from?" Trying to calm her heart, Vanessa took a steadying step farther back, away from the large figure now looming between her and the outside world. Andrew at her side, she allowed her eyes to scan over their guest. She took in his posture and dress. The stiffened spine and the manner in which his hands were tucked behind his back reminded her of the soldiers at the garrison below the settlement. His uniform, similar to that of officers in the Royal Navy, was unmistakably a seaman's uniform. When her gaze scanned his face, angular, clean-shaven, and exceedingly well-formed, her eyes lingered over the long healed scar curving around from the brow to the cheekbone of his right eye. Her innate curiosity drummed within her to ask how he had come by such a mark. But as he looked rather stern, she feared he would not only refuse to answer such a question but that it could lead to anger. Something she suspected would be terrifying coming from a man such as he. The only thing about him that seemed even slightly out of place was the loose tresses of sandy blond hair that reached his ear lobes and curved around the sides of his tanned face.

"A ship in port, I wouldn't wager. You simply can't be from the university; we are nowhere near ready to return! You were not set to arrive for a month yet and we have at least three weeks' worth of packing to do." She scanned about the ransacked tent for a suitable place to deposit her load. When she had lifted it she had been sure she could set it down long before now and its weight was becoming tiresome. As if the sailor could see the strain in her, he took two deliberate steps forward, scoped the heavy box out of her arms with ease, and, turning to the side, set it atop the crates that had been its destination all along. Once the burden was deposited, he returned to his former position and posture, as if he had never moved a muscle.

"Indeed, I am a sailor. And you are Lady Everly, I presume. I am Captain Clark. I have been hired by your father, Lord Mansfield, Earl of Leicester, to return you to London with haste. Would you come with me please?" He extended his broad hand and stepped to the side as if to allow her to pass, but she made no move to precede him. Indeed she had no intention of accompanying him anywhere without a great deal more information. Noticing her inaction, and trying in vain not to let the aggravation it caused him to seep to his disciplined surface, he cleared his throat and spoke again. "Lady Everly, I have a schedule to keep. My cargo has already been unloaded and replaced and my ship awaits only your arrival before it can turn once more from Kingston harbor for London."

"Then it will be waiting for several weeks yet. I have much left to do here. I cannot simply leave, not now. There must be some mistake. My father knows our expedition is drawing to a close he would not send you..."

"Unless it were urgent." He broke in on her tirade as he reached into the breast pocket of his coat, producing a sealed envelope and extending it to her before he continued. "He said you would likely be obstinate. I see he was not mistaken. He gave me this letter to deliver when I found you. I trust it will provide you with the necessary urgency my request seems to have failed to produce." For a moment she stood, frozen, staring at the extended letter, unwilling to reach out to grasp it. All manner of horrors raced through her mind as she tried and failed to contemplate what could have driven her father to send for her like one might send for a container of rare spices or exotic wood.

Pinching her face in a scowl, she looked back at the man who seemed completely unaffected by the terrifying possibilities the letter in his strong fingers was quite likely bringing to her. "What does it say?" Her voice was weak as she beseeched him for any kind of comfort. While he did shift slightly and his shoulders slumped a bit, his demeanor altered little as he held the communique out farther to her. When it became clear he had no information to give, she snatched the letter from his hand with force brought on by the uncertainty welling up within her. His eyes widened at her brash behavior before he folded his hands behind his back and waited for her to read whatever news lay within.

Tearing the wax seal open, she fished her father's familiar stationery out of the envelope and unfolded it. Tensing uncontrollably, she turned away from the stoic man in the door to read as she paced around the tent.

Dearest Vanessa,

I hope this letter finds you well, though I fear once you have finished reading these words this will be a hollow wish. There is much I must tell you, my dear daughter, but I find the telling difficult. It is with a heavy and broken heart that I inform you of the passing of your beloved Alfred. After a lengthy battle with Syphilis, an illness most foul and low, he succumbed on the twenty-third day of August, the year of our Lord, 1874. Only one week past the writing of this letter. His body has since been returned to the earth and his soul to heaven. We sent many letters to you concerning his health, though it would appear none have reached you as no response from you has come and you have not yet departed from Kingston. I know this news is devastating, though lessened; I have come to fear, by unfamiliarity between you and the late young Lord Everly. Take heart in the good fortune and generosity of his mother and brother Stephen. They have seen fit to continue to embrace you as kin. To lessen the loss you must now suffer, Stephen has suggested another betrothal and I, seeking only your happiness, have consented. As soon as you return to London, under the care of our man, Captain Clark, we shall see you married and well cared for. Please, daughter, I know you will rail against this, but I must insist you do as the Captain requests. I desire you here at home, with me, post haste.

Until you are safe within these walls, my heart is with you in this time of sorrow.

Your loving father,

Lord Winston Mansfield, Earl of Leicester

Swallowing with difficulty, her knees weaken beneath her. The legs holding her up lost their strength. She listed to her side and leaned heavily on the stack of empty crates Henry had just delivered, trying to breathe through seizing lungs. Alfred dead...an illness...*marry Stephen!* Her mind was reeling to such an extent it took several moments for her to recognize the hands at her shoulders. Looking up she found the concerned round face of Andrew peering down at her and filled with fear.

"Lady Everly, ...*Vanessa*," He whispered her first name under his breath. Though she insisted he address her informally, he still felt it improper, especially when in the company of others. "Are you well?" Glancing over his shoulder as he helped her back to her feet, she could see the captain, still standing rigid as ever in the doorway, though he appeared quite concerned as he watched the informal scene unfolding before him. Watched only, making no move to assist her.

"No, Andrew, I am afraid I am far from well. My father sends me news most unwanted and painful. Alfred...he...he is dead." She fought back the tears welling behind her eyes. She would not cry. Andrew she was sure would care little but Clark was a different matter entirely. She realized this was only the beginning of their acquaintance and she did not want him to view her at her most vulnerable.

"Alfr...Lord Everly, dead! How?" Andrew had known Alfred. Through her, they had become friends during her years at Oxford, and Alfred had been most excited Andrew would be accompanying his bride to the Caribbean as her assistant and protector.

"A lengthy illness has claimed him. I am now without a husband and without time. At my father's insistence, I must return to London immediately." She had been speaking to Andrew alone, but when Captain Clark responded, she once again shifted to face him, though this time impatience glared in her deep olive green eyes.

"Then I must again request you accompany me, my Lady. Now that you know the circumstances surrounding my appearance surely you will delay no longer." She could not believe his cold callousness. She had just received word her husband lay dead and buried some weeks now and he was stoically beckoning her to hurry her pace. As if he could sense her hesitation, he continued, "Madam, I have been hired to return you post haste to your father and as I have never failed to make a delivery, I do not intend to start now." His arm lowered as his jaw tightened.

Though her heart ached, her spine stiffened. She would not be so easily turned from her purpose. "I cannot simply up and go. There are arrangements that must be made and none of my personal belongings have been packed. I will need at least a week to make ready."

"A week? I'm sorry, Lady Everly, but that is out of the question. We are expected in London in four weeks' time." There was a soft chuckle to his words though his face showed no signs of mirth.

"Four weeks? Then we are already late. The crossing takes twice that." Though she was certain of her words, there was something about the look ghosting over his features that made her doubt. Raising a curious brow, she again propped her hands on her narrow hips and moved closer to him, away from the support of Andrew's arms, no longer necessary.

"I assure you, my Lady, my time frame is entirely reasonable as we reached port here in less from London not three days ago. If I am to get my ship to port on schedule we will need to weigh anchor no more than three days hence. I would prefer less. Now, please, come with me." It was clear from the hardening of his voice and his jaw he was losing all patience for her, but she cared little for his schedule.

"These artifacts we have found must be properly crated and labeled before they are to be loaded onto a ship. That takes time Captain. Not to mention the time it will take for my crew to pack their belongings as well."

"There seems to be a misunderstanding here, Lady Everly. I am not here to return your discoveries or your crew. There is only room on my vessel for you and your personal baggage. My ship is currently full of cargo whose space in my hold was already reserved and paid for. I can spare no more room than is already allotted to you." When she gasped he genuinely looked put out, as if it had never occurred to him she would not simply drop everything and rush into his ship.

"Nothing? I can bring nothing with me? That is absurd!" Re-clasping his hands before him, a slight grin pulled at the corners of his mouth for one brief second before he cleared his throat and continued.

"I see no reason why a small assortment of relics could not accompany you, but they would need to take up no more room than you are willing to spare in your stateroom. May we go now? I will have my men assist you in your packing if you need the help." He turned and took several steps toward the sunlit clearing beyond the tent. Though it was nearly October, the seasons had little change in the tropical atmosphere around them and the day was hot and humid, as it always was. When she again made no move to follow him he sighed loudly in unhidden aggravation and glared back at her. "Lady Everly, I grow weary of this exchange."

"As do I." She squinted at the large, unnervingly handsome man, sighed, and changed her tactics. "You said a moment ago you must raise anchor in three days. Then I humbly request the three days as my remainder here in Kingston, if you would permit me." She could see the argument building within him, so she quickly added, "I would of course fit the bill for your men's lost time. Kingston can be a rather hospitable place to sailors. At least, that is what I have come to understand. I spend little time there myself. I would provide them with funds for entertainment if it affords me the time to prepare my things and leave instructions. Surely you cannot begrudge me three days when I have offered to compensate you handsomely for them?"

Shaking his head, he stated, "My Ship is the Siren's Call. She is anchored out in the harbor, but there will be a dinghy waiting at the dock for you in three days' time. I will meet you there myself, Lady Everly. Do not make me come in search of you." With that, he vanished into the bright afternoon sun. His sudden departure was followed by her breath as a heavy sigh left her reeling. She hadn't realized she had ceased breathing for the last of their conversation. Vanessa wobbled slightly as she turned and headed for the only chair left in the tent. Sinking down into it, she rested her forehead in her hand as she tried to steady her racing heart. While her blood had been high during their argument, she had paid little attention to the effect his presence had had on her. But now that he was gone, she felt it acutely. As much as he intimidated her, he interested her as well. Especially the moon-shaped scar she could not sweep from her mind.

When Andrew spoke, she nearly jumped out of her skin. "Essie, you can't mean to go back with him! Not alone! I must insist you refuse. You put yourself in too much peril." His voice was low as he approached her. Despite her disheveled state she smiled warmly at her friend. "I mean it. The thought of you alone, confined on a small cargo ship with sailors only a hair's breadth from being pirates, chills me to the bone. What if they mean to take advantage? What will you do with no one to protect you, or your interests? You are a hard woman, but I fear it will not be enough to spare you if they choose to aggress." Her smile did not falter as she stood to speak to him on even footing.

"Nonsense, Andrew, I will be perfectly safe. Our Captain Clark will see to that." When she saw the doubt flood his face she chuckled again. "Honestly, did you not hear the manner in which the man spoke to me? Of me? As if I were nothing more than a crate of bananas or a compliment of fine mahogany. He sees me as nothing more than cargo. Valuable cargo if I know my father, and he will not allow anything to threaten the successful completion of his delivery. Now, would you mind gathering the team? I will need to impart instructions before I leave and I seem to have precious little time. You will take charge and complete the packing. Take the vessel that comes from the university as planned. I will take the tablets we uncovered three weeks ago with me. There is much left on them to decipher and they are small enough not to take up too much space. Now, if you would, I have a great deal to do yet today." He looked as if he might argue with her and she braced herself for the rebuttal, but his face softened and he nodded as his mouth closed. Turning, he made to leave.

As he passed into the light, he shot a wearied look back at her. "Essie, I am so very sorry about Alfred. I know you two were close, in spite of his...habits." Then he was gone, leaving her alone with his unintentional reminder of her loss. The tears she had fought off in front of the captain came rushing back with a fierce need to be shed that she could do little to slow. Hot, fat tears rolled down her olive-toned cheeks as she allowed the sobs to wash over her for her lost husband. Though, if she were honest with herself, the tears carried more sorrow for her than for poor Alfred. A marriage to Stephen was beyond heartbreaking. Nearly twenty-three years her senior, she had heard many stories of Stephen's personality, none of which were complimentary.

According to Alfred, and what little contact she had had with Stephen, he was a cold, calculating man who had designs on every aspect of his life, including those which cannot be controlled. And when life did not unfurl according to those designs his wrath was swift and terrifying. Alfred bore a rather brutal scar on his arm from one such incident. According to his tale, once when hunting with their father, Alfred, only seven at the time, had tripped and fallen spooking the game and causing it to run out of range of their rifles. Stephen flew into a rage and swung his rifle butt down on his brother's splayed arm, shattering the bone and forcing surgery to repair it. While it had been that burst of rage that had led Alfred to his calling, the tale terrified Vanessa. Now, knowing he was the fate awaiting her, her fear compounded into a knot in her chest that threatened to kill her.

The tears would not slow. Alone in the tent, she railed against life. Against her absent father. Against fate. She had been happy here. Kingston, once a den of pirates and thieves, was a place of free thought with little care or concern for titles held across the sea. The people respected action and honor and she had earned their respect, despite being a woman.

Alfred had taught her much and she had, on more than one occasion, found his medical teaching useful. To think all she had worked so hard to build here, for herself and her team, was coming to an end, and in such a way, hurt her tremendously. The thought broke her heart anew and fresh tears joined the old ones just starting to slow on her cheeks. How was she to go home and play the obedient wife? She did not know how to be obedient and her time amongst this free place had not improved her capacity. What was worse, she was certain no matter

31

how well-behaved she would be it would never suffice. Her future, once something she coveted, became a source of overwhelming anxiety.

The sound of feet on the path alerted her that her team was approaching. Though she was desolate and broken, she wiped her cheeks hastily and composed herself. Her tragedy was hers alone. They did not need to read her suffering on every inch of her. She took a deep steadying breath and rose to her feet, squaring her weakening shoulders. She turned to face the door, every bit the strong leader her team had come to believe she was, even if she felt none of the strength written on her features. Throughout the briefing, she did her best to skate around and avoid the questions concerning her sudden departure. She imparted detailed instructions for the care of the artifacts they would now have to crate and catalog without her. After giving the last of her instructions, she scanned the faces of her men. There was so much she wanted to say, but her voice fled her as the knot in her throat swelled.

Sighing, she smiled at them. "I...thank you so much for being willing to come here with me. I know I am not the easiest person to work with, but I want all of you to know that this past year has been as enjoyable as it has been fruitful. I hope to see you all safe and sound in London in a few months' time. Until then, know I am proud to have worked with you." With that, she nodded and the assembled men hesitantly dispersed. As she gathered her bags and prepared to leave for the boarding house, Andrew touched her shoulder.

"I still believe this to be a mistake. I fear for you in this, Essie." She turned back to see the concern and care on his face. A sudden pang of awareness hit her. The look in his eyes went far beyond friendship. She knew he cared for her, but she had done her best to hold his attraction at bay. Despite their closeness for the last year, she felt nothing for him save friendly affection. Sensing he was about to cross a line from which there was no going back, she turned away and took several steps farther into the tent. "Do not pull away from me, Essie. Not when I have something this important to discuss with you." Again he approached her.

Before his hand could touch her arm once more, she turned on him. "Andrew, I know what it is you wish to say." Her voice cracked and from the look of surprise and pleasure flashing across his face, she felt sure he thought her receptive. She cringed at the pain she was about to cause her friend. "I am to be married again, Andrew. To Stephen, Alfred's brother." She watched as the pleasure in his eyes deteriorated into pain. For a moment he looked as if he might rage against the death of his dream, but he instead turned and fled from the tent, only barely nodding to her as he sped away. She hung her head. The pain he felt was pale in comparison to the pain hearing her true opinion of him would have caused. She was well aware of her physical shortcomings; her father had made his opinion of her visage quite clear throughout the better part of her childhood, but even still, she would never be able to love a man like Andrew.

He was kind and caring, but she felt nothing when he drew near to her. She had always imagined love to be a physical as well as emotional state. That one's body would react to the touch, the very nearness, of its mate in a tangible and remarkable manner. She dreamed of a day when she would tremble at the touch of a hand as the heroines in her Victorian romances described. Sadly, she had not known this sensation in her life. Not yet.

Without looking back, she slung her satchel over her shoulder. Gathering her skirt, she stepped gingerly over a crate on the way out of the tent. She had packing to do and very little time left to accomplish it.

Chapter 2

Vanessa closed the large trunk at the foot of her bed. The last of her personal belongings lay organized across her bare mattress, ready to be placed into the remainder of her few bags. In the armchair by the fireplace sat the crate containing the pieces from the site she had decided to take with her. Andrew had had them delivered by Henry early the day before. A note, saying he wished her luck, was all the communication she had received from him since the awful moment in the tent when she had refused his advance before it had even been made. She had far too much to worry about to dwell on his hurt feelings, though. She was expected at the dock in just under an hour and she dared not keep the imposing captain waiting longer than he willed.

He had sent his first mate, a man no less than sixty, and an old sea dog if ever there was one, to give her the details of their scheduled rendezvous only moments after she had returned to her room the day they met. Since then she had not ventured beyond the boarding house. Several of her team had come to ask questions and say their goodbyes, but, as she was certain the captain had eyes on her, she had remained within its walls.

At first it had shocked her, the idea he would have her watched, but as the thought of fleeing had crossed her mind countless times in the last three days she eventually resolved he was simply a shrewd man and moved on to the tedious and depressing task of packing her things. She had acquired far more during her stay than she had brought with her and the resolution that some things simply could not accompany her made packing that much more difficult. As she placed the last of her clothing into her suitcase a single tear rolled down her satin cheek. So much left behind. So much not done. As she closed the clasp on the bag, a knock rattled the door in its frame. Wiping the tear streak from her face, she smoothed her dress front and opened the door. The first mate, looking as salty as ever, stood before her with a crooked smile.

"I have been sent by the capt'n., m'lady, to help with your bags. Are you ready to go yet?" He shifted to look past her into her room. Moving to block his view, she adjusted her posture to one her father had always taken when she demonstrated a lack of decorum.

"The interior of a Lady's bedroom is not for your eyes, Mr. Mortimer. I would thank you not to pry." He straightened and removed his cap, looking rather ashamed as he shifted his feet and stared at the floor.

"Beggin' your pardon, ma'am. I didn't mean no offense. Just lookin' to see what needed to be hauled out. I got two more men downstairs for that trunk whenever you're ready." There was a sadness in his voice she could not ignore. Realizing she had truly hurt the old man's feelings, she smiled sadly at his diminutive figure as he turned to leave her.

Sighing, she said, "Actually, Mr. Mortimer, I think the trunk and a few other bags are ready to go now. If you would be so kind as to fetch your men, I should be glad to have you take them on ahead. I have a bit more to see to here. You may tell your captain I will only be a few moments behind you." The old man's gapped and stained smile was warm as he trotted lively away down the hall, heading for the lobby and his men.

Moments later, he returned with two rather burly-looking men who, with no uncertain level of ease, hoisted her heavy bags and her loaded trunk between them and disappeared. Truly, if the captain's crew was comprised entirely of sailors with matching strength, she would be among giants...all alone.

Shaking Andrew's concerns from three days past away from her already addled mind, she went back to gathering the bits and bobs that remained into her small satchel. When nothing left in the room could be called hers, she stood at the door looking back at the small, comfortable space. She had, in truth, spent little time in this room but it was not the room she suddenly felt fearful to leave. The moment had come and the four walls surrounding her transformed in her mind into the whole of Jamaica. She was departing it, likely forever, and her heart was sick with the loss.

Deciding that to delay any longer would be to lose her nerve; she turned and, closing the door behind her, moved down the hall and out into the city. The day was bright and warm as she strolled through the street bazaar. All around her happy faces announced their goods, exotic fruits, and handmade baubles. She walked slowly, enjoying one last time the enchanting smells of tropical flowers and the caress of the sun's rays.

Rounding the corner, the sea became visible ahead of her, spreading out like a massive teal-blue blanket, undulating in a breeze. A strange excitement coursed through her at the sight of it. She loved the sea. Their crossing the first time, a nearly two-month ordeal, had been the single greatest experience of her life until she had gotten to the dig site and been consumed by all it offered. While history was her passion, the sea was her fascination. The excitement that shivered through her was instantly tempered with dread and sadness. She would likely not be able to enjoy this crossing as she had enjoyed the last. After all, this one was taking her from her joy, not toward it.

The entrance to the docks rose up before her and the knot that had been haunting her throat returned. She caught sight of the figure that had loomed in the back of her mind for days. Captain Clark stood, just down the boardwalk from her, staring out into the distance. For a moment he didn't seem aware of her approach, but as she drew up behind him, his head drooped slightly as he glanced back at her over his right shoulder. The scar, something she had let slip from her thoughts, flashed glossy pale in the sunlight against his tanned skin.

"Ah, Lady Everly, and on time. Wonderful. Your luggage is being rowed out to the *Siren's Call* as we speak. Mort will return for us with the boat in a moment." While she had not expected him to address her so informally, she made a decided effort

39

not to let the surprise show on her person. Crossing behind him and drawing to his left side, she leaned against the rail.

"And which one is your vessel, Captain Clark?" Her eyes scanned the harbor. There were no less than eleven ships anchored at different points around the bay and identifying his without his assistance would be nearly impossible. Suddenly a large, muscular arm extended to her side and she felt his body draw near. He leaned over her as his head eased closer to her ear. Following the line of his arm, she looked out over the bay and found an impressive clipper ship. Three tall masts reached into the sky like prongs on a trident. "She is lovely, though a bit larger than I expected. You said you had no room for my team, Captain, but that vessel could easily hold all of our trappings and our relics."

Turning up to face him, she found his jaw tightening. While she had meant her comment as a jest, a harmless jab at his earlier statements, it seemed he was not enjoying her humor. Gasping at the sudden anger growing in his chiseled face, she took a step back from him and his increasing ferociousness. "I apologize, Captain; I did not intend to upset you."

"I assure you, Lady Everly, you have no effect on me for which you need be sorry. Come. Mr. Mortimer has returned and I am anxious to get underway." Without so much as a glance in her direction, he turned and proceeded down the boardwalk at a deliberate pace she struggled to match. The bag around her shoulder was heavy, but not quite so much as her stomach. His words echoed in her head, stinging and lancing her as they lolled about. She had no effect on him. None. It would not have upset her if the converse weren't so true. He strongly affected her. She could not be sure if it was for good or ill, but she felt infinitely sensitive in his presence and to think he saw her as little more than an insect buzzing around his ears was more irksome than she reasoned it should have been. Shaking her head free of her pointless thoughts, she concentrated on trying to match his pace.

"Well, that is reassuring. My dear Mr. Andrew feared for my safety. I see now I have nothing to fear from you." A cold chuckle echoed from his broad chest as his pace slowed slightly.

"Indeed," was his only reply as they neared the edge of the dock. The small row boat was just pulling along the side as she drew up to his right. Despite her best efforts, she struggled to catch her breath; her corset seemed to be crushing the air out of her. She despised the infernal contraptions, but as they were inarguably socially necessary for a lady's dress, she was forced to abide them. Without warning, hands clasped around her narrow waist as Clark lifted her with amazing ease up and over into the dinghy. The shock on her face made Mortimer laugh for a brief moment before he addressed her.

"We wouldn't want you fallin' in, m'Lady. Though I suppose the Captain could have given you some warning." He extended his hand to her and she took it swiftly. The feel of Clark's hands on her had left her off balance and the aid Mortimer offered was greatly appreciated.

"Indeed, Mr. Mortimer. I am most assuredly *not* used to being manhandled." With a strange anger flashing in her eyes she turned to watch the young captain leap nimbly into the boat behind her. The same ghost of a grin pulled at his mouth for a split second before he nodded to Mortimer. Easing her into her seat, the first mate grabbed up the oars before him and began to row them, in deafening silence, out to the lovely clipper that would carry her home.

Attempting to seem disinterested, she peered over the side at the crystal clear blue-green water slipping by as they moved. Her impulsive side, one she too often catered to, wanted to reach into the cool, glossy ripples but she restrained herself. Flights of fancy would now have to be controlled and measured out for moments that did not include such a motley audience. Stiffening her spine with the efforts to stop her fingers from dipping into the bay, her head turned back to the captain.

He seemed even larger now than he had three days ago. His sandy blond hair was as unkempt as it had been though, with the breeze drifting over the water, the cause of its dishevelment became clear to her. His uniform coat was clean and well-maintained, as were his trousers and his boots. From tip to tail, he was every bit the formal ship captain and if it hadn't been for the appearance of the older man behind her, dressed as one might expect a vagrant to be, she might have believed her father had chartered her on a military vessel.

"Is there something about my clothes you find interesting, Lady Everly?" A slight gasp left her as her eyes popped back to meet his.

"No!" The word jumped from her before she could catch it. "I...well, yes actually. I can't help but look upon you and see the marks of service. Royal Navy perhaps?" His specter of a grin returned as he studied her with all the same scrutiny.

"Have you much experience with His Majesty's sailors, my Lady?" Heat rushed over her cheeks as her eyes darted to the ship closing up beside them. "You are quite right. I spent six years in the Navy before retiring to command the *Siren*."

"Retired? You are no more than thirty! How can you be retired?" Again, she failed to catch the words that surged up her throat. "Forgive me; it seems my tongue has lost its manners. As have I. You need not answer my impertinent questions. Your military record is no concern of mine." Fire raced across her cheeks.

"Indeed it is not, but I see no harm in answering you. I am but twenty-nine, this past July, and yes, I am retired, but I assure you the Queen received all she asked for and more in my short time in her service. Now, may I return the same appraising eye to you, my Lady?" His face was bland and unreadable, but there was something of a warning flickering in his eyes. Not wanting to back down from his challenge, she furrowed her brow and scowled across the small boat at him.

"Of course, Captain Clark. Enlighten me." His jaw tightened as his eyes scanned over her once more.
"From the lift of your chin whenever I address you as Lady Everly I would say you dislike your title or

perhaps are simply not used to hearing it. I doubt your man Andrew called you that on a daily basis, as I heard him use your first name, though he tried to hide it. One might then think it is the surname and not the title from which you shrink; that you would prefer Lady Mansfield over Lady Everly. But from the hesitation you expressed when hearing he had urgently sent for you, I would guess your father does not hold sway over you either. Perhaps the title of Professor would be found more pleasurable. You have accomplished much, especially for a woman, though you are strangely humble about it. I must confess a certain personal curiosity on that point. I would think you would glory in your advancement considering its rarity." Her scowl deepened at his accuracy. His words would sound kind if not for the cruel tone of his voice.

"I never had much use for society, it is true. Though in truth it never had much use for me either. And you are right, my father and I were never close, but my hesitation to accompany you was not out of a lack of respect for him, Captain. I love my father dearly, even if he does not return the sentiment." Her admission seemed to stun him, but she did not stop to question the change. "My hesitation was toward you, naturally. Did you really expect me to saunter innocently after you? You, a complete stranger with so intimidating a form? Though I am sure many women have, I was not prepared to be the next." Her words seemed to burn him and for a moment she wished she could take them back.

"M'Lady, can you climb up on your own, or will you be needin' a lift?" Mortimer's voice startled them both. The dinghy had reached the side on the clipper some minutes back and he had apparently been too interested in their terse exchange to interrupt. She had turned around to assess the vertical wooden ship side when, out of nowhere, hands clasped her waist again. Spinning round, she found Clark once more about to lift her. She sloughed his hands-free of her waist and glared at him, growling in her throat.

"Excuse me, Captain, but I can manage just so on my own. Your hands may remain your own."

Releasing her immediately, he took a step back and said softly, "We shall see." The teasing tone saw the fire in her cheeks blaze. He either didn't notice, or was doing a good job of pretending so, as he passed her and began scaling the ladder made into the side of the ship. Repositioning the satchel around her shoulder, Vanessa approached the ladder with trepidation. She was an excellent climber under most circumstances and this ladder would prove child's play were it not for the infernal corset digging into her on all sides. The damned thing had not once

46

let her draw a decent breath since she had set eyes once again on the captain.

She reached for the first step, looking up just in time to see him disappear over the rail at the top. Determined not to let him win this childish game, she began to climb. She had been right. The corset proved to be more than inconvenient, but as she grasped the rail at the top, he seemed truly impressed. When he moved to hoist her over, she snapped at him.

"I can manage, Captain." She struggled with her skirts as she slid over the rail and found her feet. Brushing a curly tendril of her ebony hair away from her cheek, she stood straight and looked around at his crew, all gathered and gawking as if they had never seen a woman before.

With a gruff chuckle, he said, "So I see. This way, Lady Everly. Your stateroom is in the cargo hold." Without another word, she followed him across the deck and down a narrow flight of steps below a grated trap door.

Chapter 3

The hold of the ship was dark, but the wonderful scent of freshly baked bread filling the space was intoxicating. She inhaled deeply and let the enticing aroma fill her lungs. It was one in the afternoon and her packing had left her no time for a morning meal.

"We have the best cook on the sea, Lady Everly. You'll see." Mortimer's now familiar voice whispered behind her. He lugged two of her bags, one over each shoulder, as they moved like a train down the narrow corridor. Crates of all shapes and sizes were stacked high and close around her, held back by thick rope nets that reeked of dust, salt, and old fish, and for a moment she feared she would suffocate. Just as she was about to ask how much further, the figure of the captain stopped short in front of her. The low light and his sudden stop combined to result in her running straight into him. While the impact almost landed her on the floor, he barely shifted in his shoes.

"Pardon me, Lady Everly. We have reached your quarters." Again his hint of a grin could be seen even in the darkness. Grinding her teeth, she turned and entered the door he slid open beside her. The stateroom was more like a suite. She walked into a rather large expanse with a low ceiling. There was a queen-sized feather bed along the far wall, which was most likely the hull of the ship itself, with a large oak desk at the end. A dining chair had been placed at the desk for her use, but next to the small pot belly stove along the near wall was an elegant, if somewhat worn, wing-back, thickly padded and exceedingly comfortable looking. There were a few other pieces of furniture, including a vanity and a dresser with a large, intricately framed mirror, completing the room. Oil lanterns hung around from large tie hooks on the walls, no doubt remnants of this room's former purpose, and an elegantly crafted stained glass lamp sat atop the desk, casting warm yellow light. All in all, the room was quite spacious and lovely. Far more than she had expected.

"Is the room to your liking, my Lady?" The captain's voice was low and calm and entirely too close. Spinning on her heels, she found him inches away and staring directly at her. While she wanted to make a scathing remark, the navy blue of his eyes was hypnotizing, and the overwhelming desire to lean closer to him fought against all her common sense.

"It is far more than I expected. Thank you, Captain Clark." Realizing how breathy and soft her voice had become, she looked away and took a step back, another blush coursing over her flesh.

"I am glad to hear it. Your trunk and the artifact crate will be brought down momentarily and then we will be weighing anchor. I will have the cook bring you something to eat. This rope here will signal the deck if there is anything you require, and the ones along the far wall will open cannon ports so that you may get some fresh air and see the ocean whenever you like. I am sure you will be most comfortable here for the duration of our crossing."

"Excuse me, the duration? I am to be confined?" A subtle nod of his head had her seething. "I am not a bird fit for a cage! I refuse to be locked into your cargo hold for a month!" Her indignation flared as she railed against his cold insistence, but the hot anger coursing through her veins broke off at the sight of the scathing hardness that rippled through his massive frame. Even under his well-made uniform, she could see his muscles flexing and it frightened her. Well, it did something to her, yet she could not really be sure what.

"The only way to protect you, and deliver you safely to your father, is to control your whereabouts while at sea, Lady Everly. You *will* remain within your quarters. Your needs will of course be met, but so will mine. I need most for my men to function without distraction. Now, there is a lock on this door that only I have a key to. I strongly suggest, once all of your things have been delivered, and your food is brought to you, you lock it and let it remain so until something else you require is ready for you to receive." As he spoke he moved back out into the hall beyond her door.

"This is ridiculous! I refuse to be stowed away like cargo. I am sure someone such as I would have little to no effect on your men. Just as I have no effect on you! I have no illusions of my own vanity, Captain. I am well aware of my shortcomings. My father made them quite clear to me during my youth. It is why I was given to an arranged marriage to a lower station, and why, as you pointed out on the boat from the dock, I did not leap at my father's command." Without turning to look back at her, he paused in the hall.

"Regardless of your apparent opinion of your attractiveness, I must insist all the same. Oh, and do let me know if there is anything I can do to make your trip more comfortable." With that, he was gone. Mortimer smiled sadly at her as he set the bags down.

"It really is in your best interest, m' Lady. He can be difficult, but he is an honorable man. He means only to see you safely home. If you need anything just tug the rope. I will tend to you personally." She smiled warmly at the old sailor as he, too, took his leave of her room. The door closed behind him with a hollow thud. She groaned to herself. Rubbing trembling fingers to her temple, she glanced out once more over her home for the next four weeks.

"Must you argue with everyone, Essie?" She mumbled to herself, hearing her nanny's voice in her head. She smiled pathetically as she moved to the bed and lowered her satchel to it. "Even with myself, it would seem," was her answer. Stretching her back, she rubbed her hand across the back of her neck, trying to stem the frustrated tears that tingled in her nose. She would not cry, not over this. Deciding that action was her only course, she grabbed one of the cannon port ropes and tugged. At first, it did not want to give, but with a little added force, she eased the rope down to the lower hook, opening a rectangular hatch in the side of his well-maintained clipper. The bay lay before her. Its crystal water and cloudless sky blending seamlessly into infinity seemed to make the desire to cry greater. Leaving the port open, she moved to the large wing-back chair and eased into it.

It was even more comfortable than it had appeared and smelled of coconut oils and lavender. Leaning her face into the faded fabric, she closed her eyes and tried to fall asleep. At least in her dreams she still found hope. The chair proved amazingly effective and in only moments she had drifted off. When the knocking on the door became violent, she was snapped from her encroaching nap by the frantic calls of Mortimer, just outside.

"Lady Everly, are you alright? Lady Everly?" She smiled sadly at the honest concern in the old man's voice. With some difficulty, she stood and made her way to the door. There he was, her artifact crate in hand, and followed closely by the same two gargantuan sailors with her bags and trunk between them, looking exactly as she remembered when they left her room at the boarding house. "There you are, lass, I was beginning to worry. We have the rest of your things here."

"Bring them in, Mr. Mortimer. Please set your burden on the desk. The rest you can place next to the dresser if you would be so kind." Mortimer nodded and eased into her space, but the other two men scowled at her, moved just inside the door, and dropped her trunk. Without so much as a word, they turned and left.

"I told you, lass, you are better off down here." Just as Mortimer crossed the threshold, a rotund balding man in his late forties appeared carrying a tray. "Ah, Cookie! This is our passenger, Lady Everly. Lady Everly, this is Cookie." Mortimer smiled and stepped aside as the large man struggled to squeeze through the doorway.

"My name is John, ma'am, but I am indeed the ship's cook. Captain Clark likes his food to be exceptional and varied, so we carry a fully stocked pantry. If there is anything special you would like I am sure I can accommodate you." His pudgy face curled into a smile that made her want to laugh, but she stifled the urge and motioned him to the vanity. He set his tray down and uncovered a steaming plate of roasted chicken, potatoes, and some of that heavenly bread she had inhaled earlier. "If you would, simply place the tray in the corridor when you are finished, ma'am. I will retrieve it in my own time. Dinner is served at seven." His smile holding steady, he left her as quickly as he had come. Mortimer, still standing in the hall, looked at her one last time.

"We are about to weigh anchor, m'lady. The ship may shift a bit. I would suggest you wait to unpack until we are out of the bay. It shouldn't be more than an hour." Then, he too, was gone. She slid the door closed and moved to the enticing meal waiting for her. Mortimer had not been wrong. The food was unbelievably good and she found her appetite unaffected by the fear and sadness causing her heart to ache. When the ship seemed to list, she realized they were turning. Turning toward the open ocean. Toward London. Toward home.

Once her meal was finished, she set the tray in the hall as requested and returned to the wing-back chair. Closing her eyes, she tried to dream of what her life could have been had Captain Clark never appeared. A feat strangely impossible.

The rest of her first day on the *Siren's Call* had been spent sleeping, unpacking and nervously pacing the planked floor. As desperately as she wanted her freedom, she did not possess the nerve to claim it. Frustrated and defeated, she opened the crate of tablets and spread them over the large mahogany desk placed at the foot of her bed. Inside the drawer, she found several notebooks and pens. The captain had put an inordinate amount of effort into providing her with a suitable workspace. If only he had applied as much thought to her social needs, she would not be trapped. These had been her thoughts for all of day two. She dressed early and prepared herself as if visitors would come, but it proved to be a fruitless effort on her part. A knock on her door found a tray of food in the hall, for all three meals and afternoon tea, but no round-faced John accompanying it. It seemed even the cook was told to avoid contact with her.

She tried to throw herself into her research and for a time it worked. The small stone tablets proved far more intricate than she had originally thought and their detailed cleaning consumed most of the third day, which saw her in a loose blouse and skirt for fear of an unexpected caller. By the fourth day, she did little more than brush her hair, remaining in her dressing gown. The fifth and sixth saw her hair washed, but nothing beyond her robe was freed from her dresser. By the seventh, the end of her first week, she felt as if she were losing her mind. She found herself arguing with the tablets, or worse her reflection in the large mirror, and hanging out of the cannon port over her bed trying fiercely to feel the sun on her flesh. But, as it was riding high on the other side of the ship this time of year, her efforts were an utter failure.

Solitude did not suit her and she feared if she did not escape soon she would be mad as a hatter by the time they made port. A sadistic smile curved over her gnawed lips. That would serve the captain right. Her father would not pay for a lunatic in the skin of his daughter. At least, she hoped he wouldn't.

Chapter 4

Her lunch, delicious as always, had been delivered some hour past and she sat staring at the empty tray wondering what the galley looked like. Thoughts of the galley led to memories of the hold and before long she was imagining the sun-covered deck caressed with an ocean breeze. Her boredom and fear-addled mind couldn't sustain itself on idle dreams any longer. Her eyes snapped to her dresser. She decided to follow her impulsive side; something she had denied herself for weeks. Standing quickly, she moved to the drawers, shedding her dressing gown as she went. Opening one, she stared down at the corsets inside and grimaced.

No. Not today.

Closing it, she opened the one beneath. She claimed a pair of her tailored trousers from within. From the next she pulled a lose fitting linen shirt and a sculptured leather vest. Retrieving her combinations from the top drawer, she set about dressing in her digging clothes. She had had the outfits specially made after arriving in Kingston. The work of an archaeologist was hindered to the point of pain by the trappings of society dress and the freedom the new pants afforded her had been intoxicating. Despite their comfort, she had only had the nerve to dress in such a way on dig days, reverting to her corset most of the time.

Though there would be no digging up top, she decided, clothed more like a man, she would cause less ripples and therefore receive less wrath from the captain when she was inevitably discovered on deck. At least, this was her hope as she stopped in front of her mirror. The trousers, designed to fit tight and move well, hugged her natural curves in a way she failed to notice and the vest, just as form-fitting as the trousers, accentuated the narrow waist she possessed without the aid of a corset. Scanning over herself one last time, she scowled at the loose tousle of curly, long black hair swirling and hanging down her back. Her tresses would most certainly identify her as a woman. With hasty fingers, she braided the floppy mass into a loose plait curling around one side of her head and resting on her shoulder. Smiling at her meager efforts to hide what she was unaware was impossible to disguise, she turned with determined steps and left her cage behind. Excitement quickened her pace as she sped down the hallway. She feared now she would be discovered too soon and ushered back into her cabin without inhaling the ocean air.

This fear was a sensation she had become bitterly familiar with in her youth and she dreaded it fiercely. Countless times she had been confined to her rooms, forced to listen to the laughter and music of balls being held below. He father was ever the socialite, throwing party after party in his high circles, but not once had she been allowed to attend. Nanny would try to keep her entertained, but all she really wanted was to see the beautiful people dancing late into the night. The ladies in massive, intricately made gowns swirling on their toes and the gentlemen in tails and top hats kissing their hands. She had attempted repeatedly to join in on these events but each time her father would catch her and scuttle her away just shy of entry. He tried to explain his feelings to her. How he did not want her hurt by their callous remarks, how her appearance would no doubt make them shun her. While he had not intended to damage her so deeply, his words had left her scared. Society had become something to be avoided, even feared. She was not welcome in its company. That feeling wouldn't come back to her here. She refused to let it.

Nearing the hatch, she ran up the narrow steps that led to the deck. As she emerged into the full sunlight, she squinted against its unfamiliar brightness. All around her, deckhands stopped their actions and turned to stare at her appearance from the hold. She glanced from face to face, taking in the shock and alarm written on each in turn. Turning to the aft, she spied a large elevated expanse upon which only Mr. Mortimer could be seen. Moving with haste across the boards, she climbed the ornate stairs to the platform where he stood.

"Mr. Mortimer, it is a lovely day at sea, is it not?" She smiled warmly at him, but when he didn't return it, she scowled slightly. "I needed a bit of air, Mortimer. I promise I will vanish as soon as I have had my fill. Please. My cabin is becoming a coffin and I can handle no more silent solitude." He nodded woodenly and she moved farther back, climbing another set of steps to a platform at the very rear of the ship, devoid of any other person with whom she could interact. Though she wished for companionship, she found herself suddenly fearing the type she might receive if she went in search of it. Settling for the air and the sea, she leaned against the rail guarding the drop-off, as she now stood some thirty feet above the water's surface.

The wind caressed her skin and the fresh salt air filled her lungs. Her smile was broad as she lifted her face to the sky. Lost in the warm touch of the sun, she became aware she was no longer alone. Opening her eyes, she glanced quickly to her left to find the looming form of the captain, dressed far less formally than she had ever seen him, then quickly moved her eyes back to the open ocean.

"I thought I told you to remain in your quarters, Lady Everly. Not wander my ship and peruse my poop deck." His voice, cold, deep, and clear, sounded as if he had no interest in speaking with her, but she couldn't help but feel a course of excitement at seeing him again. One she felt strangely sure was mirrored in his flesh. He had become as rare as the sun since they set sail and while she had hoped his effect on her would lessen, she was mistaken. Seeing him in shirt sleeves and a simple pair of pants painted him in a far too familiar light for her affected mind.

"Is that where I'm standing? How interesting." Her teasing tone seemed to make him uncomfortable, but he did not move away from her.

"Your appearance on the surface is likely to unsettle my men, even under ideal circumstances, but your attire just now is completely unacceptable." She turned her head to look up at him fully, finding him standing tall and straight, unwilling to even cast a glance down at her. She straightened her spine to match his posture and frowned at him.

"*You* are wearing trousers. All of your *men* are wearing trousers; at least I would hope so. Why is my appearance in them more of a grievance? I should think looking more like a man would ease their discomfort at having a woman on board, not heighten it." As her eyes devoured his profile she saw his jaw flex, but he still did not look at her.

Clearing his throat heavily, he spoke again, "More like a man? My Lady, if you think what you are wearing is less disturbing to a man's sensibilities than a dress, especially where a woman such as you is concerned, you are sorely mistaken. Where on earth did you even find such clothes? Surely they are not your own. Did one of my men provide them for you?"

Again, his cold tone was tempered with what she could only describe as excitement. "What do you mean, 'a woman such as you'? And no, they are not one of your men's clothes, they are mine. I had a tailor make them for me after reaching port in Kingston. You cannot imagine the difficulty one faces attempting to dig in the earth wearing long skirts, petticoats, a bustle, and one of those infernal corsets. These clothes proved invaluable to me over the last year. Besides, as I said when I boarded, I do not fear your men. I am most likely beneath their notice."

She sighed and allowed her body to slump against the railing, unable and unwilling to maintain his rigidity. Deciding he did not intend to look at her as he spoke, she removed her eyes from him and returned to looking out over the expansive ocean. She took another deep refreshing breath of the crisp salty air that breezed past her. Suddenly, she felt him shift ever so gently beside her and the undeniable feeling of his eyes on her flesh compelled her to speak again, though due to the heat his nearness was producing in her face, she could no longer bring herself to look at him.

"I assure you, Captain Clark, it was not my intention to disturb your crew, but I simply cannot sit in that room any longer." Feeling his spine stiffen, she continued, "The accommodations are wonderful, and I did not intend to imply anything other, but one cannot live in solitude. No man is an island unto himself, isn't that the saying? I was in desperate need of some air, the sun on my face, and the salt smell of the sea. I do so love the sea." Her tone had become involuntarily wistful as she spoke of her fascination.

"As do I, Lady Everly." There was a strange new rasp and warmth to his voice, sending warning shivers down her spine. Before she could stop herself, she looked up to find him staring down at her. Though he was not really smiling, the corners of his finely crafted mouth were pulled slightly into the shy grin she had come to see in her dreams. Fresh warmth coursed over her face.

"Do my feminine fancies amuse you, Captain?" She could barely speak under the heat in his eyes. Something was lingering in those navy depths, making a secret part of her anxious. Though she was frightfully unsure what this part wanted her to do.

"No, not amuse exactly. Surprise, perhaps. I have never met a woman of high birth who expresses herself the way you do. Nor have I ever met one who held little more than a passing interest in the sea."

"How do you know mine is genuine?" She knew she shouldn't goad him, but she couldn't help herself. This was their first conversation since the journey had begun and though it was cold, she was enjoying the discourse.

"Because there is far too much honesty and forthrightness in you to deceive me, Lady Everly. I admire that. I am glad you find the sea wonderful, and I understand your need for fresh air and freedom as that is the reason I have made the sea my home. Sadly, however, I must insist you return to your quarters. Your presence is disturbing to the men."

Her mouth dipped at the corners. She looked up at him defiantly. "I find that highly unlikely, Captain. I see little more than alarmed stares cast my way."

"Lady Everly, far be it for me to discredit your father, as you seem to share his opinion, but in this he is distinctly mistaken. I joined you here because the men sent Mort to fetch me, demanding I take care of your appearance and your presence. You are, without doubt, the loveliest woman I..." he shifted nervously beside her before he continued, "any of my men have ever seen. If you insist on needing fresh air in the future, please send word to me and I will clear the deck and have you escorted. For now, I must regretfully request you return to your stateroom before I have a mutiny on my hands."

The flush in her cheeks deepened unbearably, forcing her to break eye contact with him. Something she instantly regretted, finding the navy of his eyes surprisingly soothing to her addled nerves; absorbing her concentration in distracting curiosity. She thought for a moment perhaps he was teasing her, but there had been no sign of jest in his face or his features. Part of her wanted to check again, examine his expression in-depth, but her blush was already setting her ablaze. One more peek into those eyes might just ignite her.

She didn't want to leave the sun, or the air, but his words had been soft and pleading and she could not bring herself to argue with him. Not after he had shown her such kindness.

Sighing, she cast one last lingering look out over the blue expanse. "Very well. I shall bid you good day then, Captain Clark." On a groan, she moved to leave the deck and return to her room. As she crested the narrow stairs leading back down from the poop deck, she felt him following behind her. Turning slightly, she shot a glance up over her shoulder to find him gazing at her with that unnerving slight grin pulling his mouth off kilter. Unable to speak, she turned back and rushed down the stairs and into the belly of the ship, not missing the stares and relief on the faces of his crew. Without stopping, she ducked into her room and closed the door behind her. She leaned against it, flushed to the point of fearing she might combust. Her heart was racing. It drummed in her ears, a deafening beat in the utter silence.

He had called her lovely. And what was more, she was sure he had meant it. No one had ever, in her memory, called her lovely. Alfred had, in his limited capacity for such things, told her he found her appearance pleasant to be around, but that paled in her eyes compared to the adoration and respect her late husband had shown her intellect. Her mind had always been her source of pride. To hear someone praise her beauty, even though it had always seemed a shallow thing to her, made her heart flourish as never before. She pushed away from the door and walked slowly across her stateroom to stare out the open port hole above her desk. Conceding he must have meant it, she wondered what she was supposed to do with this new revelation. Was she to take pride in his admiration? Or was she to fear this change in her circumstances?

She had told Andrew since she believed herself a homely creature, she had nothing to fear from his men. But if his words were true, she now had much to be afraid of. She was alone in the middle of an expansive sea, trapped on a ship, with no fewer than fourteen men who apparently found her lovely. Men who undoubtedly saw women as little more than physical pleasures. Only the captain was standing between her and their aggression and she now wondered if he could protect her. Allowing her thoughts to drift to the captain found the flush from earlier returning. His eyes, dark and mysterious, filled her vision once again. She began to tremble, remembering his closeness.

Why did she react this way? She barely knew the man. In truth, she did not know him but knew of him. Mortimer had called him honorable, and she had seen his cruelty and his kindness, but she had little of his personality at her disposal. She knew nothing of his past outside of the count of years he had spent on the sea and that he bore a fearful scar from some tragic event in his history. The scar hovered in her mind like a beautifully wrapped present she was forbidden from opening. It teased her with potential. She loved a good story and one that left a scar so unique would surely be harrowing and courageous.

Smiling to herself, she wondered what his full smile looked like. If it curved the scar more tightly around those mystical night-sky eyes of his? Suddenly, she felt a consuming fear. She should not allow herself to wonder about such things. Even if he shared her fascination and longed to know her the way she desired to understand him, there was little that could come of it. Stephen loomed behind her like death. He was her future. Deciding that allowing herself to entertain this curiosity, to permit it to grow, would only cause her pain, she resolved, reluctantly, to keep the captain at arm's length for her own good. She settled down at her desk and pulled the notebook in front of her. Lifting a tablet into her still trembling fingers, she did her best to focus on the past, her future becoming even more frightening. Something she had hoped was not possible.

She sat for hours lost in the tablet, turning it over and over in her hands. With her future providing her with doubt and pain, and her present filling her with confusion and dread, her work seemed the only thing capable of giving her safety and so she indulged. She sketched the images and described the tool marks. She made educated guesses as to the purpose of each hieroglyph, though in truth, their language was still mostly a mystery. This particular people, the Tainos, had been the only culture in the Kingston area for nearly eight hundred years. But after the European migration, finding enough of their written word to create a translation was next to impossible. Still, the location of some artifacts, and the objects found with them, had allowed her to attempt just such a feat. She had of course conceded to the possibility she was entirely wrong, and that actually thrilled her. Only in her work did she find comfort in not knowing. It gave her something to strive for, something to move toward. And with the confidence she possessed in her own intellect, she felt sure she could arrive at her destination entirely on her own, given enough time. Sadly the rest of her life was far less confidence-inspiring.

When a hard knock on the door signaled dinner, she looked up from her work amazed to hear the thunder of rain on the hull. When she had left the deck only a few hours ago there had not been a cloud in the sky and the sun had been bright and warm, but the world beyond her open porthole had become dark and terrifying. Realizing rain was blowing in directly atop her bed, she sprang from her chair and rushed to close the portholes. Casting a glance out at the tumultuous sea before the wooden door sealed tightly against the hull, she could see the flashes of distant lightning. The blue water had turned to slate, writhing and tossing all around them. She had weathered several such storms on the journey from London, but she hadn't enjoyed them. No doubt the ship would pitch and yaw all night long in this squall and she cared little for the dreams such frightening events brought her.

After she finished her evening meal and returned the tray to the hallway floor, she tried to return to her work, but the ship's rocking made writing in her notebook nauseating. Declaring defeat, she packed away her tablets and settled into the wing-back chair, curling her feet under her for warmth. This storm had come from the Atlantic and with it the cold air of Europe. They were progressing north, after all, and the closer they drew to England the more chill they would encounter. She hadn't felt cold in a year and her body reacted unfavorably. Deciding she needed to light her stove, she stood stiffly and moved to the door, pulling the rope to alert Mr. Mortimer she had a need. When he appeared several moments later she wished she had simply pulled the quilt from her bed. The poor old man was soaked from head to toe and she could see, despite his efforts to hide it, that he was shivering.

"Mr. Mortimer! You look positively frozen! Are you all right?" She wanted to pull the old man into her room and toss her quilt around his shoulders, but he only smiled at her warmly.

"Aye, m'Lady, I am fine. This storms a rotter though. Beggin' your pardon, but the captain needs me at the helm. What can I do for ye?" For a moment she thought she would dismiss him, not wanting to burden the drowned sailor any more than his profession already had but, deciding it would be far ruder of her to have called him down for nothing at all than to give him the task she had initially intended, she sighed.

"This storm, as you well know, brought a chill with it. I find myself no longer accustomed to the cold, Mr. Mortimer. I was wondering what fuel I could have for that stove there?"

She jerked her head in the direction of the potbelly and he smiled. "I can have that lit for ye in no time, lass, and call me Mort, everyone does, and your Mr. Mortimer is more formal than I deserve."

"I can light it, Mr...Mort, have no concerns there. I do not wish to keep you from your duties. The fuel is all I require." He smiled and nodded, then moved into the darkness, vanishing into the cargo hold. She stood shivering in the doorway. The hold of the ship, devoid of life as it was, carried an unnatural chill. "The lamps..." She muttered under her breath. The lanterns burning on her walls had done their best thus far to hold the cool air at bay, and until the storm had landed they had succeeded.

"What was that, lass?" Mort reappeared beside her lugging a heavily laden bucket of coal chunks.

"Speaking to myself. Pay no mind. Could you bring that in here? I fear I may not possess the strength to carry such a full bucket." She knew full well it was a lie, but the quick smile that lit his face told her he enjoyed feeling useful to her. He carried the container to her stove and set it down. As he moved to open the door and start her fire, she cleared her throat. "I can surely do that for myself. Did you not say the captain would need you back on deck?" He turned for a moment with hurt written on his brow, but it soon faded into urgency.

"You are quite right, lass. The captain has his hands full with the rigging and I am needed at the helm." Standing as straight as his battered body allowed, he moved swiftly to the door and bowed low to her before disappearing back toward the hatch. Sliding the door closed, she found herself impressed the captain would aid his men in such a storm as this. The voyage out had seen the captain entertaining quests in his quarters during similar gales, barely able to stomach the sight of his men when they arrived, no more than drowned rats, to share the state of things. This Captain Clark was indeed an interesting case.

Remembering her decision from earlier, she shook her thoughts free of him and moved to the stove. She could do for herself in most circumstances, something she hid from almost everyone. Her dear Nanny had taught her how to be a whole person, not *just* a lady, and she loved her dearly for it. With the fire started, and warmth filling her space, she settled back down into the wonderful sweet-smelling chair and drifted with the sea.

Chapter 5

The storm lingered for nearly three days, but as the rain finally subsided so too did the cold. With the cool air drifting away with the clouds, the residual warmth of the Caribbean returned. Waking to the sound of waves and wind, she pulled the hatch open and looked out at the clear morning sky. The sun had not yet peeked over the horizon in their path, but its glow was setting the sky ablaze with orangey-red hues and golden fire. She leaned on the sill of the cannon port and allowed the wind to stir her dark hair about her shoulders.

"Beautiful..." Mumbling to herself, she propped her elbows on the edge of the opening and cradled her head in her palms, enjoying the natural grandeur of the sea. As her mind wandered over the crests of the waves before her, voices drifted over the side of the deck above. For a moment she listened to the sounds of men shouting information in what could only be called another language. While the words were English, their meaning was completely lost on her.

When the sound of Clark's voice, booming over all the others with its deep clarity, drifted down to her, she stiffened. He had offered her fresh air whenever she had felt the need so long as she gave him prior warning. If it was a prior warning he wanted he would get it. Spinning around on the bed, she crawled quickly to the edge and leapt to her feet, looking more like a child than a full-grown woman. Her heart raced with excitement at the prospect of escaping her cage again, only this time she would obey his rules and hope for more consideration from him in the future. She flew across her room and tore through her dresser, pulling free one of those blasted corsets and her drab brown dress. Her fingers moved with anxious speed as she dressed. As she was attempting to pull her brush through the mop of her hair, she tugged the rope that would set her free. Within moments, Mortimer was at her door.

Still trying to tame her wild hair, she slid the door open to find his familiar face smiling at her. "Good morning, m'Lady."

"And a fine morning it is, Mort. I would like you to tell the Captain that, at his earliest convenience, some fresh air would do me good." She pulled the brush free of her unruly tresses and folded her hands before her as she grinned sweetly at him. The old man's face flushed a faint pink as he returned her grin.

"Aye, Lass, I will do that, but it may be a while before he can accommodate you." Her grin fell and he seemed desperate to return it. "We had a bit of damage to the main mast in the storm. He is up in the rigging repairing the cross beam right now, but I will make sure he gives you the time you need. You can count on me." Her smile returned as she leaned in and kissed him softly on the cheek.

"Thank you, Mortimer. I truly appreciate your kindness." His face flushed almost to purple as he stammered, then turned and made for the deck at a frenzied pace. Chuckling to herself, she slid her door closed and set about the task of pulling her hair up into a reasonable facsimile of a bun, though the job had never proved an easy one alone. Nanny was the only person who had ever been able to fully tame the thick ebony sheet of her hair, and ever since the day she departed this world, Vanessa had given up perfection in lieu of passable.

Having done all she could do for her waist-length mop, she paced her room waiting to be fetched. The minutes became an hour and one became three. Soon she began to fear the day would pass without her moment of freedom. As she sat in the wing-backed chair staring out the porthole, she struggled with the wasted time. She should have been working. The tablets still had much to tell her, but she simply couldn't concentrate. She had never known this type of anxiety before, not even when she was to be wed to Alfred. She had been afraid, to be sure, but he was attractive and kind and she believed her father's promises of happiness and fulfillment. If only he had been right. Thoughts of Alfred brought a tear to her eye as she sighed deeply, sinking farther into the chair and resigning herself to having to try again tomorrow.

After giving up on a walk in the sun, her adrenalin waned and she drifted closer and closer to unconsciousness. Allowing images of the dig site and the palm trees to soothe her mind; she felt the heaviness of sleep creeping up her spine when, all of a sudden, a knock at the door sent her hurdling out of the chair. Sprawled on the floor, she struggled against the tightness of her corset to stand as the firm knock sounded again. A frustrated scowl crossed her face as she righted herself.

"What now?" She wondered aloud, and then it hit her. Perhaps it was Mortimer, come to fetch her for her freedom. When the knock returned, far louder and a bit impatient, she bolted to the door and slid it open, beaming at the spot where she expected to see Mortimer's gapped grin, but instead found herself staring slack-jawed at the delightfully firm expanse of the captain's taunt chest. Swallowing hard, her gaze traveled slowly up to his shoulders and then still farther to his face, all the while her mouth hanging open. He was back in his uniform coat, impeccable as always, and standing with his stiff-spined posture.

"Captain Clark! I...I am sorry, I was expecting Mort...I mean, Mr. Mortimer to fetch me when the time had come." She did her best to compose herself as he stared down at her with that implacable grin. She watched as his dark eyes slipped from her face to travel down the length of her body, a strange look of amused confusion painting his features. "Surely this meets with your approval. It is by far the ugliest frock I own. I can't possibly turn a head in this old thing."

"It is that indeed, but it is also perfectly acceptable, Lady Everly. Shall we head above deck?" With a sweeping motion, he allowed her to precede him to the stairs and was close behind her as she emerged into the late afternoon sunlight. The deck, just as he had promised, was completely cleared of sailors for her walk. Suddenly she regretted wearing her homeliest garment as there were no men to avoid disturbing. None save him and he had already made her lack of affect completely clear. "I thought perhaps you would be interested in a tour of the ship, and maybe some education as to its workings and mechanics."

With surprise she couldn't suppress, she rounded on him. "You are to be my chaperone?" The shock in her voice seemed to catch him off guard and she could tell from the darkening of his eyes he had not expected her to say anything of the kind.

"I can certainly leave you to your own if that is what you wish." Stiffly, he turned as if to abandon her, and without thought to her actions, she found herself reaching for his arm. Catching it in her small hands, she could feel the lithe muscles bunch under her fingertips, tension rising in the whole of his frame at her unexpected touch.

Trying to ease the discomfort her comment had caused him, she continued, "I did not mean it that way, Captain Clark. Of course, I would love a tour, and I can think of no one better to educate me on the workings of a ship such as this than its captain. I merely thought perhaps there might be more pressing matters for you to attend to that would far out way my need for fresh air." The tension in his muscles seemed to lessen everywhere but where her hand still rested on his forearm. Realizing her touch was undoubtedly unwanted she started to remove it, but before her fingers could break the contact, his large, work-roughened hand, descended, holding her in place.

"Shall we begin then?" He wasn't smiling, not even his ghost of a grin shown on his face, but somehow she knew his spirit was light. Smirking slyly, she cocked her head to the side and nodded. He lifted her hand and tucked it under his elbow, bringing her along his left side for their stroll. "Well, Lady Everly, what would you like to know about the *Siren's Call?*"

Vanessa blushed by his side. His demeanor had changed so much from their first meeting. Her arm linked with his was sending shivers over her flesh. What was more exciting, *he* had done it. Three days ago he could barely look at her and now he made to walk with her the way dear friends or courting young ones do. Despite the awkward tension in her limbs, she turned and together they began to stroll from one end to the other. While the clipper was a good-sized vessel, at a normal speed it would take only moments to travel from front to rear, so his pace was more than leisurely.

At first, they only strolled. She waited for him to begin the lesson he had offered her and yet he remained silent. Deciding she would have to break the stillness, she cleared her throat, but the questions fled from her before she could get them out. At the sound from her, his pace slowed even further and she felt his posture shift and knew he was looking down at her. Meeting his gaze cautiously, she found his face, stoic though strangely soft considering his ruggedly angular bone structure, bent from his shoulders and focused on her.

"Yes? Is there something you wish to ask? I must admit I was expecting a torrent of questions from an intellectual such as yourself, Lady Everly. Have you lost your interest in the sea already?" There was a slight teasing tone to his words as they curled his lips. Unable to stop the chuckle in her throat, she smiled at him.

"And I was awaiting a torrent of facts and stories from you, Captain Clark. It seems we were both doomed for disappointment." His arm shifted slightly closer to his core, squeezing her slim wrist against his rib cage. The act, though small, sent a flush over her. He was simply magnetic. Chiding herself for her adolescent reaction, she stiffened and let her eyes slip from his face to the large mast beyond. "Shall we start with a ship's necessary vocabulary? This morning from my window..."

"Cannon port. Or port hole, if you prefer." His correction made her chuckle again and the tension between them eased considerably.

"From my cannon port, then, I overheard some of your men barking orders at each other and I confess, with all my education, I understood none of it." She sighed slightly as she scuffed her heels over the deck boards, still staring up and into the mast at the front of the ship.

"And I must confess a loss as to where to begin on this point, my Lady. My men were working from fore to aft this morning. Are there any terms in particular you wish me to define?" His eloquence was astonishing for a sailor. Mortimer tried desperately to sound as proper as possible when he spoke to her and yet his ignorance was clear in dropped syllables and misused terms. The captain on the other hand spoke as her peers at university had. Wondering suddenly if he had been privileged to a formal education, something rare among the lower classes, she smirked to herself; another question to file away should their conversation turn personal. Redirecting her thoughts back to his query, she searched the rambling shouts in her memory for specific terms. Finding one she had heard several times, she brought her eyes back to his, which had not once left her.

"Yes, what exactly is a "bobstay"? I heard that word several times and there seemed to be anger concerning it. Did someone lose it?" He chuckled softly in his chest as his eyes finally drifted away, looking forward.

"The bobstays are ropes, Lady Everly."

"Well, now I simply feel foolish. To ask such a ridiculous question has completely defeated me, and only moments ago you mentioned my intellect. How disappointed you must be." She cast her eyes to the deck as hot shame washed over her face. Though she honestly had not known, hearing the simple truth embarrassed her.

"Not at all. They are special ropes, if that eases your discomfort, specifically used to shore up the bowsprit. My men were working on securing them at dawn, as the storm had dislodged several. You are an early riser indeed, Lady Everly, to have overheard that exchange. I am impressed by you yet again." Her heart fluttered at his simple remark.

Grinning coyly, she asked her second question. "And what, exactly, is a "bowsprit"? As your answer has created another unknown for me to ponder." He stopped entirely and she found they had made their way to the very front of the ship. "This is the bow, correct?" He had not yet managed to answer her last question before the next flew from her.

Chucking in his throat, he said, "It is indeed." She expected him to say more, but when he paused she spoke instead.

"Then am I safe to assume that the bowsprit is somewhere near to us?" Again he chuckled and squeezed her hand against his side, sending a ripple of excitement through her. A strange energy seemed to be vibrating within her as their exchange grew friendlier with each chuckle and grin they shared.

"Correct. The bowsprit is that beam there, extending out from the fore. The figurehead is directly below it. The bobstays are the ropes that aid in its stability, see them here, anchored to the deck?" As he pointed casually around them to the lines wrapped snuggly to cleats on the floor beneath her feet, she furrowed her brow. "What troubles you, Lady Everly? Have I gone too fast?" His question had an unmistakable tinge of sarcasm and she felt his tease in the whole of her heart, causing its beat to increase.

"Not at all, Captain. I was just sure this portion of a sailing ship was called the *bow*, but you just referred to it as the fore. I am now at a loss as to which term is appropriate for me to use in conversation, should the need arise." He suddenly snorted, holding in his full, hearty laughter and she couldn't help but laugh herself at his effort.

"My dear Lady Everly, you may call it whatever you wish." From that moment on their exchange was light and informative. She learned much, from the definition and location of the "mizzen mast" to the uses of a "jib". When he pointed out the crow's nest, encircling the very top of the main mast, she shared her wish to see the view from such a perch. He again only barely stifled his rich, deep laughter. She wished he wouldn't. Despite the fact that she was sure he was enjoying their conversation as much as she, he was putting considerable effort into restraining his smile. Nothing more than a smirk had managed to show on his face in the entirety of their discussion.

After three laps of the deck, she found them once again standing over the hold hatch. Releasing her hand for the first time since he had tucked it under his elbow, he stood before her, his slight grin beaming down at her. Though it was a faint thing, it sent restless ripples down her spine, and she blushed. "I confess I have very much enjoyed this time in the fresh air and it saddens me to think it is done. I thank you, Captain, for the permission to take this time. I suppose I should retreat below deck so that your men may return to their duties." Her voice, filled with sad, wistful truth came out faintly on her breath. When he made no effort to respond, she nodded rigidly and turned to enter the belly of the ship.

As she took the first step down, he cleared his throat behind her, drawing her eyes to his. She was not prepared for the look that ghosted through their dark blue depths and she found her gaze darting away from the provocative glow dancing over his darkly tanned and expertly crafted features. When her eyes landed on the moon-shaped scar she felt her chest grow tight. While she imagined that, to some, the scar was a source of discomfort and perhaps even fear, she found herself again enthralled with the possibilities of what story lay behind its creation. Some rash part of her wanted to ask but she simply couldn't. She didn't have the nerve. He did not speak until she brought her eyes back to his.

"Lady Everly, I was wondering if you would dine with me tonight. I have also found our conversation quite pleasant and I am not of a mood to end it, as yet."

Smiling broadly, she hurriedly accepted his invitation. "I would like that very much, Captain. Will you send for me? I think perhaps I would like the time to change. This dress is simply atrocious and I no longer wish to be seen in it." With the soft rumble of contained laughter filling his chest, he nodded his agreement to her terms.

"I shall send Mortimer for you in an hour's time. Until this evening, my Lady." He bowed slightly at the waist before he turned from her and made for his cabin. His back toward her and his form in retreat, she did the same. Her blood was racing through her veins, the excitement over dinner's possible conversations consuming her thoughts.

Chapter 6

At just past six, Vanessa stood nervously in front of the ornate mirror agonizing over the unruly length of her curly ebony hair. She had changed swiftly into her favorite dark green riding dress after returning to her quarters. Dinner was promptly at seven every evening, but he had given her less than an hour to prepare for the meal she was eagerly looking forward to. This meant either they would be taking it early or that he desired a pre-meal conversation. She buzzed inside with anticipation at the prospect of spending more time with the intriguing captain. Part of her struggled with her new sensation of desire. She had felt attracted to men in the past, but never had the feeling been this potent. Even worse, she was betrothed, a fact she feared Clark did not know. There was, in truth, no hope in cultivating a relationship with him, but she was a slave to her impulses. She found pleasure in his company and, with all the sadness and uncertainty surrounding her, the little pleasure she could find she hungrily consumed.

Sliding the last pin into her loosely bound hair, she took a step back to admire herself. From the moment he had called her lovely, she had made an attempt to see what he saw, and it was starting to work. She had a new appreciation for her long slender legs, tall frame, and narrow in-swept waist, accentuated beautifully by the wonderful rich olive satin she adored. She had debated with herself about wearing her favorite dress, fearing that the party cut of her neckline, revealing the expanse of her naturally tanned chest, might be a dangerous choice considering her current circumstances. But caution lost. She hoped he would appreciate seeing her at her best. Though she had indeed conceded the fact that she could be lovely to some, she had little idea just how striking she was. The dark olive green of the tightly bodiced dress matched her eyes perfectly and flaunted her curves with a scalpel precision that would slice any man to the core.

As she pinched her cheeks to bring some rosy color to her face there was a slight knock on her door. Smiling at her reflection, she slid the door open to find Mortimer. His eyes went wide the second she came into view and she flushed as his jaw flopped open.

"M...m'Lady, you are beautiful!" His stammer made her blush deepen. Embarrassed by his brash comment, he pinked as well and cleared his throat, looking away from her with effort. "Excuse my manners, miss. The Captain is ready for you; at least he thinks he is."

"He thinks?" She couldn't help but flutter at the old sailor's reaction to her, feeling utterly lovely for the first time in her life.

"Beggin' your pardon, ma'am, but no one can be ready for you. Not in *that* dress." His shy smile made her giggle as she stepped into the corridor and pulled her door closed. Nodding to the still-flushed first mate, she followed him to the hold stairs. At the foot he paused. Turning to her with concern on his face, his eyes drifted over her fleetingly before he cleared his throat and said, "Move quickly, miss. The less the men see of you now the better."

A sudden apprehension hit her with his words. She hadn't thought of the moments between her room and his. The idea of being seen by his crew in her current state terrified her with possible dangers. Nodding jerkily, she grabbed her skirt and made ready to hurry. Mortimer's brow furrowed as he turned to the stairs and made quickly up. She followed at the same pace.

As she crested the hatch she found all eyes on her. They had stopped their tasks when Mort had emerged and were still focused on the spot, and now on her. She could feel the eyes on her flesh, along with the tension that suddenly washed over the deck at her appearance. Looking around frantically for Mortimer, she found him already at the Captain's door, wrenching it open for her. Ducking her head against the hungry stares scouring her body, she bolted across the deck to the opening, sliding within and out of sight. Mortimer closed the door as soon as she passed through and from the other side, she could hear him barking at the men to lift their jaws and get back to work. Her pulse was fierce in her veins and she felt out of breath, her chest so tight she couldn't inhale properly.

"Most people knock before entering." Clark's deep melodious voice seemed miles away in the din of her heartbeat. Scanning the room for its source, she caught sight of his blonde tresses over the top of the single wing-back chair in front of his potbellied stove, door open and filled with flame. In the orangey light, she recognized the pattern of the chair as a mate to the one just below in her stateroom. He had given her one of his own. She watched as he stood and rounded on her. The slight grin that seemed a permanent fixture of his face whenever she was near faltered the second she came into view. His jaw went slack for a moment and then tightened into a frown. All at once she wanted to scream as the thought that he did not find her attractive raced across her face. He apparently read her concern clearly and immediately spoke against it.

"Lady Everly, you really are trying to cause me grief. My men cannot handle seeing beauty like yours. Now I must worry over you constantly." As he spoke he drew around the chair and closer to her, reaching out one hand for hers. Her fingers shook as she extended them to him. He took them, holding them gently as he placed a light kiss on the back of her slim hand. "You are truly lovely, my Lady. That color suits you." There was a rasp to his voice which set her cheeks on fire and the soft rumble in his chest caused her pulse to thunder all over again.

"It is not every day one is asked to dine with the captain." Though she had meant the comment to be light, an effort to break the tension welling within her, the tremble in her soft breathy voice only seemed to cause more. Sighing, she frowned. "I am afraid I have made a mess of things indeed, Captain Clark. I would volunteer to return to my cabin and change into something less disturbing, but I fear walking past your crew again." Her eyes fell to her hand, still clasped lightly in his, and she swallowed the lump building in her throat.

"Nonsense. You look perfect exactly as you are. I will handle my crew if it comes to that, though I have to hope it does not. Come, sit. Dinner should arrive shortly and I am eager to continue our conversation." His grin returned as he released her fingers and brushed his knuckle under her chin, causing her head to lift. His friendly tone eased the unbearable tightness along her backbone, threatening to snap her spine if allowed to persist, and she exhaled on a smile. He led the way to his small dining table and pulled her chair out for her, taking the seat opposite hers for himself. The table was set with all the elegance of a dinner party for nobles and she had to blush, thinking he had gone to all that trouble just for her.

"This is a lovely table. Please say you did not do this just for me, Captain. I have eaten on dinghy plates with dirty forks for a year now." Laughing nervously, she lifted her napkin and placed it across her lap. He chuckled huskily in his throat.

"Lady Everly, meals are one of the few things I take quite seriously. I assure you my table looks as it does now for every meal. Though I will admit it is nice to have more than one place set. Mortimer refuses to eat with me. He claims he is too afraid of damaging my flatware to attempt it." They both giggled at the thought.

"He is a dear. I was afraid he might faint when he came to fetch me this evening. He has taken such good care of me." There was a flash in his eyes hearing her speak of her own beauty.

"I am glad to hear you have finally come to terms with your own "vanity." That is how you put it the day you joined us, is it not?" She had to look away from his eyes as they were filled with a fire she feared would catch her up. As if she willed the interruption, a knock sounded on his door, breaking the spell between them.

Looking away from her, he did not rise but called out, "Yes, come in John." At his command, the door swung open to reveal the ship's cook brushing, backside first, into the room carrying a heavily laden tray. Two large silver domed plates and a wine bottle teetered as he swung his heavy body around. Focused solely on his delivery, he moved to the table and had almost finished depositing his plates before he caught sight of her. She blushed again as his round face seemed to light up.

"That will be all, John, thank you." The captain's voice, filled with impatience, startled him and he jerked himself around and rushed to the door, casting one last look at her beauty before disappearing. Grumbling slightly at the brash behavior of his cook, Clark stood from his chair and lifted the bottle of wine. "Would you care for some?" She smiled sweetly and nodded, extending her delicate violet glass for him to fill. His glass was already full of some other liquid and so he promptly re-corked the bottle and set it on the table. Before returning to his seat, he lifted the silver domes. "I hope you like swordfish, Lady Everly. One of my men managed to hook one today and I grow weary of salted meat."

The smell wafting from the large red steak beneath her nose made her salivate. Smiling wickedly, she lifted her fork and readied to tuck in as she spoke. "I do indeed, Captain. The food on your vessel has been impeccable, but I agree, the cured meat grows tiresome, no matter how well prepared." She waited for him to carve his first bite before following suit. Their meal continued on in silence until both plates were cleared. He left the table for only a moment to pull a rope and within seconds John returned with a new tray, two smaller domes resting atop it. Exchanging the empty for the full, and beaming at her the entire time, he departed and Clark revealed two delightful tarts. Vanessa cheered softly before tearing daintily into her dessert.

As he stood to refill her wine glass for a third time, she giggled and smiled up at him, her face flushed from the alcohol. He paused to grin down at her lazy expression and she felt words surging up her throat. The rational part of her mind which understood what was socially acceptable in these situations begged her to catch the question before it leaked from her, but the wine had robbed her of the ability. With a rasp that seemed to make him shiver a bit, she asked, "How did you come by that scar? I find it haunting my dreams with possibilities and I desperately wish to hear the tale." Had she been sober and allowed such an impertinent question to slip from her she would have been appalled. But muddled as she was, she simply sighed and smirked up at him expectantly.

Clearing his throat, he sat back down and reclined in his chair, gazing at her. "Are you sure you wish to hear such a tale just after dinner? It is rather harrowing and is likely to upset your sensibilities." She laughed full and loud, something else she would have never done had the wine not eliminated her inhibitions. She was impulsive even on her best day, but she was in rare form sitting across from him in the dim light of his private quarters.

"I am absolutely certain. I adore a good story, and a unique mark such as yours is sure to be riveting in explanation. My sensibilities are much firmer than you know, Captain Clark. Something I would love to prove to you." Her chest tightened as a slight blush heightened his tanned cheekbones.

"And what will I receive in return for my tale? I feel after such an admission I will require compensation of equal value." There was something overtly provocative about his tone but, while she recognized the danger, the excitement rising in her drowned the warning bells.

Her half-closed eyes glazed over as she pursed her lips at him. "Your compensation shall be one of my secrets. A question of your own to be freely asked and honestly answered. Does this bargain fulfill your need?" Her wicked tongue flared and his eyes flashed across from her.

"Terms accepted. My scar," he turned his head to give her a clear view of it for a moment before returning his gaze to hers, "is the aftermath of an accident from my youth. When I was a lad of eight my family was making a trip across the English Channel. Our vessel, a ship not nearly as large as this, came upon a sudden squall. The wind lifted so suddenly the crew was unable to bring in the sails. The boat listed to one side. One of the tie lines snapped, sending several crates sliding across the drenched deck. I was where I was not meant to be and became pinned between the crate and the rail.

The crate was crushing me, breaking one arm and bruising several ribs. As I tried to climb out the crew was attempting to pry the crate away from me. I managed to wiggle free and climb on top as another gust hit the ship. The railing splintered and sent the crate over the side, carrying me along with it. The scar is the result of my head landing on the container as we hit the tumultuous sea together. I clung to that box, barely conscious, until the crew managed to fish me from the drink. My parents feared I would never again return to water. We traveled over the ocean often, you see, for business and personal reasons I should *not* like to discuss, and a terrible fear of the water would have made each pass horribly stressful for all of us. But they were mistaken. The experience did not deter me from the sea but rather drew me to it. That event spawned my passion. One could argue that this scar made me the captain before you."

As he finished his tale, he lifted his goblet and took a long drink of whatever he had chosen to have with dinner. She could do little more than sigh. She had devoured every word of his tale, finding every syllable entrancing. He replaced his beverage and grinned across at her enamored look. "Did that satisfy your curiosity, Lady Everly?" She nodded lackadaisically and propped her dark head in her palm.

"Your tale was far better than any of my imaginings, Captain. Though, I dare say, you have far from satisfied my curiosity with respect to you." His breath caught a little at her obvious flirtation and even she seemed to realize just how improper her current state had become. Blushing, horribly embarrassed by her words, she sat up straight and hung her head. "I feel I have lost my mind and my manners. I beg your pardon. The wine has gotten the better of me." She almost whispered her apology, consumed by guilt. It wasn't that she hadn't meant what she had said. She did. He was becoming far more fascinating to her than any man, any person, she had ever met, and she was dangerously close to falling deep into infatuation, if not beyond. "Perhaps I should retire. I fear my manners will only falter more if I remain and I have already done irreparable damage to your meager opinion of me."

"Nonsense. My opinion of you, my Lady, is still as infallible as always, and we struck a bargain, remember? You are not dismissed from my table until your end has been fulfilled. As for your manners, I have spent the last twelve years in the company of the crudest men England has to offer. Your slight slips of the tongue cause me no grief." Reluctantly, she lifted her sorrowful gaze to find that enticing smirk etched once more on his handsome face. Her growing feelings wrapped around her chest, strangling her damaged heart. The knot under her bosom hardened into a rock, making her ache with each breath she struggled to take. Flushing even beyond the wine, she averted her fiery gaze but did not lower her head.

"If you are truly not disgusted, as I am, by my behavior, ask your question. I will stay as long as you will allow me to." Again her words betrayed her true feelings. Unable to even acknowledge this falter, she simply sighed at her own impertinence.

"My question shall mirror yours." Her brow furrowed as she lifted back to his eyes.

"I bear no scars upon my body for you to inquire over." At her allusion to the perfection of her flesh, his grin grew wicked and she gasped.

"Thank you for that image, my Lady, but I was referring, of course, to your ability to ask about the very incident that sparked my lifelong obsession with the sea. I wish to know what brought you, unmarked as you are, into the arms of the past as your chosen field."

Despite how horribly embarrassed she felt over the last few moments of their conversation, the chance to share her own harrowing tale sparked a light in her that he seemed to find fascinating. Sitting up a bit straighter, she sighed and let her eyes drift off into the shadows of his room beyond his alluring face.

"My tale is perhaps as harrowing as yours and, though I bare no mark to remind me of it or to create obsession in others who look upon it, I still believe it is worth the telling." She cleared her throat and sat back in her chair, struggling against the restraint of her corset for comfort, still focused on the hidden spot in the corner. Her eyes fogged over with recollection, she lost herself in her history, preparing to share the tale of her own personal creation.

"Perhaps by coincidence, perhaps fate, I was also eight when the course of my life was altered. I was, by all accounts, a mischievous child. My mother died when I was exceedingly young. Too young to even recall her face. She died attempting to bring what would have been my younger brother into this world. Tragically, neither survived. My father, unable to cope with her untimely death, walled up his heart, closing me firmly out. I was placed into the care of a string of governesses that stayed for a short time, each in turn, before leaving for greener, less obstinate, pastures." Recalling her misbehavior brought a faint smile to her face before she straightened and continued.

"I was particularly fond of slipping away without permission. One afternoon, my governess was taking me for a walk in the wooded area bordering the rear gardens of our manor. I suggested we play a game of hide and seek, but when she closed her eyes to count I took off on my own. I wandered farther than I ever had. Admiring the clouds, I took a faulty step and fell through the earth, taking several feet of ground with me. I fell quite a long way, nearly twenty feet, into a cave previously unknown to my family. My ankle was hurt badly in the fall and I found myself trapped, unable to climb out. In truth, I was barely able to stand."

She shivered remembering the cold dark. "It must have been terrifying for you." Her eyes drifted to the luminous blue of his in the dim candlelight. He was taking in every word she uttered just as she had consumed his tale. Warmth spread over her body under his gaze, before she sighed longingly and continued.

"At first, yes. I was lost in the dark. I shouted until my voice left me, but I had fled too far from my companion to be heard. Crying at the helplessness of my situation, I curled up in the center of the room I was in, surrounding myself with the sunlight still able to filter in from above. Slowly, my eyes adjusted to the dimness and a most wondrous thing happened. All around me, images began to appear out of the dark. Paintings of beasts and scenes of domestic simplicity were everywhere I turned. I began to wonder who had painted them and chronicled their lives on the rock around me. Questions took the place of my fear. Who were they? How long had it been since they had lived here? How they had come to be in this place that from my vantage point had no other exit? These questions became my friends as I was trapped in that cave for nearly two days before the search party found the hole through which I had fallen. My father, himself, pulled me from the darkness, and despite his chill towards me, I have loved him ever since."

"After several weeks of rest, I made a full recovery from my injuries, but the curiosity spawned in that darkness never faded. My governess, the one I had managed to escape, was let go for her ineptitude, so my dear Nanny became solely responsible for me. She was my dearest friend and had absolute faith in me so when I told her I wanted to go back, she did not hesitate. Taking only a lantern and a notebook, I ventured back into the cave many times over the next two months, sketching the images and writing down my questions and musings. One day, my father caught us leaving. He became very cross with Nanny and to spare her from his anger, I confessed that it was I who had instigated our excursions each day. I showed him my notebooks and shared my interest in an effort to save her."

Her tale paused as the memory of what happened next seemed to curl her entire body into a smile. "His reaction was surprising. He suggested I send what I had discovered to a friend from his youth who had become a professor of history at Oxford. Within a fortnight we had a visitor. My father's friend had come to see my cave. I showed him and we had long discussions about the people who had marked our land long before it was ours. He knew who they were and how they had lived. He was able to answer all of my questions and I wanted to be just like him. He was responsible for convincing my father I deserved far more than a society education and I had more to offer the world than becoming a "*good lady wife*"."

The phrase brought bitterness to her voice as the idea conjured images of Stephen and the future that awaited her in the haze of her mind. Sighing deeply, she looked down at her own small hands in her lap.

"He sponsored me when, at sixteen, I made to enter University. It was quite the scandal." Her voice lowered as a small laugh rattled her rasping tone. "No woman had ever been admitted prior to myself. As it stood, I wasn't enrolled in the traditional sense at first, only auditing classes for which the professors graciously examined my work. After nearly two years of this arrangement, I was given a proper enrollment much to the dismay of my peers. Still, I made it through, and head of my class, too. On top of jeopardizing his career on my behalf so I could study, it was also he who put my name in as the leader of the expedition from which you gathered me. I would not be what I am if not for him."

"I do not doubt he backed you, but I also believe that you have earned all you have achieved. So, you do have a harrowing tale of your own. You have told me much, Lady Everly, and I believe I am beginning to understand you."

As he spoke, he stood and moved around the table to her. Extending his hands, he paused before her, his face hidden in shadow, waiting for her to react. She swallowed back the lump his new nearness was forcing in her throat and reached her suddenly trembling fingers to his. The second there was contact; he clamped her hands with gentle firmness and pulled her quickly up to stand before him, only inches apart. She stared nervously at the navy blue cravat before her, unwilling, and unable, to look him in the eye at present. When, without releasing her small shaking fingers, he lifted her chin with his knuckle, she gasped. All that stood between them was empty distance and time. She wanted to span the distance with the whole of her, press her hands to his chest, and feel his heartbeat. She was dying to know if it had kicked into a veritable tempest just as hers had the moment their flesh connected.

She desired, but she could not act. An image, unwanted and cruel, of her father standing with Stephen hovered in her mind like an angry hornet and threatened to sting her if she made even the slightest motion toward the captain. Whimpering slightly, she whispered, "I think perhaps I should retire, Captain. I am afraid I am losing my grip on myself and fear what might come." His slight smile returned and she watched with rapt attention as he drew a breath, a prelude to speech, but he would not get the chance. The entire cabin seemed to shift, leaning dramatically to the right and throwing her already wine-damaged balance completely for a loop. Unable to stop her body, she began to flop toward the floor, only to feel his powerful arm snake around her waist and haul her against him.

Had he attempted to kiss her he would have found no resistance as she could think of nothing else, wrapped tight to him as she was, but he immediately released her brushing past in a huff. Swearing under his breath, he marched with angry strides and yanked the door open. There in front of him, he found the man he had been intent on yelling for only half a hair's breadth from knocking on the door himself.

"Mortimer! What the devil is going on?" There was a frightful sternness to his voice that set off warning bells in Vanessa's muddled mind. Watching poor Mort try to stammer his answer, she remembered what it had felt like to be the object of that tone. How she had backed down from a confrontation for fear of what this captain could be capable. Seeing it happen before her eyes to another was even more distressing as she had no recourse or comfort to offer the beleaguered man.

"Rogue gust, sir. Caught the main sail. We have it now, don't you worry, but there is a bigger problem!" Beyond the door, Vanessa could hear shouts and calls. The whole of the crew seemed to be in uproar. "It's Connor, sir! He's gone over!"

Chapter 7

"Connor?!" Clark went rigid in an instant. From her position, still teetering from her near fall, she watched as he quickly tugged his navy cravat from his neck and tossed it clumsily over his shoulder to the chair she had just vacated. His fingers began popping the buttons of his starched military coat free as he turned back to her.

"I am sorry, Lady Everly, but I think it *is* time for you to retire." His face had turned to stone, framed with a concern that made her chest tighten within her corset. As his coat slipped from his broad shoulders he handed it to the frantic Mortimer and strode past him. She watched the line of his back, visible now through the thin white linen of his simple shirt, move away from her and ground her knees together at the beauty of it. God, how he made her ache. "Mort, take her to her quarters!" In two steps he was racing away from them toward the crowd of sailors gathered around the rail on the starboard side. Even with the main mast, they hung over the railing, all bearing frantic, agonizing looks and helpless postures.

She jumped, surging after him as if she could help; a ridiculous notion in her current state and attire, but it mattered little at the moment. As she cleared the door to his cabin she managed to catch sight of his impressive, muscled frame just long enough to watch as he launched over the side of the ship into the dark nothing of the sea.

"No..."She stumbled for a moment as her heart lurched. He was gone, lost over the side. Every muscle in her body yanked at her, tugging her forward with unnatural speed. She launched into a run at the mass of sailors crowding even tighter at the site, now searching the pitch for, not one, but two lost comrades. Only feet from the group, hands clasped her shoulders. She tried to wrench herself free, but they held fast, far stronger than she expected. Then, they weren't just holding her, but pulling her backward, away from the one place she wanted, *needed* to be.

"Release me!" Her voice was harsh and visceral as she rounded on the terrified face of Mortimer. "Let me go!" She was screaming at him, and tears she hadn't realized had begun to flow down her face. He looked equally afraid, but he did not free her.

"I must return you to your quarters, lass. It was his order and I feel that it is best. Please, come with me."

Despite the panic on his face, his voice was surprisingly calm. Her anger surged. How could he be calm? How could he casually escort her from the deck when, in all likelihood, the captain was lost forever? Her mind sputtered and churned, still fogged by the wine and too much emotion to function. He tugged on her once more and she began to drift with him, her steps wooden and uneven over the boards.

"No! I am not leaving until I know he is returned!" His grip had lessened when she had become complacent and she broke free easily and turned back to the crowd, ignoring his pleas. Reaching the backs between her and the rail, she began pushing against them, shoving the burly men to whom they belonged out of her path. Had she stopped to think about the danger she was putting herself in she might have fainted, but there was only one thought on her mind.

It seemed the men were also too consumed by concern for the lost members of their band to care at the moment about her presence. Parting gradually as she pushed and prodded, they broke open a small expanse of the rail for her to lean over, farther than safety would dictate, and stare into the nothing hidden below the hull.

Darkness and the sound of waves were all her senses could manage to recognize and the panic in her heart turned into desperation. For a moment she thought to fling herself over after him. Sadly, she was at best a fair swimmer and even if she were able to find them in the dark, treacherous sea, what would she do? She did not hold the strength to save them. Frustration twisted her lovely face, turning its buttery golden to a pallid pale. She found hopelessness, her constant companion, returning to her bearing a new source.

Something draped over her shoulder. Something heavy and thick. Her eyes darted around to find Mortimer standing with her at the rail. He had wrapped her in the captain's large uniform coat. She grabbed it greedily and pulled it tight around her. She was not cold, but it was his; still filled with his marvelous heat.

"You are trembling, lass." She nodded and returned her eyes to the black before her. He turned and joined her in her search, having, thankfully, given up on shuffling her away to the make-shift stateroom so long as the captain was missing.

"Grab the lanterns, men! Spread out! They are down there somewhere, so let's give them light!" Mortimer's voice rang out in the rapt silence.

Instantly, the men around her fanned. Grabbing torches and lanterns from around the deck, they spaced themselves at the railing and held the lights over the side.

Seconds felt like hours. Time had slowed to a crawl in the strangling panic circling her heart. She had never felt fear like this, agonizing and deep and perpetual, as if it would never end. The thought that he might truly be gone forever was too much for her to handle and so she fought against it. Slowly she began to mumble to herself, chanting softly, "He has to come back..." over and over again. Mortimer stood beside her, a friend in the dark.

The sickening terror brought into clear relief something she had felt but had not yet come to terms with. Clark had become vital, essential to life. In one day he had turned from the captain into *him*. The only man in her life she had ever seen as necessary. Not even her father, a man she loved despite his indifference toward her, rated as necessary. As the thought rushed over her the tragedy of her life joined it. Why had God forsaken her? Was it not enough to bind her to the cruel and uncaring Stephen, but He had to take from her this, *him*, as well? What had she done to lose both her freedom and her love?

Her heart kicked. In her panic, a truth had surfaced. A truth that hurt her far more than she thought any pain could. She loved him; had fallen desperately in love with the mysterious and elusive Captain Clark. It had happened so fast, so quietly, she hadn't seen it approaching. Only now, faced with the very real possibility he was gone forever, did she feel the truth of it. New tears fell.

"He is strong, m'Lady. The best swimmer I have ever seen. He will find Connor and return to us. I feel it in my bones." Mortimer's voice was soft and comforting beside her. His trembling arm draped around her shoulder as she shook with her tears. He was right. Clark was an amazing man, strong, confident, and brave. Surely he would not be lost to something such as this. As hope attempted to bloom in her breast, she took a deep stabilizing breath. Turning her tear-streaked face to the old sailor beside her, her eyes carried a silent plea. He squeezed her shoulders tightly.

"If I had a woman such as you weeping for me not even God, Himself, could stop me. The captain is no fool and stubborn to boot, even more than you, m'Lady. He will not die so easily. He will come back to you, lass." As he finished, she wiped her tears from her cheeks with the lapel of his coat.

"Here! They are here!" Shouts from behind her called her away from the promise Mortimer had just given. Hope surged up her spine as she raced with the others to the voice calling out to them. As she drew near she could just see his head, his blond hair wet and dripping over his blessed face, lifted above the rail. She froze joy and panic at war for her heart. She wanted to race to him, thankful that he lived, but she couldn't move, too enraptured by what she saw. He had gone over and returned, the body of Connor flung over his broad, strong shoulders, climbing up and out of oblivion a hero. He was soaked to the bone, the white of his blouse translucently clinging to his defined frame. She was still too far away to take him in in detail as he laid the limp form of Connor on the deck. Then her view was gone, the other sailors encircling to block the scene now unfolding beyond her sight. She took a step forward, intent on pushing her way into the crowd again when hands returned to her shoulders.

"He has come back, just as I promised; now I need to get you below before he catches sight of you and I have to hear about it. Come on. You can speak with him tomorrow, lass." His hands began guiding her toward the hatch. At first, she struggled, but the joy welling up inside her at knowing he was alive, not just alive but a hero, made her compliant. She allowed Mortimer to guide her away, through the hatch and down the dark hall. As he slid the door to her cabin open, she turned to him. Smiling wanly, she sighed and kissed him on the cheek. The fear she had been smothered by was gone, and her heart felt light as a feather. "Goodnight, m'Lady." His warm smile was the last thing she saw as he slid the door closed.

How could she sleep? She could barely breathe, too nervous to even sit down. She glanced over at the blessed wing-back. The image of him standing from its mate made her smile. *His chair.* The smell of coconut oils and lavender surrounded her. She inhaled deeply. After a moment she realized she was too far from the chair to smell it. The odor had been strongest in the beginning and even then she had to bury her face into the padding to smell it as strongly as she did now. The days since had seen the scent fade to no more than a whisper in a crowded room, available to her only at the calmest moments just before she drifted off to sleep curled in its cushions. How was it so strong?

Looking around her she searched for the source until she felt the weight of the coat about her shift. Tucking her nose into the collar and inhaling, she was consumed by the aroma. His coat exuded the aroma she had come to adore with all her heart. *Him.* It was the smell of him she had fallen in love with. Moaning lightly, she wrapped the coat tighter around her and moved to the chair. Sitting as comfortably as the corset would allow, she fell into her feelings. She loved him, his smell, his eyes, his body, his honorable and brave heart, his past...everything about him, even the things she did not yet know, pulled at her, begging her to run to him. To go and drown herself in *him*.

The knock on her door several minutes later woke her from the most wondrous dreams. Standing lazily, she swayed, still half asleep to the barrier. Her hair had come free of the pins holding it and fell all about her shoulders, still covered in the blissful weight of his coat.

Pulling her door open, she looked out into the hall with half-closed, happy eyes and found the captain standing there. He had managed to get free of his wet clothes, but his hair was still damp and disheveled. The shoulders of his new, crisp white shirt were dotted with wet drips, and his eyes glittered in the singular glow of the sconce near the door she always kept lit. His mouth was drawn tight, a mix of exhaustion and what she could only describe as hunger etched in the lines of his features. She gasped at the sight of him, having only seconds ago been imagining him sharing moments with her they would never be free to experience. The sound of her enraptured intake was not lost on him. His grin was quick and warm and she blushed terribly under the look.

"Captain! I am glad to see you well. I was terribly frightened for you." Her voice cracked under the strain of holding in her feelings. She wanted to shout at him, curse his impulsive courage, whisper her love, fall into his arms, and everything in between.

"Yes, Mort said you refused to leave the deck until I surfaced. I gave him an order, Lady Everly, and I expect my orders to be followed. It was not safe for you up there, especially when I was not present. You put yourself in danger and I cannot abide that."

Her brow furrowed as she met his gaze. "No more danger than you threw yourself into! You could have lost your life tonight, and what did I risk? Not nearly so much as you and we have both surfaced safely. Your men were more concerned for you than for my presence, anyhow." Her anger waned as his grin broadened, though still did not break into a true smile. "Please spare Mortimer your anger. He did try, but I proved too determined for him and he is simply not capable of tossing me over his shoulder and hauling me away. Which, I assure you, is what would have been required to remove me from the scene." There was a devilish light in his eyes that made her stagger. Damn her impulsive tongue.

"Indeed, I shall have to remember that for the next time, I give you an order you refuse to follow." The tone of his deep voice had slipped into a raspy whisper and she felt her flesh burst into flames. She could not breathe, consumed by impulsive notions of reaching for him, flinging herself into his arms and begging for his affection. Unable to do anything more than gasp at his provocative statement, she stared at him. A rumbling chuckle echoed in his broad chest. Her hips turned to stone, aching and screaming, for what she did not know. His hand lifted, brushing a wayward strand of her divinely soft raven hair from her brow and over her shoulder, infinitely careful not to touch her. "I have come to retrieve my coat, though I see it is in use."

She blinked up at him in confusion. "I beg your pardon?" Another bout of soft rolling laughter rattled within him as he took a small step closer to her. She watched his hands lift to her shoulders as he brushed the whole of her tresses over her back. She tensed at the thought of being touched, but his fingers stayed just out of reach of her flesh. They drifted to the collar of the coat, still draped around her shoulders. Her blush deepened as she bowed her head. Sloughing the garment off one shoulder, she pulled it around in front of her, still holding it tightly to her chest and breathing in the delightful smell one last time. His hands lowered to just beyond the swell of her breast, where they gripped the fabric lightly, and her breath hitched.

"May I?" His tone was dark and decadent as his hold on the coat tightened. She could not face him, not with the heat rippling through her cheeks. She nodded slowly and released the sweet-smelling fabric to his grip. "Goodnight, my Lady. Sleep well." As he spoke, his knuckle brushed lightly under her chin, lifting her flushed face to his.

"I was sleeping quite well before you knocked, Captain." The words had slipped out. She grimaced at her lack of self-control. The fog of alcohol had lessened to the point that she now barely felt it, so this slip could not be blamed on the wine. No, his magical eyes were guilty of this slip. She felt as if he could see through her, into her; see the truth she was struggling to hide within.

"In your dress? And my coat?" His eyebrow rose teasingly as he finished and he leaned forward, coming even closer to her in the flickering yellow light. She could not answer him, only whimper at the thought that he knew what she had done. "Interesting." Realizing she was dangerously close to leaning into him, she took a small jerky step back into her room, one he followed with his own, remaining ever so close to her. Panic started to well within her. He was advancing and she was helpless.

"And in your chair, it would seem." She stammered, taking another more deliberate step back. His eyebrow rose again, but he did not advance through her threshold. "The mate to the one in your quarters, I saw it earlier. I had not realized you had parted with anything for my sake. Thank you." Her voice was weaker than it should have been, her mind too focused on evaluating every move of his face, every shift of his weight, for danger.

"In truth, all of your furniture was once in my cabin, my Lady." She gasped, glancing over her shoulder quickly to her bed and realizing that it, too, had once been his. Swallowing back her irrational desire to scream, she struggled with her next move. One she had better make quickly or things would take a turn from which there was simply no going back. She wanted his nearness far too desperately to restrain herself if he were to advance again. Looking back at him, her eyes lingered on the damp tendrils of his sandy blond hair licking at his eyebrows.

Pulling a shock of her own hair in front of her, she began distractedly stoking the length of ebony down her torso, her hands brushing over her own breast, absentmindedly. Remembering why his was wet in the first place, she blurted out, "And how is your Mr. Connor? He looked rather limp when you hoisted him over the rail." He had been too intently watching her casual caresses when she had spoken. His glowing night eyes popped to hers so suddenly, she was compelled to speak again for fear of collapse. Releasing her hair, she continued, "I...hope he is still with us?"

There was the hint of frantic distraction in her voice and he recoiled slightly, as if he could sense how uncomfortable she had become. Standing straighter and slipping back into the hallway slightly, he cleared his throat.

His voice still kind, though a bit firmer than it had been, he said, "He will be fine with a little rest. The rigging is no place to be when a rogue gust hits, and he was not properly lashed. I have changed his assignment for now. I trust he will be more careful in the future." Once finished, he looked to her for more questions but she had none to offer. For several agonizing moments, they simply stared at each other. Realizing she was lost, he smirked and bowed low.

"Goodnight, Lady Everly." Turning as if he made to leave, he paused. "May I collect you for a walk tomorrow? If you feel up to it of course?"

Answering a little too quickly, she said, "Oh, yes please, Captain. I would like that very much." She blushed as his ghostly grin widened, and then he was gone, vanished into the dark of the corridor beyond. Breathing for what felt like the first time since she had found him there, she slid the door closed and leaned heavily against it, staring at the lovely feather bed she had slept in for a week and a half. *His bed. His chair. His desk.* Everything about this cabin she loved was his.

Guilt flooded her. She had no right to hope. No right to love. No right to draw near to him knowing full well that it could not be. What else was she to do? He drew close to her and every cell in her body cried his name...a name she did not know. Shame burned in her buttery flesh. She didn't even know his first name, nor did he know hers. He had been Captain Clark for the whole of their acquaintance.

"This is absurd." Her own voice sounded foreign to her ears as it whispered into the solitude of her cabin. To get closer to him would only cause her pain. She had to stop, to keep her distance no matter the cost. However, she wasn't really sure how she would manage such a task considering how joyous her heart became in his company. Besides which, she wasn't even sure he wanted her to come closer. He had told her once she had no effect on him, and while his behavior of late had made her start to doubt, it still loomed between her and her feelings like a row of sharp spikes.

Shivering against the new cold, having lost the warm weight of his coat, she changed quickly into her nightgown and slid into his bed. She had feared sleep would not come with her mind racing with doubts and confusion, but she had been mistaken. Almost instantly she was living other lives, other futures, which did not include Stephen. Lives that lead her each time into the arms of the elusive Captain Clark. Lives that saw her filled with happiness and contentment. It was a dangerous thing, to allow such fantasies to take up residence in her heart, but lost in sleep she was powerless to control the hidden, secret desires of her soul.

Chapter 8

Over the next three days, she found her singular promise to keep her distance becoming a hollow vow. Each day he appeared at her door ready to walk with her at length on the deck of his ship. While the chill of autumn was creeping in with the new harsher winds that billowed, she felt warmth radiating through her as she strolled with him. She learned much. The ship had become her home and she ardently studied its ins and outs with the same scrutiny she had shown her private rooms in her father's house growing up. She knew each piece by name and the purpose of each line and tie.

She had also learned much about the man. She discovered his naval history as he shared tales of battles he had engaged in during the War Between the States. How he had become a captain only two years into his service due to the death of his superior and that he had flourished in his new position, running secret, perilous missions up the embattled coast of the Carolinas.

Each story only heightened her fascination. He had seen so much in his short time in His Majesty's service and, after the war was ended, as a reward for his loyalty and dedication, he had been offered a high position that would have made him a political figure in London rather than a leader at sea. A life he claimed to have no desire to live. Against the advice of everyone he knew and his mysterious family, he refused the position and acquired the *Siren* and has been wonderfully content ever since.

He had maintained their story for story agreement, insisting on a piece of her for each of himself he relinquished. She had shared her experiences at Oxford and bits and pieces of her childhood, though, in truth, she felt he was cheated with each exchange. His stories were full of danger and intrigue while hers were full of her mischief and tales of lessons and accomplishments made in the quiet of a lecture hall.

She only wished he would speak of his youth. Each time she asked a question about his family or his life before the Navy, he would share enough to answer her query, but not enough to paint even a partial picture of the life he had lived. In truth, she didn't much care who he had been as a child. It was the man walking beside her, holding her arm close to his chest, which thrilled her and filled her dreams with ever more sinful exchanges. Images of which flashed in her mind each and every time he would squeeze her closer or smirk down at her the way he always tended to.

Their walks had changed as well. While the first was a solitary stroll, the second day had seen the crew in their places, busy adjusting and repositioning the sails with the fickle breeze. She had hesitated at the top of the stairs, but he assured her she was safe. He confessed rather shyly that the ship had lost valuable time as a result of her freedoms and while he did not wish to deny her, he could no longer afford to keep his men below for an hour or so each day. They had already lost too much wind. Her tension was high at first, but his words rang true as she barely noticed eyes on her as they moved. By the end of their walk, she felt perfectly at ease in the presence of his men, though she doubted they felt the same.

As they stood at the bow on the third day, he confessed softly he had grown weary of her drab dresses, and despite his fears, he would very much like to see her comfortable in her trousers again. The heat that washed over his face as his eyes fleetingly brushed down the length of her body beside him made her heart stop. She had leaned into him, wanting to fall head first into the deep royal of his irises. It had been he who pulled away from her advance, though the pink in his deeply tanned cheeks had intensified. The night he came to retrieve his coat she had felt hopeful he wanted to draw near to her the way she longed to be close to him, but ever since that night, he had maintained his distance. His comment on the dinghy rang in her ears as truth, even though he did blush more often and he refused to walk with her without holding her forearm against his ribs. There was a new formality to him that stung her slightly. Her logical mind understood the need, but her impulsive side wished he would be the aggressor so she could give in and be blameless.

Standing beside him just after luncheon on the fifth day, leaning limply against the rail on the poop deck, she breathed in deeply. The sun was bright and the air, though a bit cooler than the day before, was sweet and light as it whispered through her loosely bound hair. It stirred the curly tendrils that had sprung loose all around her face and they tickled her cheeks as they moved. She was so grateful for his permission, being rid of that blasted corset chiefest among them.

Reveling in her freedom, she stretched her arms over her head, enjoying the way the leather vest shifted over her abdomen and tugged tight across her bosom. She sighed lazily to herself as her eyes drifted with the clouds above. His chuckle beside her drew her gaze. He was watching her, a strange look of sadness etched into his features, considering the light grin curling his lips.

Brushing one of the long silky spirals on her cheek over her ear, careful not to touch her flesh, he mused, "You remind me of a contented house cat, my Lady."

She laughed lightly at his allusion. "I feel rather like a content house cat, Captain Clark. Thanks to you I can breathe without pain. I would love to stand face to face with the person, no doubt a man, responsible for corsets. I would, most likely, bring shame on my family with the words I would say. But, oh, how wonderful it would be to say them." He stifled a laugh with the back of his hand as his eyes devoured her one last time before returning to the horizon.

"I have no doubt that you would, my Lady. I dare say at this point there is little you could say that would surprise me." His whole body seemed to rise and fall with silent laughter. She snickered at him.

"I am sure if I truly tried I could surprise you, Captain. My father used to say there was no end to the trouble my tongue could cause." His body tensed as it brushed along her side and she chuckled out loud for the both of them knowing he would not.

"Perhaps this is forward, my Lady, but I can no longer bear to hear you call me Captain." His eyes found hers and she smiled up at him, her feelings bubbling to the surface, not that she was interested in containing them.

"And what am I to call you, if not Captain Clark?" She bit her bottom lip as his cheekbones tinted pink. God what a glorious sight to see a man such as he, strong and large, blush like a green lad.

Clearing his throat, he struggled to maintain eye contact with her but failed, as if it pained him to gaze upon her. Casting his eyes back to the water, he mumbled, "Tiberius. Call me Tiberius, my Lady." Her smile faltered. His first name was now hers to know.

As friendly as they had become, she would have, under any other circumstances, expected to be on first-name terms long ago. But not with him. The captain had proven himself to be as shrewd and guarded a man as ever she had met. For him to offer that small bit of himself was tremendous, and she had come to know him well enough to see it for the revelation it was.

Gasping, she turned her eyes from his profile. Watching it tense with anxiety was hurting her heart.

With a rasp to her soft voice, she returned his gesture with her own. "Vanessa."

"What was that, my Lady?" His eyes fell on her once more. She couldn't see him looking at her. She couldn't bring herself to face that look. She could feel his eyes moving over her face, however, scorching the flesh as they caressed her.

"My name, Cap...Tiberius, in exchange for yours. Call me Vanessa." She swallowed as her small voice finished her response.

"Vanessa. It is a lovely name for a most lovely creature. Vanessa." The sound of her name in his melodiously deep tones sent shivers down her spine. Feeling heat rush through her hips, she chanced a look at his beloved face. Standing over her, his head was lowered from his shoulders and she tensed, drawing in a sudden breath with anticipation.

"Vanessa..." No more than a whisper, her name had become a plea, a sweet demand. Licking her suddenly dry lips, she began to ease up onto her toes...*so close...so very close...*

Screams rang out behind them. Cries of pain and panic from each man working the lines created a chorus of terror. Spinning on their heels, both she and Tiberius turned in unison to see the source of the sudden ruckus. Every man was racing in a singular direction, though away from or toward the danger she could not be sure. Agony was etched on each hardened face and the scene of a dozen imposing sailors looking so frightened sent crippling fear through her even as she and the captain turned in the self-same direction and joined their race.

Reaching the rail of the quarter-deck, she looked over to find a large pool of blood smeared into a trail leading to the base of the mizzen mast. There, being propped against the wooden column was a young man, his shirt gaping at the side and allowing an incredible amount of blood to spill over the boards.

"Vanessa, go to your cabin at once. I need to see to this." She heard him, but his words did not slow her. She had the knowledge to handle this. She was heading for the stairs, and the injured man when his strong hands clasped her shoulders. Large strong fingers dug into her flesh as they tugged her to a stop and spun her around. Tiberius towered over her. "Where do you think you are going? I need you below. This is no place for a woman."

Wrenching free of his grasp, she returned to her course. "Nonsense. Alfred was one of the best surgeons in London and he taught me much. If you wish your man to live I suggest you leave me be, Tiberius." She clicked her teeth at him as she jumped the last two steps and launched at the wounded man. Perhaps her sass was unwarranted, but she refused to butled off, not again. Sliding in the growing pool of blood at his side, she barked at the men surrounding them. Looks of shock and confusion twisted their normally stern faces.

"Lay him down. Flat, yes...just like that. Now, I need water, needle and thread, and cotton cloth. Hurry!" The men simply stared at her, their jaws gaping as the sailor sprawled prone before her, bled to death rapidly. Losing her patience, she shouted, "Now! He has precious little time for you to gawk at me!" Her anger seemed to rouse them. Three men peeled off from the group to fulfill her wishes as she pulled her sleeves up.

Her fingers trembled for a second at the edge of the bloody tear in his shirt. Just below the layer was a wound of unknown magnitude she had pledged she could heal. Her tongue, in a desperate play at proving herself to the captain that haunted her dreams and saw her as little more than a lovely bookworm, had placed a great weight upon her shoulders in the form of a promise. One that, in all likelihood, she could not keep.

Taking a stabilizing breath, she pulled the shredded fabric away, tearing it open from neck to waist, revealing the horrendous slash across the young man's side. The wound, deep and fierce, brought bile halfway up her throat. She had seen bad before. One of the diggers had put a pick ax through his thigh at the site just over four months ago and she had stabilized him while another had run to town for a doctor. But this was considerably worse.

Clearing her head of all thoughts but what she knew needed to be done for the sailor at her knees, she began examining the wound.

It was a strange sort of gash. The edges seemed burned and, though it wasn't exactly a slice, it bled like a knife had cut straight through an artery. Within seconds the man who had gone to fetch water returned. Taking the bucket he extended her, she looked up at the two burly barrel-chest older sailors across the body and said, "Hold him." While the look in their eyes told her they had no idea what she planned to do, they nodded woodenly. One placed his large hands onto the injured man's shoulders and the other braced his hip and arm. Tipping the bucket, she drowned the wound. It looked almost like a burn, only burns didn't bleed and this one bled incessantly, and from everywhere.

"How did this happen?" As she applied pressure to the location where fresh blood bubbled to the surface, she looked for the face of Mortimer, frantic and pale beside her. "Mort! How did this happen?" She repeated her question, before looking back down at the mess still needing attention. Strips of cotton filled her vision. The man sent after the wadding had returned. Her brow furrowing, she took the cloth and set some of it aside, the rest she folded quickly and replaced her hand with the batting.

"He was manning a rigging line with it snapped. Those ropes are powerful tight, Miss. It backlashed on him. Damn near split him in two...sorry, m'lady, I didn't mean to swear." Despite the gravity of the situation, his concern for her female sensibilities amused her.

Snickering, she said, "It's quite all right Mort. It did indeed damn near split him in two. So, this is little more than a rope burn, good Lord. I need that needle and thread! Now!" The batting was beginning to work, and the bleeding slowed, but she needed to close the opening in the vein before any more of his precious liquid escaped him.

"Here! I have it here!" The man who only days ago had been hauled over the side unconscious, Connor, slid in the pool of blood beside her as he extended the needle and spool of thread. His hips cracked against the deck, but he stifled his groan for her sake.

"I need you to thread it for me; can you do that, Connor?" He blinked at her, as if unsure what to do next. Or maybe it was that he hadn't any idea she knew his name. "Connor! Thread the needle...please." He was still frozen, unable to move. She heaved an annoyed sigh. She couldn't do it herself. She couldn't afford to lessen the pressure on the wound to take care of it, but it needed to be done.

"Move aside, Connor. Let me have that." Tiberius's large hands landed on his shoulders, shifting him away. Crouching down next to her, he took the needle and thread and readied her suture. "Like this?" She blinked up at him, too busy to admire his fortitude. Taking the loaded needle from his fingers, she held his gaze.

"When I remove the cotton it will, in all likelihood, resume bleeding. I need to get the vein closed as fast as possible. If it starts bleeding from another location I will need you to apply pressure there until I am finished. Do you understand?" She waited for him to nod, then pulled the cloth away. A small spurt erupted from the opening before she could pinch it shut.

There was a gasp from every crewman now crowding around the scene. Even Tiberius seemed to recoil from the site. She wanted to as well. Despite all of Alfred's training, the sight and smell of blood turned her stomach and made her chest ache. Poising the needle, she took a deep breath and steadied her nerves before she began. With calm hands, she plunged the needle in and pulled the stitch. Then another. With each in and through, less of the red brine-smelling liquid leaked from the man, no more than twenty and pale as lily petals, before her. Finishing the last, she bent closer to the wound than she should have liked and snipped the thread with her teeth, tasting the man on her lips.

Studying the entire gash, she found no more locations of profuse bleeding. "Reload the needle. I need to close his abdomen next." She sat up a bit straighter as she spoke to him, rubbing the back of her blood-covered hand across her sweat-drenched forehead. As Tiberius took the needle his fingers brushed lightly over her red-stained hands. Her veneer faltered as his eyes pierced her. He nodded slightly and went back to the needle now in his grip. Breaking contact with him, she looked over at Mort. "I need you to move a cot into my room."

"I beg your pardon?" Tiberius's voice was almost shrill as he questioned her current request. She rolled her eyes and scoffed in her throat.

"His bleeding is stopped but he is by no means in the clear. He will need constant attention until the threat of infection is passed, and I will need to change the dressing every few hours. He is not out of the woods, Captain. The choice is to either put him in my room with me or to move me into the bunk room. I will leave the decision to you." She watched the horror flood his face and snickered. "I did not think that would be acceptable. Now, the needle, if you please. Mort, I will also need a stretcher of some kind, something stable with which to move him. The less jostling the better, if you understand me."

She cleared her throat, feeling his fiery gaze burning her flesh as he stared at her. She couldn't look up at him, couldn't return the eye contact he was so obviously demanding. Instead, she began slowly stitching the young sailor's gaping slash. Inch by inch she closed the garish wound, the whole time musing to herself that if he lived through this, it would be a most impressive scar for him to share with the females he entertained in ports of call in their future.

She had just started the last stitch as several men returned with a makeshift gurney. Snipping the

138

thread with her teeth one more time, she looked up at the frightened faces all around her.

"All right, lift him gently. All together now." Once he was loaded onto the gurney, she stood slowly beside him. Folding his hands across his chest, she sighed with her whole body. "Gently carry him to my quarters." Turning to the two men behind her, she said, "I will need all the cotton cloth you can spare, cut into strips, no more than four inches wide and as long as you can manage, and several more buckets of fresh water, if they can be spared." They nodded and followed the stretcher into the hold. She walked shakily to the rail and cast her eyes out at the water.

"Vanessa..." His voice was right behind her, so close to the back of her head. The horror of the last few minutes, something cold knowledge had allowed her to temporarily block out of her mind, consumed her and at that moment she desperately needed his comfort. His men gone, all retreating below deck to see to their injured comrade, she turned and pressed against him, burying her face into his firm chest. He gasped at first and then wrapped his arms around her, squeezing her as if it would be enough to wipe away the recent past. She could sense his breath, hear his heartbeat, and feel his lips pressing into her hair. She wasn't crying. Not exactly. She was still too caught in her own adrenalin. After seconds that felt like lifetimes, she smiled against the strength of his muscled chest.

She whispered into his flesh, "I should go and tend to him. He will need me if he is to live through this, though there is no guarantee he will." She didn't really want to leave the stalwart comfort of his muscled grip. His smell was overwhelming and delicious and the feel of his arms was the closest thing to home she had felt in months, maybe years, but if she did not break from him now she might never be able to. He sighed into her hair and eased his arms from around her. Without looking into his face, too afraid of what might be lurking there, she slipped from his grasp and retreated down the hatch and out of sight.

Chapter 9

Terrance was a fighter. That was his name. She had learned it from Mort after she had arrived in her quarters. He was an attractive lad, perhaps a bit sharp for her, though his strange pallid color left much to be desired. The fever had come shortly after he had been brought to her room and it burned hot for three days straight. Tiberius had been upset with the idea of her sharing her space with him, but after seeing his second mate consumed with fever he seemed to resign himself to the need. He did insist a curtain be hung, cordoning off the portion of her room containing her wing-back and her pot-bellied stove for him, and the rest for her private use. The stove had not been allowed to cool since the day he was carried in, burning hot non-stop as his chills caused violent shaking and she feared the tremors would undo her stitches and cause his prolific bleeding to resume.

She had spent hour after hour by his side, wiping the sweat that beaded constantly from his brow and forcing water down his throat. His bandages and dressings were changed almost hourly as she feared the onset of an infection. She was well aware one often accompanied wounds that were not properly cleaned and his fever was a tell-tale sign one already raged within him. At least he had remained unconscious almost the entire time. She had no laudanum to give him and the pain from the injury he had sustained would certainly have caused him to scream and writhe in agony. An occurrence she was becoming more and more sure would have been beyond what she could manage to tolerate.

As it was, she was becoming weary of his constant need for attention. While she truly cared if the poor man lived or died, her nerves were shredded and she had not gotten more than forty-five minutes of sleep at a time in all three days. Her only consolation was the visits from Tiberius she received randomly throughout the days and nights. Each only lasted minutes, but somehow filled her heart with enough fresh hope and joy to sustain her. He claimed the visits were to see to his man, and indeed he often asked after his condition, though most of his inquiries were for her wellbeing. He claimed she was beginning to look worn and, while it was true her health and color were starting to pale, his was taking a far greater turn for the worse.

His crew was minimal for his vessel size, as he desired to grant each man the greatest pay possible, but it also meant each sailor was already working to the fullest extent a reasonable captain, of which he could certainly be ascribed, could expect. As a result, he had picked up the duties of the man lying prone on the cot in her quarters. He did this in addition to his responsibilities as captain and it was beginning to show. He had three days' worth of beard growth shadowing his handsome features and his eyes had become drawn and sunken. The light that flashed in the dark depths of his navy irises had all but gone out and there was a new rasp to his voice she could only attribute to exhaustion. It was clear to her that, while she was getting bits and pieces of scattered sleep, he was getting next to none. His double shifts consumed all of his time, save the precious moments he shared with her.

Though the embrace she had exchanged with him after the frightening ordeal had filled her dreams with even more wonderful intimacy, it had been fleeting and, despite the overpowering desire she had to repeat it, his exhaustion and her distraction had not allowed the event to transpire. He was again distancing himself from her physically, though he was showing far more concern for her emotional well-being than ever before. He could not take her up on deck anymore, as neither of them had the freedom for such pleasures. She was confined to her cabin to tend the wounded Mr. Haddock and he was obliged to climb into the rigging each and every day.

On each visit, he expressed his regret at this turn of events, a certain longing in his dulcet timbre, but was confessedly unable to alter them at present.

In the wee hours of the fourth day, long before the glow of the rising sun crested the horizon, she was wakened by Terrance's grumbling as he attempted to sit up. She jumped from the wing-back faster than her breath and her balance afforded, as she hurled herself at him. She had to stop him; he was in no condition to stand on his own. Landing hard on her knees at his bedside, she huffed slightly.

"Terrance, please, still yourself. Your wound is not yet healed enough for movement."

"M'Lady! Where am I? What the devil is going on? What has happened?" His shock at her appearance by his bedside faded fast in the face of his confusion. No doubt he had lost all memory of the accident itself and she was quite sure, aside from flashes and impressions from the last three days, he held no recollection of them either. He allowed his body to go limp and flop back to the cot, too weak to hold his weight propped on his elbows any longer.

"The rigging line nearly severed you in twain. The wound is closed now, and," she placed the back of her hand on his forehead, "it appears your fever has broken. You will live, Mr. Haddock, though I am afraid there was nothing I could do to prevent the scar you shall bear. I apologize, but you will carry that mark for all your days to come. In a few more, the stitches holding you closed shall no longer be necessary, but I dare say we will be long in the Thames before you will be right again. As it is, you should no longer need my constant care."

Standing, she smiled down at him and moved beyond the curtain. Tugging the line to signal the helm she was in need, she sighed with relief. She had spent the last seventy-two hours on edge, fearing he would be lost and what consequences that might bring upon her. Now that he was finally on the mend she felt a huge burden lift from her shoulders.

"You have saved me!? M'Lady...I...I thank you, but...how?" His voice was breathy and soft, but surprisingly strong as it drifted through the curtain to where she leaned against her door frame. It called her back to him. "Could I trouble you for some water, m'Lady?" She snickered a little as she resumed her post next to his cot; though this time she landed much more softly on her knees, wanting to spare herself a repeat of the pain that had only just given way from her start earlier.

"Of course, sir." Giving him a drink from the ladle hanging on the bucket of water by his bedside, she continued, "As to how, you may not know this, but my late husband was a brilliant surgeon in his life. He taught me much and I had several occasions in the last year to put his teachings to practical use, healing wounds and treating sickness, though I will admit your injury was by far the most gruesome I have yet witnessed. I thought sure I would lose you there for a while. Tyb...Captain Clark will be glad to hear you are on the mend. With your fever broken and your strength returning, he will no doubt have you moved back to the bunk room. As for me, I think that might be best." As he drank the whole of a third ladle, a knock sounded firmly on her door.

Excusing herself from his bedside, she answered to find Mortimer standing hopeful and terrified at the same time before her. Her quick smile seemed to relieve all of the tension holding him rigid. "So, lass, does that mean our man is on the mend?" His voice was giddy as his concern warmed her heart.

"It does indeed, Mortimer. Come in and see for yourself. Our master Haddock will soon be right as rain, though a little worse for wear on the eyes, I'm afraid." He returned her smile as he moved past her with a bow. He slid through the curtain to his mate, and so she gave them a bit of privacy, at least as much as the flimsy barrier would allow. She set about preparing a bundle of cloth bandages to accompany him to the crew's quarters as she was sure he would be leaving soon, no longer needing continuous care. Their conversation turned a bit ruckus, laughter and cheers ringing through her space, and she was forced to enter the curtain to calm her patient. Smiling at Mort, she cleared her throat. "I think that the captain will now insist he be moved to his bunk. He cannot move quiet yet on his own, but he is more than capable to tending to his own bandages now."

Turning her face to Terrance, she continued, "I will check in on you, of course, but I believe your pride will give you the strength to see to yourself. Now, Mort, fetch some men to aid him. As I said, he cannot walk on his own yet, but I am sure the men will be as pleased as you were to see him up and about. No doubt they feared I would lose him." Though he shook his head in argument, she could see the truth of her words reflected in his eyes. Most men found little faith in the competency of women, especially when such serious circumstances existed.

"Aye, lass. They will be right proud of you in this." Grinning down at Terrance one last time, he nodded to Vanessa and took his leave. Within moments he returned with the same two massive men that had lugged her trunk down from the boarding house. There was a change in them. They actually attempted to smile at her as they entered her space and lifted Terrance, cot and all, and carted him off. Mort collected the bundle from her and soon butled after them, leaving her in blessed solitude for the first time in days. Her bed veritably screamed her name the instant her door closed and she caved to its demand for her company as soon as she freed herself from her clothes and donned her nightgown.

Sleep came fast to her wearied body. It was just past noon when a thunderous knock woke her from the most blessed sleep she was quite sure she had ever had. On the other side of the door, she could hear the voice of Tiberius, her beloved captain, calling her name with concern in his tone. Smiling, she climbed from the bed and pressed against the door, unable, in her current attire, to open it for him. "Captain, I am awake now, but as I am not properly dressed at the moment I must beg your indulgence for a few minutes to right this situation before I can allow you entry." She could hear him stifle a gasp from the other side and her heart fluttered at the sound. The idea that images in his mind of her in nothing more than a dressing gown affected him so was intoxicating.

"Aye, Vanessa, I shall wait as long as I need, and again, call me by my name, not title. I am Tiberius to you. At least, I hope I am." She rushed to dress. He was at her door and she wanted more than anything to see him. She slid into her trousers and a blouse. Forgoing her vest, she hastily pulled her hair back and finished tucking in her shirt tail as she slid the door open. He turned to meet her smile and returned it with that selfsame ghost of grin he always had for her.

"I dare say, my dear, you look far better with a few hours of good sleep on you. Your color has returned and your eyes no longer carry the weariness they did last evening when I paid you a visit." He nodded as he entered slightly into her quarters, reaching for a strand of her hair she had failed to collect in her haste. He allowed the length to slip between his fingers before releasing it to once again graze her breast. As it fell a tremor seemed to move through him and she found it contagious. Reaching out one massive, muscle-bound arm, he tugged firmly at the curtain still hanging from the ceiling, freeing it from the nails with which it had been secured and returning her stateroom to its former size. Wadding the sheet over on itself, he turned and tossed it back through the door before he bent and retrieved her cooling lunch tray from the floor just outside.

"Ah, I see John has kept his schedule. Place it on the desk if you would, I will see to it when you have left me." Her request would bring him fully in the room, somewhere he had not ventured as yet. She moved to the side as he reluctantly entered farther into her space. The pink that highlighted his cheeks was endearing as he almost tiptoed through her room. "I dare say you could do with a little good sleep yourself Tiberius. You look positively dreadful." He laughed, full and hearty, but as his back was to her she was denied the smile that accompanies such mirth. By the time he turned back to face her, his visage was stoic once again.

"It seems my crew agrees with you, though I dare say they were a bit more political in their assertion. How very blunt you have become, Vanessa. They came to me just this morning, having agreed to share the void Haddock has left in our business so that I no longer feel it necessary to bear the load alone." She smiled warmly as she drew slightly closer to him. Her hand lifted as if to brush over his arm, but she lowered it almost immediately, suddenly sure he would shrink from her touch.

"They care for you, as do I, though they fear being sacked if they approach you too honestly, whereas I carry no fear of you at all." He took a step toward her in the empty quiet of her space.

150

"Do you, now?" His tone had shifted as it had the night he had dove over the side after Connor, but this time she did not back down. Leaning forward slightly, she stared into his eyes, as if daring him to act.

"Indeed," was all she was able to say, and even that was little more than a whisper, though not because she was afraid. She was attempting to tease him and his slight gasp and uneven backward step told her she had succeeded.

Clearing his throat with some difficulty, he turned and headed for her door. "Well, I came to say that I am most pleased with the significant improvement in Terrance, and it is owed to you. You have done the *Siren* a great service and I am indebted to you. I should let you rest, you have earned it, and so have I. I shall give you a day or so more to refresh yourself and then, with your permission, I should like to provide you with your necessary fresh air." He opened her door and moved into the hall. Turning to look over his shoulder at her, he winked, pulling his moon-shaped scar around his midnight eye a little tighter and causing her breath to catch. "Thank you, Vanessa. I am proud to have you aboard."

Then he was gone. Her body was on fire, tingling and tensing to surge after him. Sighing, she turned back to her lunch, growing cold on her desk. Even though the meal had been sitting for nearly an hour it was still delicious. Once she had cleaned her plate, she placed the tray in the hall as usual. As she eased her door closed, the need for sleep crept once more up her spine. Back in the feather softness, she closed her eyes again and felt his arms circle around her, pulling her into him. The feeling from days earlier had not left her flesh and as she drifted into dreams, the thought of his lips on hers consumed her heart in a way she had never known before.

Chapter 10

She did not wake for dinner, nor for breakfast the next morning, sleeping soundly till almost noon. Her eyes drifted open on a sigh, the sound of waves and a shanty song about a savior maiden drifting through the open cannon port on the chill air. She felt so much better, rested and refreshed, so much different than the past few days. She slid out of bed quickly, making her way lightly to her dresser and rifling through her drawers for the day's clothes. She was certain as soon as he awoke he would come for her and she was bent she would be ready. She dressed with haste, the chill air speeding her along. The fire in her stove had burned out and her cabin had taken on a cold that made her nose and fingers ache.

Relighting the fire, she decided to busy herself with the work she had neglected for over a week. Trying to focus her mind on the relics, she whiled away an hour in what felt like seconds. Stretching her arms over her head, the door to her room burst open. Connor ran up to her, completely out of breath and in a panic the likes of which she had not seen. His face had lost all its sun-kissed color and his eyes were a wide and hollow gray, fear surging like an incoming tide within him. "Connor! What has happened? What are you doing here?"

He was completely out of breath and as he reached her he doubled over, struggling to catch his wind.

"Cap...captain...hurt...need..." She did not need to hear anymore. She rushed past the poor young man still trying desperately to finish his now superfluous statement. The hall seemed a mile long as she ran.

Bursting through the hatch, she called his name, "Tiberius!"

"He is here!" Mortimer was standing over the figure of a man slumped against a crate farther down the port side ahead of her. Her pace never slowed as she crested the hatch and turned toward them.

"I am fine, Vanessa, it is but a trifle." Tiberius's voice was strained. He was attempting a light tone, but the unmistakable tint of pain hung on his words. Clearing Mortimer, he came into view, leaning to one side against the crate. She gasped as she took him in. A large shard of wood, just over an inch in diameter and nearly six inches long, splintered and fractured along the end, protruded from the meat of his right shoulder, just below the seam of his shirt. There was surprisingly little blood, considering the depth, and she teetered between laughter and tears.

"That would not be my description." She sank to her knees next to him to get a closer look at the new emergency she was summoned to solve. *Could she not have one day?* "How did you manage to do this? I thought you were going to get some rest. Take a day to recover? Can I not have one day of peace?" She smiled sadly down at him as he returned her grin and shook his head.

"I told them to leave you be, that I could pull it out on my own. Seems I cannot resist a high weather day in the rigging. I apologize, Sweets." His humorous comment coupled with his new endearment towards her made her blush. "But, as you are here now, would you be so kind as to show me a bit of your, now famous, attention? You have proven your skill and it would seem I am in need of it." He grimaced with the pain of being skewered and her smile quickly faded.

Sighing with equal parts frustration and flattery, she said, "If I must. Mortimer, Connor, get him into his quarters. I shall need a few things as well."

One of the large men from the day before stepped forward. "We have already sent for water, cloth, and a needle and thread, ma'am." She turned and smiled at him, nodding her approval.

"Lovely. And a bottle of rum, if you would please." He blinked at her as if she had grown a second head and was attempting to argue with it. She sighed and continued, "Not for me, for him. Mr. Haddock was unconscious when I was tending to him, but the captain will be lucid, at least he will be without the rum, and the pain will likely be more than I can bear to inflict. Alcohol will deaden his senses enough to make the work that must be done bearable. Now, Rum. Thank you." He stood for a moment in shock and then scuttled off to fill her unorthodox request. Huffing, she turned and hurried in the opposite direction toward his cabin.

Pushing through his door, she almost ran into Mortimer as he was turning to leave. "Oh, Mort, you're leaving? I thought perhaps you would stay and help..." Before she could finish, two more men brushed in behind her, deposited their load of supplies, and then retreated. The second paused in front of her to hand her a bottle of rum, three-quarters full. He snickered at her shyly before following his friend out. Connor, having helped Tiberius into a dining chair, exited next, leaving only she, Mort, and the injured captain behind. Mort smiled, bowed, and disappeared without a word.

"I told them to go. I thought you would feel calmer without an audience. Now, what should we do first?" In spite of the hunk of wood protruding from his shoulder, his tone had turned strangely provocative. She shook her head and moved closer, centering the bottle in her hands and extending it to him. "I think not, Sweets. I don't drink. Call it a lifestyle choice."

She raised her brow at him and held the bottle farther out. "But I insist. Surely a little alcohol will not hurt you. You had something to drink the night I dined with you, did you not?" He took the bottle and promptly set it aside on the table.

"Nothing more than water, lass." She almost growled at him. Groaning in her throat, she moved closer and lifted the bottle again, thrusting it into his firm chest, unable to miss the way his pecks taunted and shuddered under her touch.

"You refilled my wine three times and all you had was water! You certainly are a cad! I demand you drink this, and now. Retribution for the embarrassment I brought upon myself that night." Her anger lapped at her cheeks as he did little more than smirk and chuckle. Gritting her teeth, she tried a different approach. "Tiberius, please. All kidding aside, you must drink. The process of removing that

157

spike will be most unpleasant and, though you are a very strong man, the pain will be intense." His hand reached out and wrapped around the bottle, and hers holding it. Pulling her a bit closer to him, he flashed his eyes.

"Vanessa, dearest, I have not had a drop of alcohol since before I entered the Navy. I cannot break that vow now. I can handle the pain, I promise." The softness of his voice, and the feel of his fingers brushing lightly over her own, sent shivers down her spine. Releasing the bottle, she pulled her hand free and took a small step back. Her face darkened with concern.

"You may well be right, but have you considered that I cannot? The thought of causing you that much pain hurts my heart, Tiberius. Do not make me watch you suffer in silence." He watched her for a moment before sighing and removing the cork from the bottle with his teeth. The tip of his tongue inadvertently lapped at the rim and caused the space between her hips to throb. Casting one last sad look at her over the mouth, he put it to his lips and took a long, deep draw, his face bunching against the taste. He grunted in his throat before taking another, longer drink.

"Beware, my dear. Liquor has an ill effect on me."

"I have never met a man on whom it did not, Tiberius. I can handle anything you throw at me so long as it is not the furniture." She snickered, but he did not return her mirth.

"Vanessa, I'm serious. There is a good reason I swore away from alcohol so long ago. I fear what I will say to you...what I might do if..., but what is done is done." Stuffing the cork back into the bottle with his good hand, he returned it to her nearly empty. She gaped at it. Even a drunkard would lose himself at that amount and he hadn't had a drop in over a decade. As she set the bottle aside, he shifted uncomfortably.

"Remove your shirt."

"Heh, I had no idea you could be so forward, my Lady. Such impropriety..." He tisked her even as he acquiesced. Grimacing as he tugged his whole arm free, the shirt fell loosely from his injured shoulder and hung on the shard. Focused on her task, she moved forward and slit his sleeve from wrist to splinter with a knife from the table, successfully removing his shirt entirely. With the garment freed, his torso, bare and beautiful, spread before her. The gasp escaped her before she could hold it in. He was magnificent. Finely crafted muscles coursed below taunt, tanned flesh and a dusting of light brown hair.

Her mouth went dry as her eyes traced the lines that marked his body. Scars, of all sizes and shapes, swirled on his flesh. He was a relic. A monolith. A piece of art covered in hieroglyphics and symbols begging her to read them. She wanted to trace each one with her fingertips, learn each curve and grove of them, and run her tongue along their pale smooth flesh. The need was so great she trembled with it.

"I am sorry I frighten you. These scars are the result of years at sea. Terrance is not the first sailor to be caught by a lash line." As he spoke, he gestured to a rather wide mark along the left side of his rippled abdomen. She could do little but lick her lips. "My body disturbs you. I beg your forgiveness..."

"Frighten? No. Fascinate, perhaps, but not frighten." Her voice had all but left her as she reached for him. Before her fingers could brush along his skin, his hand caught hers.

"Talk such as that will soon become dangerous, Sweets. The rum is already starting to cloud my mind. In moments I will not have the strength to refuse such a bold invitation. Perhaps you had better begin." He squeezed her fingers bracingly before moving them toward the supplies arranged on the table beside them. There was a dare there, but she only nodded woodenly. She peeled her eyes from his flesh and looked down at her tools. Frowning, she moved away to the door and opened it wide, calling for Mortimer. Connor appeared instead, ready to help.

"I need you to fetch my kit. It is in the top left-hand drawer of the desk in my room. Please hurry." Instructions delivered, he headed to the hatch and she returned to Tiberius. His eyes had already begun to glaze over and his jaw had gone slack, causing his grin to slide to one side, making it strangely even more alluring. Grasping the large piece of wood, she looked down at him. "Brace yourself." She did not wait for him to respond. With a firm jerk, she pulled hard on the large splinter, freeing the bulk of it from his meat. A plethora of smaller shards remained in the now open hole in his muscle and blood began to ooze slowly from the wound that had been plugged only seconds ago. He groaned loudly.

"Next time, give a fellow a chance to follow your instructions, will you?" She could hear the pain in his voice as he tried to hide his discomfort with a forced chuckle. Frowning, she blew a tendril of her ebony hair away from her cheek and drew closer to the wound. Trying to focus on the task at hand and not the entrancing scent of him that enveloped her senses at this distance; she began to pick at the remaining pieces. Starting with the largest, she pulled them one at a time free of his wound. When only the very small ones remained, she looked back at the door. "Where is that boy?"

Puffing the curl away again, she returned to the door and opened it. Leaning out, she stared at the hold hatch for a long moment. Giving up, she meant to try and get more from his flesh, when her name echoed across the deck. Ignoring Connor's impertinence at the use of her first name, she turned back to him as he ran to her. Handing her the case, he was once again out of breath. For such a healthy young man he seemed to get winded exceedingly easily. For a second she wondered if he suffered from some malady of body, but that would have to wait. Taking the case, she did not address him but returned immediately to her more pressing task.

The man she faced when she returned was no longer entirely the captain. The rum had set in and she could see it on him like a uniform. His face had become flushed and his eyes had a glare to them that was hot and bordered on violence. "Tiberius? Are you well?" For a moment she feared he would be sick, and then his posture changed, but he did not speak. Deciding he was too far gone for conversation, she moved close and unfurled her kit on the table. Pulling her tweezers from the pack, she crouched close to his shoulder and began to pull the tiny splinters from him. As she bent over his shoulder, only inches away, she heard him groan deep in his chest, and the sound, so utterly masculine and obvious, made her hips tense and her heart beat faster. With his groan, his head lowered over her, his nose burying in her hair as he breathed her in deep.

She gasped as she leaned back. He was looking at her like a starving animal would eye its prey and it turned her blood to lava. Danger filled the inches between them and she recoiled at the realization of it. Before she could stand, he reached out and brushed the back of his fingers across her cheek. "You are so beautiful...achingly beautiful, Vanessa. I *ache* for you."

For a moment she leaned into his touch, his words ringing in her ears like music, but it couldn't last. His mind was muddled by the rum and she soon remembered his warning. He was not himself. The affection was not truly his and she could not in good conscience make it hers. Trying to keep her mind on her task, she grabbed his hand, pressed it lightly to her stomach, and stood beside him.

Leaning over to get the needle and thread, she attempted to stifle his advance. "Tiberius, please, the rum has you. Try to remember yourself. You told me once I had no effect on you. Don't you remember?" She was making a play at distraction, but even in his clouded state, he was not falling for it. Pulling free of her feeble grip, his hands spanned her waist as he pulled her to stand in front of him.

"Ah, Sweets, what I said was that you had no effect you need apologize for. If *you* can recall. You affect me greatly; have since the moment I laid eyes on you." His broad hands tightened around her narrow hips and then began moving up. As they slipped over the edge of her leather vest his groans and their pressure increased. All she could do was whimper at the feel of him on her.

She had dreamed of this...well not this precisely, but of him holding her tightly, his hands on her. In her fanciful dreams, he had not been dulled by rum. *The rum*. None of this was him, but rather the liquor and pain mingling to cause his body to seek comfort and she was sure no sailor knew comfort greater than the arms of a woman.

"I need to finish my work, Tiberius. Release me. Please." Her voice had become soft and pleading and it only seemed to agitate him more. His hands continued their northward exploration and she gasped as they drew to a stop at the base of her breasts, so close to her tender flesh she could feel the heat from his fingers licking at her. She bit down on her lower lip so hard the tingle of tears wrinkled her nose.

"Ty..." Before she could exhale, he tugged her forward, causing her to lose her balance. She was tumbling toward his lap, falling into the waiting strength of his arms. To catch herself her leg slipped from between his knees and widened her stance. While it worked to halt her before she landed squarely on his thighs, it left her in a most awkward position. She was now bent at the waist, exceedingly close to his face, and straddling his thigh between her own. The sensation was strange and wonderful and terrifying as she tried and failed to right herself. He was too strong and as he did not want her to move away, she simply couldn't.

"Say my name again." There was desire in his raspy tone as he brushed his nose over hers. Without thinking, she licked her lips and he groaned. His chin lifted and she knew what was about to happen.

Despite how fiercely she had desired this very moment, she blurted, "Tiberius," before his mouth could take hers. As she had hoped, it stopped his approach, even reversed it. His head leaned back far enough for him to be able to meet her glistening gaze.

"Not *that* name. The short one you just called me." She was mesmerized by his eyes, so different and yet still filled with him.

"Oh...I didn't mean to call you Ty. I see I have insulted you. I was trying to say your full name but I...lost my balance and cut the word short. I am sorry." She was trying again to get free, to put at least a bit of space between them. While her logical mind knew he was not in control of himself and he likely meant none of what he had said since the rum had touched his lips, she still desperately wanted it to be the truth. Given too much demand she would surely crack and she could not allow that, not knowing how badly it would hurt when the reality of London loomed before her.

"Do not apologize. I have not heard that nickname in years. My brothers used to call me Ty and I like it very much. It suits your lips. Call me Ty, Vanessa. Won't you please?" Again his grip tightened and he began to pull her back to him.

Placing her hands over his just below her breast, she stilled his advance. Tugging gently, she managed to pry his fingers from her ribs and hold them in the small space between their chests.

"Essie." Her fingers still clinging to his, his hand lifted as he cupped the sides of her face, winding the wayward tendril resting against her cheek around his pointer as he pulled her closer. "My nickname in my youth was Essie. I offer it to you in exchange for yours." A mistake, she knew. This admission, this permission, would only make things more tense between them, but she couldn't help herself. Rum or no, she was close to him and that was where she wanted to be more than she had ever desired anything in her sheltered little life.

"Essie..." No more than a whisper, her pet name on his lips sent surrender shivering through her and he grunted its acceptance. Now holding her face in calloused yet gentle, hands, he drew her back to his mouth. She closed her eyes, intent on letting what was to come, come, but as his breath brushed over her cheek an image of her father and Stephen standing together, seemingly staring at her in disgust, filled her mind. *She could not do this.*

His attention focused on the kiss looming between them, his grip faltered and she managed to quickly slip free of it. Taking a distancing step back, freeing the thigh she had been inadvertently squeezing between her own, she separated from his hands and immediately felt lost without them. While she knew she must, she still regretted the need. Sighing, she focused on threading the needle still clasped in her shaking fingertips.

"I need to stitch you up, Ty. Now behave yourself, this is important."

"I have had far worse, Essie dearest. The only thing I need right now is you." His voice sounded almost violent with need and her heart leapt into her throat at his admission. Reminding herself it was only the rum, she scoffed halfheartedly at his words.

"Ty, now really. To allow rum to steal your good sense so completely is a shame. Were you sober you would be appalled at your own words. Restrain your tongue."

"I'd rather occupy it, Sweets. Could you help me with that?" Her body became licked by flame. Rum or no, he could light her up. She whimpered a sound that only made him more agitated. *Get a hold of yourself,* she demanded inwardly.

She hesitated as she finished loading the needle. She would need to draw close to him again and he still looked at her as a cat would look upon a mouse. "I must close the wound, Ty. Allow me?" The last was not a request but a firm demand and he seemed to understand. Grumbling, he righted himself and averted his eyes from her.

Pursing her lips, she moved around his side far enough to where she felt sure it would be too awkward for him to seize her and knelt. Even with the wound, she looked at it again. Without the large piece of wood holding it open it had collapsed in on itself, becoming nothing more than a hole, even smaller than a sovereign. "Three, maybe four stitches and we will be finished, now, hold still."

"Yes, of course, only, *we* will not be finished. The wound will be finished, but not this. I...ouch!" She could not let him continue. Plunging the needle in a little too fiercely, she managed to silence him. Trying to focus on her work, she ignored his arm slipping from his lap to hang limply between her knees. As she tugged the second stitch tight, it slipped around to the outside of her leg and fanned lightly over her hip, but she brushed the sensation aside, too intent on her task to be bothered.

As the third stitch pulled closed, she bent into him, her face brushing over the taunt brown flesh of his muscled shoulder to snip the thread with her teeth. It was a mistake. The second the thread popped, his

169

arm snagged her like a fish in a net. Hauling her swiftly up and across steel-hard thighs, she found herself draped helplessly in his lap, fully encircled in his arms and only a breath away from his delicious mouth. The smell of coconut and lavender consumed her as if it flowed from his pores and she shuddered at the emptiness that sprang up in her core.

"Ty..."

"Essie, I want you. I need...Essie...your beauty haunts me. I can no longer live only holding you in my dreams. No longer satisfied to walk with you. Let me..." His mouth descended. His lips brushed over hers but did not take. Back and forth, he allowed them to caress her plump pout. Then her cheek. Then her forehead. She began to shake with her own fierce need.

Unable to pretend she did not want this with everything she had, she sighed her permission. Before his lips could return to hers, there was a pounding from the door. Mortimer's voice, tinged with worry and impatience muffled through, asking for an update. The interruption was enough to free her from the moment and she managed to slip out of his grasp. As she moved away he stood and wobbled after her, his giant hands landing on her shoulders, both to catch her and to brace himself. "Essie, stay

170

with me. Let us pass what remains of this voyage together. Let's ease each other's loneliness, at least for a time..."

She pulled free of him, indignation and desire at war in her eyes. His offer was vulgar and crass, but part of her wanted to accept. At least then she could be with him without the guilt of betraying her father, but she knew it would be folly. She loved him and to have him and then walk away would only destroy her, especially knowing he would have her replaced within moments with another lass in port. A woman whose sole profession was to ease the loneliness of sailors.

Smiling sadly at him, she turned her head toward the door and shouted to Mortimer he should enter and her work was done. The grip on her shoulders tightened painfully. "Don't leave me, Essie. I need you." She hesitated before she met his eyes. The light there was bright and consuming. So much so, she had to cast her eyes away. A mistake as now she was staring at the beauty of his etched body once again. No part of him could not send her into a tizzy and she swallowed her whimper in her throat.

Struggling to find her voice, she said, "What you need, Ty, is some rest. The rum is to blame for your behavior and I will not hold you accountable. What has passed between us need go no farther than this room. This moment. Let me help you into bed." Mortimer was approaching over his shoulder and she prayed he would hold his tongue now that they were no longer alone, but she was mistaken.

"Only if you promise to join me. Say you will, I beg you..." He attempted, in his ill-balanced state, to sweep her into his arms again, but he faltered, falling against her. Mortimer sprang forward, relieving her of his weight before they crumbled to the ground together. A circumstance he would surely have seen as advantageous.

"The rum has stolen your captain's senses, and mind, it would seem. Help me get him to his bed. Sleep will right him." Mortimer nodded, a strange smile tugging at his lips as they shared Ty's considerable heaviness between them and helped him to bed. In spite of Mortimer's presence, he tried three more times to pull her into him, the last managing to accidentally free her hair from its pins. It fell about her shoulders and onto his pillow and he turned into it, babbling about how he wished to bathe in it, to feel it sliding over his chest. Her face lit on fire as she gently tugged her tresses free of his greedy hands and turned away. As Mortimer finished seeing to him, she returned to the table and hastily reassembled her kit. She shivered uncontrollably from his words.

"He is out, lass. Come. Let's get you out of here." His arm draped lightly about her trembling shoulders as he guided her from the captain's room. Once outside the cool air kissed her burning cheeks and she felt the tightness in her heart ease. "I am grateful to you, m'Lady. I am starting to wonder what the *Siren* will do without you." Seeing her upset, and no doubt feeling the tremors in her body, he tried to comfort her. "It was only the rum, lass. The captain would never say any of those things if he were in his right mind. No doubt he was so taken with drink he will not remember a vulgar syllable in the morning and it will all be but a memory."

If only his words were a comfort. Nodding and forcing a smile, she left the deck for her room. Mortimer's words had sliced her like a sword. She didn't want his words to be the drink; she didn't want him to have no memory of them. She wanted those moments to have been real, to have meant something to him as they had to her. Sadly she knew they did not, would never, and she cried. Buried in his pillow, she wept for the love that would only ever cause her pain.

Chapter 11

The moment she closed her door she fell into hysterics. She had never wanted to believe an ardent lie so desperately in her life. The rest of the day had been spent buried in his chair wiping tears from her ever-reddening cheeks and wishing the journey would end, he would come to her, or death would take her, as the horror of not knowing threatened to drive her mad. Worse yet was the memory of his flesh, so delectable the mere thought made her mouth water. The tales and stories etched on his skin teased her. The feel of his flesh in her hands, even the taste of his blood in her mouth was a torture.

Too upset to even eat, she had ignored the knock on her door at seven signaling dinner. Her bed felt colder than the air as she climbed in, unable to hope for pleasant dreams, but they came to her anyway. In her mind the clock rewound. She stood in his room, allowing herself to be tugged into his bed, granting him the company he so passionately demanded; his words true and heartfelt. In her dream, his hands did more than span her waist, more than graze her cheek. His fingers explored her, caressed her in ways she had never imagined and she writhed in her sleep to deepen the touch. More than once in the dead of the night she mewled herself right up and out of the dream, hot sweat beading on her flesh and an aching throb spreading through her hips. Each time she calmed herself and fell back to the pillow, only to seconds later be again in the throes of his passion. Consumed once more.

Waking early the following morning, her dreams left her desperate to see him. A thing that could easily break her heart in two if he were cold, but the minutes ticked to hours as she paced and it began to dawn on her he may not come to her at all. Perhaps he had shamed himself beyond repair and she would spend the week remaining in their journey alone in her room with not but her dreams to keep her warm. After lunch, she tried to work, but it was useless. She had even rung the bell, summoning Mortimer to her, but when he arrived her nerve failed her and all she could manage to do was ask after his wound.

She did leave her room once to check on Mr. Haddock, but even he seemed to no longer need her. While his injury had been most grievous, he was healing swiftly. He sat in his bunk reading when she appeared and did little more than glance at her and say he was well before returning to his pages. *A fine how do you do*, she thought bitterly as she returned to her prison. She should have been grateful he did not gawk at her as he had before. It might have been a comfort to know all the crew had come to see her as so much more than simply an alluring creature made for sport, but it did not. Not so long as Clark avoided her.

As she slid the door closed far harder than necessary she sighed, forcing her tears back. She would not cry again. Not yet. Not until there was no hope left. Turning to lean against the roughhewn wood, she spied a strange note folded on her desk. Her breath caught in her throat. The hope she was weakly clinging to burned brighter as she took tentative steps toward the missive. It was a page from her notebook, torn free. Grabbing the paper, she spread it open and read the words greedily. A sparsely written memo, she held an invitation to dine that very evening, in his hand no less. He had come and she had been absent. She cursed her boredom, but the prospect of dinner warmed her.

She spent the remainder of the afternoon trying to prepare for her appointment. She stood before her mirror at ten till studying herself for any flaw. Her hair was as neatly coiled as she could manage, held back by her pair of intricately carved jade combs. A gift from Alfred on their wedding day, they matched the light flecks in her eyes perfectly. Examining further, she smiled, her skin glowing creamy olive in the lamplight. *Flawless*. There could be no error, not tonight. She was straightening her vest when a loud roll of thunder rattled the lamps on the walls. She had foregone her dresses for her trousers, remembering the way his eyes seemed to shimmer when she moved in them. The sounds of a storm stilled her pounding heart. It wasn't fair that a gale should take her freedom like this. Resolving she wouldn't allow it, she left her room alone, not waiting for her escort to appear.

The sailors turned in unison to see her emerging from the hold but soon returned to their work as if she were nothing more than another of their lot come to join the toil. Mortimer, on the other hand, rushed to her as she moved over the deck boards towards his door.

"M'Lady, It's not time for you...he isn't..."

"Ready?" She smiled coolly as she brushed past his concerned expression, continuing with intent to his room. "Have no fear, Mr. Mortimer; I shall defend you if he rages." With that, she pulled the door ajar and stepped through with nary a knock to alert him. Part of her hoped she would catch him unaware and perhaps steal a glimpse of him in his shirtsleeves. *Or less*.

The wicked thought curved her lips as her eyes adjusted to the bright light of every lamp and candle in his space lit at the same time. Her first tuck-in with him had been lit by little more than his open stove and a single candelabrum in the center of his table. The day she stitched him there had only been the afternoon sun filtering in through the large stained glass windows creating his far wall. Each time the room had held a multitude of deep, dark shadowy pools where light did not reach. Now, bathed as it was, she could see the whole of his space and it was even more expansive than her own, though strangely sparse. There was the table in the center of course, and the chair and his small twin cot of a bed, those pieces she knew, but the small bureau and the built-in trophy cabinets were new, at least to her eyes.

Perhaps what spoke to her more were the voids where furniture had once sat and did no longer. A space perfectly suited to the desk below opened to her right, while a large area under the windows, dwarfing his miniature bed, was ample space for the lovely queen she had occupied since climbing aboard. His room gave off a stark and empty feeling without his things. *Perhaps that is why he kept the lights always dimmed*, she thought fondly before she caught sight of him. At the rear of his room, he was pulling his uniform coat on over his powerful body as the door behind her banged closed. Turning to glance over his right shoulder to see who had entered, she watched as the scar that made her thighs ache pulled taunt around flashing eyes. Without buttoning his coat, he took several steps toward her and froze. His eyes, greedy as they were, ran over her flesh, taking in her attire with confused interest.

"Do my trousers disturb you now? Just days ago you were extolling your desire that I should wear what I pleased. I rather took that to mean you liked them. Was I mistaken?" She could not help the teasing grin that pulled at her plump lips. She frankly didn't care at the moment if he liked her trousers; the sight of him was distracting beyond measure. He stood before her with his coat undone, spread wide as his hands rested on his narrow hips, the flat muscles of his impressive chest tightening under the thin white of his undershirt while a look of bemused excitement and confusion consumed his angular features. Her eyes lingered at the edge of his collar bone, visible now as the weight of his hands tugged at the bottom of his shirt, and the scar which curved up and over it before disappearing around the side of his thick, corded neck.

As if he could feel the damp spreading within her knickers, he cleared his throat, and quickly sloughed off the coat he had just been donning. Tossing it to the tousled bed behind him as if it meant little, he moved across the room to stand before her.

"Not at all. I just...I expected you to indulge in pomp and circumstance as with our last dinner. I see I was mistaken. You look lovely. And you are right. I do have a certain...fondness for your trousers. I do not, however, have a fondness for those who do not knock. I was only moments from sending for you, Vanessa dearest. Why have you come, barreling in as it were, unescorted and early?" Were it not for the smile flickering in his eyes she might have thought him cross with her, but as it was she giggled lightly as she made her way to her customary seat at his table and pulled her chair back.

Settling in with an unladylike flop, she sighed merrily and, with a false air of irreverence, examined the table, already laden with dinner plates. "There is a storm coming, Tiberius *dearest*," She savored the way his frame tensed as she returned his sentimental touch, "and I did not wish to walk through the rain to your door. Oh, and do spare Mortimer your wrath, bless his soul, he tried to stop me." She was the one being cold now, and she had spent all day fearing this from him. She suddenly felt ashamed of herself. Coy did not suit her.

180

"Ah, well, no harm done. I am pleased to see you, though I gather from your tone I do indeed owe you an apology. My behavior yesterday was appalling, though I did try to warn you." His face darkened as he spoke of their last meeting. She tensed. He was about to destroy her and he had no idea. On his confession that it was merely the rum she would crack and crumble and he had no way to know. Wanting to spare herself the pain of hearing it from his lips, she ventured to do it for him, as if somehow it made it less real if she said it.

"Rum has foul effects on even the best men, Captain. I do not hold you accountable for the falsehoods you peppered upon me in your muddled state. The drink did all I required and the side effects were, in truth, quite minimal considering. I release you from the embarrassment you feel. Think no more on it and neither shall I." Bile rose in her throat as the lies leaked from her lips. She wanted to scream at herself, scream at him that she did not feel as she claimed, but instead, she gave a hollow false smile and sat back in her seat, self-loathing creeping over her clammy flesh.

"It is true, my Lady, that the rum loosed my lips, and that I said things I am ashamed I could not contain, but I would not venture so far as to say they were lies. Not entirely..." There was an endearing shyness to his words as his tone slid from strong to wistful. His eyes fell from her face to the table. She couldn't move. He had not been false, had not lied. Her heart kicked.

Softening her cold tone, allowing the hope in her breast to color her words, she reached for his hand as he moved to lift the domes from their meal.

"Then...may I still call you Ty?" Her fingers grazed his knuckles and his hand froze before turning over quickly and catching her.

"So long as I can continue to call you Essie, *dearest*."

A wickedly decadent smirk curved over his lips. A whimper escaped her. She had thought perhaps he had no memory of that part of the conversation but it would seem he did. Kissing her knuckles gently, he released her and removed the domes. Sliding into his chair, he lifted his fork and cut into the fish fillet, steaming and fragrant before him. She followed suit and before long they were engaging in a most innocent, if not strained, conversation. His discomfort and her defenses seemed to wane as the evening progressed. When dinner was finished and her tart was done, she leaned back into her chair and sighed with satisfaction.

In the new quiet, the sound of rain, pouring and pounding against the quarter deck over their heads could be heard. "I see the rain you saw coming has finally arrived, and fiercely, too." He stood quickly and moved with speed to the side of her chair. She watched with rapt attention at the grace he could muster, having just eaten such a large meal. She expected him to move past her to the door to look out at the rain, but instead, he stood in front of her, his large, tanned hands extended for her to take.

"My dear," His voice was almost a whisper. Her mouth flopped open for a second before she snapped it shut and swallowed. She reached for his hands and instantly she was lifted before him. His smell consumed her and her head grew light. She wobbled and his arm circled around her waist, hauling her against his broad, muscle-hardened chest. She had only been there, pressed against him, once before and then she had been too consumed by grief and fear at the gruesomeness of what she had just done to fully appreciate the sweetness of it all.

Her palms fanned open over his heart as she leaned her forehead against his chin. He rubbed that stone chin over her flesh, gently, coaxingly and she shuddered, falling into him completely. A deep sigh racked her body as she whispered, "Ty, dearest..." Then she felt it, his lips pressed to the smooth satin of her skin. They were softer than she would have guessed and there was a slight hot wetness to them that made her groan.

"Essie, love. I am sorry I was so vulgar. I will not take back what I said, only the manner in which I said it. Can you forgive me?" His cheek lowered against her temple as his grip on her tightened. She sucked in his scent, deep into her and smiled longingly into his nape. His flesh was warm there, warm and lush. Her rash nature took hold as she dragged her lips, dry and hot, over that luscious spot. His groan was deep, rumbling against her suddenly aching breasts; his hands slipping over her vest and gliding to the sides of her contained bosom.

"Do that again, love." His voice was little more than a hot breath on her skin, but his request shook her to the core. Obliging him, she trailed hot light kisses once more over his collarbone, her tongue slipping free of her lips to taste the scar she had set her sights on earlier. "Dear, sweet, merciful, God...Essie I..."

As if the prayer he had just uttered had alerted the divine to her wayward actions, the very floor beneath them listed once again; an exact copy of the last moment they shared like this after a meal together. The similarity was not lost on him either. Uttering a curse under his breath, one only a true sailor would dare to use, he lifted her face to his. "Forgive me, but I must see to that." His eyes were dark blue flames, with all the heat and intensity of the sun welling in their navy depths and she sucked in a hard breath. His head lowered and for a moment she thought he would grant her the kiss she had been fantasizing about, but instead, he slipped from her.

Deliberate, almost angry steps carried him to his door. The second he opened them she was thrown into terror. It was not merely rain that the thunder had preluded, but a squall, fierce and violent. Lightening strobed in the darkness and hard cold rain blew so far into the cabin she could feel it peppering her trouser legs some ten feet away. Standing in the door as he was, his shirt soaked through in seconds, but it was not the rain, or the lightening, or even the almost constant rumble of demonic thunder that had her frightened. It was the panicked calls and cries of the men trying desperately to fight the storm that startled her.

The boat listed again, sending her against the table, and he into the door frame. Turning to her, he barked, "Stay here!" before leaving, plunging into the raging gale to join his men. She moved with shaking steps to the open doorway, instantly feeling the ice-cold rain penetrate her clothing all the way to her combinations. Soaked through in seconds. They were grasping wildly at the lines that swayed and lashed in the angry winds. The mizzen mast was barely visible through the thick rain sheeting across the flooding deck. A wave struck the ship broadside and the spray washed over them, sending some onto their backsides and sliding across the boards before they could regain their feet and return to their posts. Over the din of the downpour, she could hear a sailor shouting inches from Ty's shoulder that they couldn't bring in the mizzen main sail. At once she understood and it froze her blood in her veins.

The wind rose again and the ship listed even farther to starboard. A set of crates lashed to the port rail broke free of their nets and slid across the deck, narrowly missing poor Connor by inches. She stifled a scream as he dove out of the way, the crates coming to a halt only feet from the opposite side of the ship than where they had begun. Men raced to secure them, the lines they had been holding going free and whipping about in the storm. Her eyes followed them up. The largest sail on the mizzen mast lay wide, full canvas, while every other she could make out had been pulled in, secured until the worst of the gale had passed. As her eyes lingered over the crossbeam, she saw it. A line knotted and snagged in the rigging was stalling all their efforts to furl the sail. One more gust and the *Siren's Call* could be lost to the sea, along with her entire complement of souls.

She watched as the men battled with the ropes, yet none of them took to the nets to fix the true problem. They had not seen it, did not know. Bracing herself against the ferocity of what lay beyond his door, she bolted into the storm. She ran for him, grasping his arm as her boots slid over the boards.

"Ty! Ty, the line…" She was trying to direct his eyes into the rigging when they focused on her.

"Jesus, Mary and Joseph, Essie what in hell are you doing out here?! Get back into my cabin this instant! This storm is no place for a woman!" He all but sloughed her off and returned to his futile task. Anger rose within her. She would not be so easily silenced. If he would not listen, could not see, then she must act. Brushing the wet tendrils of escaped hair from her face, she ran for the nets. Flashing one last unseen glare at him, she started her ascent.

The nets were taunt but still gave under her weight. It took several faulty holds for her to master the means and manner necessary for her climb, but she was an excellent scaler. Within moments she was high in the rigging, climbing to the narrow end of the net. The wind picked up again and she flopped to one side, losing her grip with one hand and her footing all together. *That must have been how young Connor lost himself over the side*, she thought, as she struggled to regain her position. Her fingers were going numb in the cold rain, and her palms ached due to the harsh rope tight in her grasp. She refocused her efforts and began again, setting her weight more firmly with each new hold, an effort to prevent the same from happening to her.

Light gusts swirled around her head, freeing her hair as she climbed. She watched, helpless, as the combs she had used to secure it fell to the deck. One struck the largest of the burly pair, a Tibilt, by name, in the head. She saw the impact, but instantly refocused on her climb. She did not see him search for the object that struck him. Nor did she see him follow the path the pale green Jade adornment had taken, finding her almost to the crossbeam and running dangerously low on netting to climb. She did not hear him shout to the captain or know that he led Ty's gaze to find her where she climbed, but she was aware of what happened next. Clark's voice, deep and angry, ripped through the storm. Her name sounded more like a curse than a moniker echoing through the heavy rain. She looked down, meeting his rage-infused gaze momentarily, before frowning and returning to her purpose.

She was too close to stop now, too near her goal to falter. At the end of the now meager netting insight, she reached numb fingers to the lines that held the beam stead, pulling fiercely to lift her weight. The rain had nearly drowned her in her climb and the added heaviness of her clothes had increased tenfold. Her palms screamed in pain, but she bit her lip and hoisted her body up and onto the beam. Sliding forward until her hips lay on the wood, she pushed up to get a look at her new challenge. Her thighs hugged the beam as her toes, damp in her water-filled boots, hooked over the pole behind her. Spying her goal some ten feet ahead, she leaned forward again and pulled her body along, inching her feet behind for stability.

Another gust kicked the ship in the teeth and she rocked hard to one side, her hips sliding off to the left. She clung frantically to the wood, her only saving grace was her boots still had a hold. Righting herself with much effort, she flopped back atop the pole. Her breath was a burning pant, harsh as sandpaper on her throat. She had begun to shake, though from the cold slicing her clean to her bones or the nearness of death should her grip falter again, she could not be sure.

She was inches from her goal. Looking back, she caught sight of a sailor halfway up the net she had scaled only moments ago. Ty had sent a man to save her. She might have been flattered if it wasn't so utterly insulting to think she needed saving when she knew precisely what she was up to. Reaffirmed in her quest, she continued. As she drew within arm's reach of the line she stretched her long slender frame to its fullest trying to snag the catch as soon as possible. While she did manage to grab the offending rope, she realized too late she should have drawn closer first. Tugging hard she managed to free the knot, but the force, extended over her elongated and poorly balanced length, sent her body flopping over the side.

The rope in her hands was all she had as she slapped against the rain-hardened canvas. It was rather like slamming into a brick wall she mused sarcastically as she drifted out and back again, the second hit nearly stealing her wind. How perfect it would be for her to die like this. He would be right to have told her this was no place for a woman and she would be the only party at fault. Deciding she would not give him the satisfaction, she reached a hand higher on the rope. The weight of her body was more than her grip could afford with only one hand and she slid farther down the line. The pain in her palm was excruciating as her other hand re-gripped the cord. Her name, etched in panic, drifted up to her. *No, she would not go this way.* Gritting her teeth against the violent burning, she reached again. Then again. Hand over hand she inched her way back to the beam.

Her body ached and shook. Her strength was failing. Soon she would not be able to return the way she had come. Expending too much of the precious little energy she had left, she dragged her body back onto the crossbeam. She slumped limply over it, panting painfully to regain her power. She could not go back, it was too far and to turn around would be even more dangerous than climbing up had been. Looking farther down the beam, her tired gaze found the mast, wide and dark, about a body length ahead of her. An overbright flash of lightning glinted off the mast, highlighting black metal. An iron spoke protruded from the pillar.

Inching closer, she waited for another flash. Within seconds she was rewarded with the sight of other such spikes, evenly spaced along the mast. Climbing grips. She inched forward again. The timber within reach, she growled against the pain as she gripped the iron and flung her aching, heavy body over. For a moment she dangled before her foot found a rung to rest upon. Sighing against the burn, she found another rung for her other foot and hugged the mast tight. Steadying her breathing, she lowered her body weight to the next and then the next. Foot by foot she sank back to the deck.

A few feet from the ground, hands grabbed her waist. She was pulled free and lowered to the boards. Her body screamed but over its wails came cheers. The entire crew was gathered around her, each hurrahing her and trying to pat her shoulder in triumph. She had done it, had freed the impediment.

The adulation was fervent but short, and then the men fanned out and proceeded to bring in the sail that had previously resisted them. She staggered on shaking legs. Wiping the back of her hand across her brow, she caught sight of Ty standing a few feet from her. In spite of the anger that had sent her into the nets, and the rage that had spurred her on, she smiled wide at the sight of him, but he did not return it. His scowl only deepened. She stiffened her spine as she stood up before him. Fighting the pain that shuddered through her, she rose up to her full height. If he was going to rail she would meet him head on.

"My quarters, Lady Everly! Now!" Her formal title. Oh, but he was angry. Her anger rose in kind.

As she swished past him, intentionally lifting her chin defiantly as she drew even with his shoulder, she matched his tone, "As you wish, Captain Clark." If he wanted to rage at her she would oblige him, only she would not do so in complacent silence. If he wanted a row, she would give him one.

Chapter 12

She could hear the visceral growl rumble low in his chest as he fell in behind her. He hovered in her shadow like a bear, ferocious and primal, as she stepped through the still-open door of his cabin. The door slammed behind him and despite her rage, she cringed at the sound. His hands, hard and cold and not the least bit gentle, landed on her shoulders and spun her about. Her body screamed at the forced action, she was so terribly sore, but she stifled the cry of pain in her throat. She would not show him weakness.

"What in the bloody hell were you doing!? You reckless, flippant girl! You could have died! And what then? Had you even considered the danger?" His face was twisted and contorted by anger and despite how terrible and frightening he had become, she felt her belly swirl. Furrowing her brow and jutting her chin stubbornly at him, a gesture that had him flinging his hands in the air in frustration, she returned his glare.

"It had to be done! You know that full well!" She could shout, too, lest he forget.

"But not by you! If you had only let me handle it!" His hands reached again for her shoulders but she swatted them away. She grimaced as the pain in her palms railed at the impact.

"Don't you dare! I *tried* to tell you! *Tried* to let you know what was wrong and you *dismissed* me! As if I were no more than an insect bothering your ear!" The pain in her hands would not subside and she whined in her throat as she looked down at the raw flesh gleaming pink. He huffed as he drew close to her again. He reached for her wrists, but she pulled away, still acting like the obstinate child.

Growling, he modulated his tone, "Goddamn it, Essie...let me help you." The last words were more a plea than a command, and her hands ached so much. Groaning under the insult of it all, she thrust her tattered flesh at his chest. His fingers were surprisingly gentle as he turned her palms to his eyes.

"Jesus, Essie. Look what you have done to yourself." Her eyes flashed emerald rage at him and he sighed through gritted teeth. "Seethe all you like, Sweets. If it pleases you, hate me, but sit down first so that I can bind your wounds." She attempted to tug her hands free of him, suddenly wanting to refuse his kindness, but he held her fast and the effort only caused her more pain.

Grumbling, she flopped down into her chair and he rested her knuckles on the table before turning for the bureau. She steamed in her soaked trousers and vest as he returned with a small tin. Pulling the lid free, he dipped his fingers into a silvery salve and hovered over her reddened, raw palms.

"This will hurt, Sweets." There was concern in his husky voice.

"So be it." Her anger was still fresh. His brow furrowed deep as he turned back to her hands. He hadn't lied. As he smoothed the concoction over her abused flesh the burn deepened into an agonizing torture. She grimaced in spite of herself and he winced for her. How dare he be gentle. He had no right to steal her anger away from her with kindness, and she struggled to hold onto it. After a second, the pain eased. The salve had a blessed numbing effect on her stripped flesh and she sighed as the burn lifted.

"There now, isn't that better?" He was trying to be kind, but all Vanessa could hear was condescension. He was speaking to her as if she were a child.

"Do not think for one moment I am through with my anger, Captain. Helping ease my pain does not erase the insult you have laid at my feet. Nor does it absolve you of your guilt!" Her words seemed to sting him as he released her hands and recoiled from her, now a viper, readying to strike. He stood from the table and stomped away. He knew what he had done; she could see it written on him as if she had scrawled it herself.

"You had no right to put yourself in that much danger!"

"I had the *only* right! It is my life to risk and what could be more worthy than saving the lives of your crew?" She ground her teeth at his back, as he refused to turn and face her. "If I had been one of you *men* you would have patted my back as they did!" At this he slammed his fist into the wall, rattling the baubles and nick-knacks within the cabinets.

"But you are *not* one of my men!" His voice turned to gravel and razor blades, raw and cruel and filled with fear.

"A fact I well know! I am nothing more than a woman. A feeble-minded creature, incapable of higher thought or self-control, which must be tamed

197

and enslaved!" He growled full and loud, not even trying to hold it in his chest, but she did not stop. "I spent my youth at the end of my father's chain until he saw fit to hand it to another man. When he died my father gave it to you so you could drag me home by it. All so he could turn around and give it to the likes of Stephen..."

Her voice cracked. She had said too much. Gone too far. In defense of her self-control, she had entirely lost it, giving him a truth she had not intended for him to know.

"What?!" He rounded on her, his face painted with shock and panic.

She could not meet his eyes, not with her terrible fate exposed so bluntly. She stood from the table and turned away from him, a sigh racking her body as she hugged her arms around her for warmth. She was so cold. Raking her hair over her shoulder, she squeezed the icy rain from it as she continued, her voice entirely deflated and utterly weak.

"My father has decided that another Everly should be in my future. Alfred is barely in the ground and he has sold me off again. I really am not more than a slave." Her voice shattered with the threat of tears. She had thought the same since the day he had delivered the terrible letter, but until now she had not said the words aloud. Sadly it seemed she was not strong enough to hear them. She wished in vain she could pull them back, but it was done.

"Stephen Everly! You are to be *bound* to Stephen Everly?!" His voice scorched her flesh.

"That is my regrettable fate." Her chest deflated; her voice becoming a hollow faint thing that drifted like far-off music through the room.

"You cannot marry that man! Surely there has been some mistake..." She chuckled, though there was no humor in it. Raking her damp hair back over her shoulder, she turned to him. Her eyes threatened tears as she lifted her gaze to his. She did not expect to see the same heavy threat on him she battled in herself.

"I see you know of him. Trust me, it is not my decision, but I have no choice. As for the truth of it, you delivered the ill news yourself, in that very hand." She pointed limply to his fingers, which he lifted to his face, staring as if he could not recognize them as his own.

"Only by reputation, which is all too well for my taste. He is a cad, a philanderer, and a brutish fiend, notorious for his violent nature where women are concerned." He drew closer to her as if he couldn't stand to keep away any longer. She watched his approach greedily, but as he drew near she pulled away. She had no right to want him. The future ahead of her was somehow more real now that he knew it, more frightening and closer than ever. "You cannot marry him." He reached for her but she shrank away from the warmth of his hands.

"You are repeating yourself, Ty. Besides which, I do not have a choice, as I have said. I am but a woman, remember? Incapable of making my own decisions and requiring the men in my life to make them for me." She knew her words would burn him, but they burned her too. The worst part, it *was* her truth, always had been. For most women, especially those of high birth, it was their truth as well.

"You are so much more than that. So very much more." His voice was rough as he slunk up behind her. She sensed him reach for her, but his fingers made no contact, hovering over her shoulder as if afraid to touch her.

"You say that but you do not really feel that way..." It was little more than a whisper from her but it elicited a shout from him.

"Bloody hell I don't! Bloody Buggering hell, Essie, are you *trying* to hurt me?" He turned from her, stomping off to the other side of the room. Her anger returned. Spinning on her heels she watched his retreat with hurt eyes.

"Did you, or did you not say to me, not ten minutes ago, that the deck was no place for a woman? The implication of which is that, as a woman, I am incapable of knowing where I do and do not belong? Regardless of your intention, you employed the same control over me my father has for years." He twisted to look back at her, pain and hurt warring with anger and something like hunger in his gaze.

"Shite, Essie! I was trying to...I only wanted to....you are the....GRRR" There was a new, strong Scottish brogue to his words she had never heard before as he stomped around the table, his thoughts broken and incoherent as he tried and failed to find a defense to her claims. Catching her eyes in his, he surged. In an instant, he was on her, around her. His arms wrapped her up, so tight it threatened to break her in half and the feeling was wondrous. His left hand fanned out over her shoulder, while the right cradled her cheek and drug her to his mouth. His lips consumed her.

At first, his kiss was brutal and she pressed her hands limply against his chest as if to free herself, but as he softened, so did she. She moaned in his arms and he wrapped her tighter, nipping lightly at her bottom lip. She gasped, parting her mouth, and his tongue dove between her white teeth to caress hers. She slipped her hands up to his neck, burying her fingers into his hair and dragging his mouth closer, increasing the depth of his taking beyond even his demanding pressure.

His fingers tangled in her hair, tugging her head back as his lips trailed hot wet kisses down her throat.

"Essie dearest...you are delicious. Caramels and cream. I could feast on you forever..." His tongue trailed over the hollow of her neck and she shivered. "In fact, Sweets, I think I will." His teeth nipped her collarbone, sending her hips jerking into his. The hand on her back slid down to her rear, digging into her flesh and grinding it against his stone thigh. They moaned together as he lifted back to her mouth.

The world stopped at his fingertips. Ended in his arms. The days she had spent wondering if he cared, doubting her own need, were silenced. Much as she craved this moment, fear crept up her spine.

Panting into his hot, wet mouth, she whispered, "Ty, I cannot do this..." Even as she said it he kissed her again and she dove into his mouth just as he plunged into hers, unable to contain her aching need.

"Oh, but I think you are, love, and quite effectively, too." He pressed her hips to his and let her feel the ardent length of his manhood, swollen and stark. She groaned as she ran her kiss-plumped lips over his cheek to his jaw. "I want you, Essie. I want to hold you, feel you, taste you..." He found her mouth again. So desperate were his kisses. He had called her delicious, but it was he she tasted and delicious didn't seem a strong enough description of the flavor. He was salty sweetness, saltwater taffy, her favorite.

"Tell me you want me. Say it. Oh God, Sweets, say it..." She growled at him as she pulled away.

"But I don't want." His eyes seemed to scream, panic and grief flaring in an instant before she continued, "I *crave*. I crave you like plants crave water. But it matters little what needs I have. My future is set. I cannot do this." She pressed her forehead to his and whimpered. He moved his hands over her body, constricting around her as if he feared she would flee from him, but she hadn't the strength nor the will.

"Nothing is set, Sweets. Every fate can be changed." His eyes were closed as he whispered the words. His breath came in small warm pants against her face. For a moment she just inhaled him, wishing time would stand still, leaving her in his arms forever.

"Sadly, you do not know my father. Once he has given his bond, it is done." The tears peeked in her eyes. She didn't want to cry, but held so close to him as she was, and knowing they could never be more than they were right now, she could not stop them. A sniffle escaped her and his head snapped up. A sad, consoling sigh ran over his flesh as he kissed her eyes, stealing her tears.

"We have time. Can we not indulge in each other? Share our knowledge and let the fate you fear wait for us?" For a moment she grinned at the thought, but the feeling soured. He could do that, couldn't he? He had offered that very thing the day before. Requested she consent to an affair with him knowing it would end as soon as London appeared on the horizon. She was nothing more than an indulgence, he had said it himself. Shame rose within her like a brush fire.

"Am I just a momentary pleasure to you? A tool to while away the hours, the days, until you return to port and I am gone?" As soon as the words left her she wished she had held her tongue. His face fell. She had hurt him beyond measure, though that had not been her intention. His arms, once holding her so tight to him it hurt, went slack and slipped away.

"You can't believe that? How little you think of me." He turned from her, apparently unable to look her in the face any longer. "I think perhaps you should go. I want to hold more than I have ever wanted anything in my life, but..." He pushed his knuckles into the table so firmly it groaned under the pressure. She gasped at the anger in his voice.

"Ty, I did not mean to hurt..." She took a timid step toward him before he spoke again.

"Just go. I think it best we say goodnight." New tears flooded her eyes. Without a word, she turned and fled from his room into the storm. By the time she reached her door, her face streamed with both her hot tears and the cold rain falling thickly from her hair. It was over. She had damaged him beyond repair and now she would suffer the consequences of her own making. Despite how improper his offer had been, it was all she could afford to accept. She knew that. The days between here and London were all she had and she was a fool not to take advantage.

As she clicked the lock of her door and peeled her soaked clothes free of her shaking body, she wished she had agreed. Wished she could go back and kiss him until he took her. Never again would she know that sweet pleasure and her heart shattered with the truth of it all.

Chapter 13

She traced her finger along the satiny skin of his moon-shaped scar. His dark gaze carried the same glow she had seen in his cabin earlier as his fingers followed the lines of her body. She sighed as his lips drifted down to caress along her collarbone. The touch of his work-roughened hands on her flesh ignited a shiver deep inside her that seemed to radiate out from her core until every limb, every inch of her flesh, quivered under his fingertips. She moaned lightly into his ear as his teeth nipped at her shoulder. As she whispered his name into his hair she heard the distant tones of his voice. Somewhere beyond her, hidden in the darkness, was the sound of him calling her name. Strange considering the fact that his tongue was drifting over the swell of her breast.

Opening her eyes in an effort to focus her hot, lustful thoughts, she struggled to listen. The stars were so bright as they lay, a tangled mass of limbs and flesh, on the empty deck of the *Siren*. The cool night air swirled around them as they held each other. Then it came again. So faint and yet so real. His mouth was occupied with her breast and yet she could hear his strong deep words. *How is this possible?* She wondered as she arched into the wet seeking touch of his tongue.

"*...Essie...*"

"Ty?" Her mind struggled to focus. Something touched her face. A soft feathery feeling that sent her head reeling. Just a whisper of a touch, it felt more real than the lips drifting down her abdomen. *A dream.* This was nothing more than a dream.

The moment her consciousness made the realization, the sensation of Ty in her arms faded. Darkness and silence filed in around her and a chill consumed her body, having lost his warmth and affection. Another light touch on her cheek. It was real. Someone was with her. She couldn't open her eyes, still too far in the grips of sleep to confront her visitor. Trying to shift her weight, an ache lit through her. After she had fled from him she had changed into her nightgown and curled into his chair to cry at her loss. For hours she had stared at the glow from the stove before she had drifted into a restless sleep. Now she awoke, still curled into the chair and very stiff.

"Essie..." Ty's voice. *Ty.* He was here with her. Joy sparked in her sore, bent body. She needed to open her eyes. Needed to see him there before her, flesh and bone and blood. Groaning against the ache in her back, she pressed down into the chair and willed her eyes to open.

The faint glow of the lone lamp was the only source in her room. It's soft aura highlighted the hard planes of his face, glinting in the indigo eyes that made her weak. His fingers brushed over her cheek once more as his grin deepened into a look that had her struggling anew to sit up straighter.

"Ty...what are you doing here? How did you...?" Her eyes darted to the door. She was sure she had locked it after fleeing from him.

"I have a key, remember, Sweets?" His hand cupped the side of her face and despite her shock at finding him watching over her as she slept, she bent into the touch.

"I didn't think you would want to see me again...after...Oh, Ty, I didn't mean to hurt you." New tears peeked in the corners of her eyes. His slight grin faded as his thumb brushed the glistening droplet from her cheek.

"It hurts me far more to know you have shed tears for me. Their trails on your lovely face cause me far more pain." A sigh escaped him as he leaned farther into her, resting his forehead against hers. She closed her eyes and breathed him in deep. Allowing her chest to fill with his beloved scent. "Why?" It was barely a whisper, but she heard it, felt his need for an answer to her core.

"I was afraid, Ty." Her voice cracked as she lifted trembling fingers to brush over his jawline as he caressed hers. The grumbling in his chest made her hips tense. The soreness that followed drew her attention back to her position. She became aware of the chill in her arms. The blanket she had wrapped around herself earlier in the night as she had curled into the chair, had slipped off. Without the cover, her exposed flesh had gone cold. Her bare shoulders and low-cut neckline had not protected her from the cool night air. Her nightgown was thin and cotton and...*She was wearing a nightgown!* The sleepy sluggishness vanished instantly.

Sitting up a little too quickly, her sudden movement caused him to lose his balance and fall backward onto his heels. "Ty, I am not properly dressed!" The ridiculousness of her ardent concern was not lost on him as his deep rolling chuckle filled the dim space between them.

"I know, Sweets. Trust me, I am acutely aware." She tried to turn away from his molten gaze, but he held her fast. "Why? Why would you say that to me? Do you really believe you mean so little to me? That I could be so callous? Is that what you fear?" His voice was firm and demanding as he held her face to his. She swallowed down the lump which formed in her throat, but she could not speak. "Sweets, please tell me! I can't stand this!" His eyes glistened and she could hear the pain in his plea. Whimpering she sighed and leaned against his fingers.

"I'm sorry, Ty. I swear I never meant to hurt you. I just...I can't..." His lips grazed over hers as he took a deep breath. She shivered at the caress. "I am afraid of myself, Ty. Afraid I wanted to say yes. That I still want to say yes. To spend what little time we have in your arms, but I fear what will happen to me if I do. I fear I would not be able to let you go." At her confession he wrapped an arm around her waist, pulling her halfway out of the chair and against his chest. His breath, hot and sweet, caressed her before his lips took hers. His kiss was gentle at first, but as she arched into his arms it deepened. With a groan, he pulled back from her mouth and gazed into her eyes.

"No. My answer is no. I couldn't just hold you and let you go Sweets. Never." At his confession she moaned and leaned into him, seeking another kiss. He granted her request, pulling her completely free of the chair and into his lap. Groaning into his mouth, she wound her slender arms around his neck, sinking into him. She did not resist as he lifted her into the air and began moving through her room. It wasn't until she realized he was drawing near to her bed that her fear surged. Pushing against his shoulders, she tugged her mouth free of his tender kisses.

"Ty, we can't. I can't. I don't..." He lowered her to her feet and turned her body to his, wrapping his arms around her and kissing her again. Despite her fear, she bent into him, molding her flesh to his and causing a groan to echo through his body. Hers began to tremble as his hands found its flesh, hidden only by the thin layer of the nightgown. The warm strength of his fingers tracing her spine caused her to moan into his mouth before she pulled back again. As much as she wanted this moment, she feared it. What if she disappointed him? Fell painfully short of his expectations?

"Yes you can, Essie. Please don't pull away from me now. I need you too much." His words kicked her heart. She wanted to cave to his demanding hands, to live the dreams that had haunted her every night since they met, but she couldn't as long there were secrets between them. As much as it pained her, she pulled away from him and took a step back. Turning from him, she wrapped her arms tightly around her core.

"I have no knowledge of such things, Ty. I have never..." She could not finish her thought. The sound of his shocked gasp behind her stole her words. Silence stretched between them for seconds that felt like days. Terror gripped her. Would he turn from her now that he knew her truth?

"Never? But you were married. Essie, I don't understand..." He hadn't left her yet, but there was so much confusion in the deep husky whisper behind her. Sighing, she hung her head.

"Oh, Ty. It is true three years ago Alfred Everly took me as his bride, but not once in our marriage did he make me his wife. I stand before you as innocent as the day I married him." His arms found her now, wrapping around her, tight. She fell into the embrace as if she feared she would cease to exist without it.

"I don't understand. How could any man marry you and not take you as soon as he was able? I doubt I would have made it through the carriage ride home." His breath was on her neck, but he did not claim her. Her revelation seemed to have slowed his demanding hands, though it did not stop them. Deciding she needed to tell him everything, she turned in his arms to face him, though she could not meet his eyes.

"At first I thought he was as nervous as I but after several weeks I grew to fear it was because of me. That he didn't want me. When I could no longer take the doubt within my heart, I confronted him. We talked well into the night. Alfred...," she paused, sighing before she shared a secret she had never told another soul, "preferred the company of his peers, if you get my meaning. The discovery nearly killed me, but he opened his heart to me. Stephen was beyond cruel in his suspicions and Alfred wanted desperately to please his mother. He begged me to stay with him. To pretend to be his wife so that he could face his family. In exchange I would be free to pursue my education, and then my career, as I willed. He even gave me permission to discretely take a lover, but I found no desire to. I have never wanted a lover ...until now." She met his gaze for the first time, fearing what she might find. She had expected disappointment or confusion, but the unhidden desire that burned fiercely in his eyes was breathtaking.

"You must understand...I have nothing to offer you. Nothing but me. No experience, knowledge, or expertise with which to match yours. I am naive and ignorant, having nothing but myself to give, and even that would be fleeting..." He hauled her body roughly against his as he dove into her mouth. His tongue swam over hers as he backed her toward her bed. His thighs, hot and hard, forced her legs to move, taking steps back until her calves pressed against the rails.

"All I want, all I have wanted since the day I laid eyes on you, is you, Essie. To have you offer me your innocence is beyond anything I could ever dream. And I have dreamed of this, Sweets. Of seeing your face etched with pleasure I have brought you..." His voice trailed off as his mouth nuzzled into the fragrant junction between her soft shoulder and sensitive neck. She gasped as his teeth grazed over the tender hollow between her collarbones.

Her voice, little more than a raspy whisper, husked, "I do not know pleasure..." She leaned her head back as his kiss grazed lower and lower. His fingers gripped her shoulders, arching her farther. His moistened lips brushed over the swells of her breasts peeking out just above the ties still holding her wispy nightgown in place.

"I swear to you, Sweets, you will. I intend to make you infinitely acquainted." The gruff husk of his voice from the cleft of her bosom was accompanied by the feel of the first ribbon slipping loose. At her gasp, a rough growl of need rumbled against her, but he released the tie from his teeth. She lifted her head to find him gazing at her, a plea for permission screaming in his dark blue eyes. Despite her trepidation, she reached surprisingly steady fingers to the ribbon he had been edging free. In one smooth, sure motion she tugged it sharply, ending the first of her ties. The top of her gown gaped, revealing the soft toffee edges of her peaks.

"Bloody hell..." was his only response to her consent as his mouth found her newly revealed flesh. She arched greedily as his tongue grazed lightly over her aching peak, unable to stifle the whimper of sheer pleasure it elicited. As he drew her wholly into his mouth her frame jerked. Nipping at her lightly, he lifted her into his arms and placed her shivering body on to the bed. Lowering down beside her, he groaned deeply, still devouring her olive flesh.

As his arms slipped from under her, his fingers, strangely trembling, he loosed the remaining two bows between her breasts. Propping up on his elbow, he slowly traced the slight gap, now untied. His fingertips were hot coals on her skin as they slid under the loose fabric to drift over the whole of her chest. Soft, gentle caresses made her body scream his name. She writhed under the feel of him, but he continued his slow exploration. When at last he flayed the thin white cotton away from her she moaned. No one had ever seen her flesh before, not like this. His body tensed beside her as his messy blond head lowered. Her hands, trembling and unsure, slipped into his hair as his mouth took her swollen, throbbing peak again.

The violence of her shudder caused him to roll his body onto her side, pinning her arching frame to the mattress as his kiss deepened. The sheer thrill of him tasting her was almost painful. Her need began to pulse, full and desperate. She had never imagined it could feel like this. Hot puffs of air on her wet flesh caused her hardening peaks to constrict even further and a pained cry leaked from her open mouth. With a wet pop, his lips released her breast and found her mouth. Letting go of her fear in exchange for her desire, she dove into him, tugging him fiercely against her and pressing her hips to his with insistent need.

She *needed*. The empty ache in her core began to throb, causing her body to quake. *Now*. She *needed* him *now*! As he kissed her deeper and deeper, his hands began to lower her gown. The more of her soft, silken flesh he revealed the more gently he touched her. In spite of the frantic craving sweeping through her, he seemed to be studying her as she would study an artifact. With precision and care, he lingered over her curves. When he tugged the top of the gown over her hips, she tensed instinctively.

Growling low and deep against her abdomen, he whispered, "Hush, love. Trust me..." His lips circled around her belly button and she gasped.

"I do trust you, love, but...I...I am going crazy..." Her voice became little more than a pleading squeak as she finished her broken statement. Her fingers dug into his shoulders as he chuckled against her stomach. He ran his fingers lightly under the rim of her gown, still barely clinging to her hips.

"Perfect..." With that, he gave a swift tug and freed the thin garment from under her. Pushing up onto his elbow again he slid the white fabric off her legs and tossed it aside. She lay, completely bare and utterly helpless before him. Shame filled her at the realization of the exposure. In a futile effort to hide the shivering satin flesh he had exposed, she crossed her arms over her chest.

"Do not hide your beauty from me, Sweets. Please." She released a sigh as he gently pulled her arms away from her body. His eyes, sparkling like deep sapphires, traveled the length of her so slowly. She began to writhe as if he were physically touching her. His gaze carried all the heat of a flame and he was consuming her like fire given dry grass.

"My God, Essie. You are magnificent... delicious..." As if to prove his point, he tasted her, running his tongue over the ridge of her hip bone, and her body snapped up, nearly folding in half. A violent motion and one completely beyond her control.

He rolled on top of her, bracketing her to the soft mattress and seeking her mouth. She had lost her mind. All her senses were overwrought and even the slightest touch of his fingers was enough to find her jerking and writhing without restraint.

"Give me your flesh! Yours in exchange for mine!" Her voice had gone low and husky. Fierce need pulling her desires to the surface. She craved his body, the look, feel, and smell of it. She wanted to taste him as he tasted her. To trace the scars that marked his beautiful skin, with all their mystery and intrigue. Saying the words was not enough to quench her frantic need. Her hands flew to his shirt, tugging without grace or control to free the fabric from his shoulders.

"Easy, Sweets. Easy. I am yours." There was a sensual curve to his lips as he grinned above her.

Staying her hands with his, he made short work of his shirt, tossing it carelessly to the side to join her nightgown. She growled at the bronze expanse of his rippled abdomen suddenly glowing above her. Her hands devoured him, running over each muscle and every mark as she whined and mewled her joy below him. He allowed her to explore him. He hung over her, his face tensing and flexing with each stroke of her greedy fingers. Groaning, he found her mouth once more and she wrapped her arms around his waist, pulling him sharply down to her.

The ache within her reached a fever pitch and she could no longer stand his teasing touch. Grinding her hips against the rigid length of his manhood, now pressed staunch and alert within his trousers, she growled into his mouth. Little more than a wild animal, her body took on a devious darkness as she begged him for his. With every move, every caress, she demanded him and he began to moan under her touch. An evil smile curved her lips against his as she realized she was bringing him pleasure. In spite of her lack of skill, she was pleasing him. Purring in her throat, she intensified her efforts.

As if not wanting to be outdone, his hands returned to exploring and teasing her sensitive, soft skin. When the tips of his fingers brushed hot over the tops of her thighs, she sucked in a ragged breath. He laughed against her, brushing higher into the small shock of ebony curls. She trembled as he continued to stroke the sensitive flesh of her hips.

"Open for me, Sweets. Open wide. I long to touch you..." She whimpered softly at his wicked demand, even as she moved her thighs. As she fell open below him he kissed one tender breast and then the other, before his finger ran fleetingly over her slickness. Feeling the wet heat there he growled. "Dear God, Essie..." His fingers ran over her again, though this time there was firm strength to them. He rubbed through her, stroking her secret place in a way she had never imagined. Her body began to tense and twist under his touch. Electricity coursed over her flesh as she flushed and pimpled. She had never felt anything like it.

"Ty...I...don't stop...I..." Her mind swam in a sea of bright lights. Her body became a tumultuous sea, heaving like waves in a storm.

"Tell me, Sweets. Say it. Tell me what you want." His mouth was drifting lazily over her stomach as he teased her brutally. Her body locked tight. Every muscle pulling taunt all at once. It was excruciating and blissful, beyond anything she had ever dreamed. She wanted to pull his hand away even as she arched farther into his touch. A guttural incoherent sound roared from her as she broke into a million tiny pieces. Each shard of her screamed in unison for him to take her, and so she shouted it, too.

"I want you!" He chuckled as he continued his assault. She couldn't breathe, couldn't think, couldn't see. Her world had become pure sensation, pure pleasure; all fuzzy edges and bright undulating colors.

"You want me to do what, Sweets? Tell me..." She growled. He knew she was naive, knew she had never, and yet he wanted her to tell him exactly what she craved. Oh, but he was cruel. Bending into his continued touch she groaned.

"I want...you...inside...me!" In an instant he was at her mouth, his fingers having finally ended their torment of her overly swollen apex. He plundered her lips, her tongue, nipping at her between ragged hot breaths. His hips lifted over hers as his hand worked to free the fall of his trousers. Her fingernails raked over the slabs of glistening muscle lining his spine. So desperate was her need of him that it had become violent, painful. He slapped against her thigh, hot and hard and heavy.

"Now!" She cried as she clung to his waist, pulling him down onto her. She pressed her head back into the pillow, her eyes staring at nothing as he nuzzled into that sensitive spot along her nape she loved for him to touch. Through the crack surrounding the cannon port, she could see the glow of dawn. This day she would be his. This day she would be complete. The thought made her tense in anticipation as his arm curved around her hips, lifting her to receive him.

Before he could arch her back far enough to give her what she begged for, a loud ringing split their blissful silence. She barely registered the sound at first, but when he went still and tense, she took notice. The bell, loud and sharp, was clanging frantically, without rhythm or purpose, and yet he was pulling away. He no longer arched her hips to his, his weight no longer holding her steady.

"No!" She couldn't manage a coherent plea, her mind too muddled with passion for more.

"I have to, Sweets. That's the emergency bell." He sounded as if he were in terrible pain as he shrank away from her open body. His eyes, full of grief and regret, drifted down her flesh.

"Now? Why? Ty, please...You can't mean to leave me like this!" She clung to him, digging her fingernails into his flesh as if she could overpower him and forcibly bring his warmth back to her. He groaned and swung his legs over the side of the bed. Kneeling beside her, he leaned over and kissed her gently as he tugged her hands free of his shoulders.

"Believe me, Sweets, there is nowhere on Earth that I would rather be than here, but I am the captain. I must see to this, and whoever is ringing that bell had better hope this is really an emergency. Else he will be swimming back to London. I will return as soon as I am able. I promise." As he stood from her, she caught sight of his manhood, still rigid, protruding from his trousers. She whimpered at the sight of him, knowing how close she had come to truly feeling him. Turning her face into her pillow, tears filled her eyes. God truly hated her. It was the only explanation that seemed to make any sense. Why else would every rich, potential moment be shattered by catastrophe? As she sobbed she felt his weight return. He leaned against her shoulder, cooing, his deep voice coated in fear.

"Essie, I swear I will come back. Please don't cry. You *will* be mine. Today. Not even God can stop me from having you." He kissed her sweetly on the top of her head, and then he was gone. She listened, shaking from tip to toes, as he moved around her room. Seconds later, she felt the blanket she had left in the chair drape over her fevered flesh. Then the door opened. A sigh full of agony and impatience echoed from the opening and then nothing. The door closed and she was alone.

She wiped the tears from her face as she sniffled into her mattress. She had been so close to knowing him. So close to the perfection of his arms. Her body finally began to calm and with the calm came her rational mind creeping back to her like a dog that knew he had been bad. With her intelligence returning she begrudgingly admitted he really had not had a choice. As important as she was to him the *Siren* and her crew must take precedence. Her sobs subsided and she began to sit up when her door opened again.

Panic sent her spinning on the bed, desperately trying to cover any exposed flesh before she saw Ty standing in the opening. His eyes filled with longing as he took in her bare beauty once more.

"Dress, Sweets. We will need you." A frown marred his face and his voice had turned strict and filled with what she feared was panic. As soon as he finished his demand, he immediately disappeared behind her closing door.

Chapter 14

"We have come upon a shipwreck, lass." Her eyes darted from the deck to the sea. Scanning the horizon around them she squinted, trying to find the sight he had alluded to. "It's there." His arm extended to her right and she followed his pointed finger to a set of small dark blobs bobbing on the waves about one hundred yards off the port side.

Crates and splinted wood stuck from the sea like briar brambles from the ground and there, nestled in the center of the quagmire, were two lifeboats. Larger than the dinghies being lowered to the surface before her, the white-washed boats drifted lifelessly among the ruined remains of their mother ship. No heads, no arms, no signs of life seemed to make themselves known and for a moment she wondered if they were vacant scraps. Empty chairs at a dinner party marking the forgotten or lost. Her throat tightened painfully. To think she had thought God was punishing her with the bell when in truth only providence could explain how they had come upon this wreck at all. If indeed there were survivors it was a miracle they had come by to find them.

"My God! I wonder what happened?" From the look of the wreckage, the ship had not merely sprung a leak and sank beneath the waves, but shattered like a glass thrown against stone.

"Not sure, lass. If there is a living soul in those boats maybe we'll learn the cause. The men will haul the boats back. God willing, there will be people in them worth more than bait." She cringed at his allusion, knowing full well that if they found bodies within the bobbing vessels they would ultimately become little more than food for the sharks.

It took the better part of an hour for the crew to row out to the wreckage and attach a lead to the boats. By the time they managed to pull back along the side of the *Siren,* it was mid-morning. And yet the chill of night still clung greedily to the air around her. Pulling his coat closer to her core, she watched as Ty moved about on the deck directing his men in their efforts. As much as she wanted to appreciate him, the weight of the tragedy unfolding made it impossible. She had stood and watched all their dizzying activity waiting and dreading the moment she would be needed.

As the first sailor crested the railing with the form of a man draped over his shoulder, Vanessa sprang into motion. Her moment of use had come. Despite the warmth and comfort of his coat, heavy and familiar around her, she sloughed it off and tossed it to Mortimer as she turned and headed for the stairs. In moments she was standing impatiently waiting for the sailor to lay the man in his arms down so that she could tend to him. Before the crewman could give her the chance, he spoke.

"There is no need. This one's gone home, m'lady." His somber tone was quiet and labored as he lowered the poor man's body gently to the deck. Her heart sank. The boats contained bodies, but were they all no more than empty vessels now? The young man stood over the body for a moment in reverence before he moved to the railing and went over again for more. Ty had gone over as well. He would take part in every aspect of this rescue, of that she had no doubt. She only hoped his courage would hold strong as she might need him if things continued in the tragic tone they had taken on so far.

One by one, bodies, young and old, were hauled up onto the deck and lined along the far side. She moved from one to the next checking for any signs of life. The dead were moved to the side to make room for more. Ty had Connor collect the personal effects on the bodies for the families waiting in vain for their loved ones to return. There would be no funeral, no burial. Once he finished, the bodies were carried to the side and heaved over.

It was brutal. Vanessa understood the need, but not the method. She did not have time to dwell on it though. The bodies were piling up. Each lifeboat had room for nearly twenty-five and they both appeared to have been at capacity when the vessel had shattered upon the waves.

The sixth victim, a man in his late fifties, had a faint pulse. Her first survivor! "This one's alive! Quick, move him to the aft! Bring water!" She watched as Tibilt hoisted the heavy-set man with all the care of a mother carrying a newborn and moved him to the shade below the quarter-deck. His skin was blistered and cracked from his time in the sun, but he was alive. Realizing she could not tend to him while others waited for her attention, she called Mortimer to ladle water between the poor man's cracked and bleeding lips as she returned to the line of bodies still to be checked.

When she finished checking the last from the first lifeboat, she sighed, deep and sad. Of the twenty-three forms hauled over the rail, only four still contained evidence of life. Two of these were barely clinging, but the first survivor was starting to rouse. The men were exchanging the first lifeboat for the second when she saw Ty helping the gentleman into his cabin. Her curiosity peaked. It would be several minutes before the first victim from the second boat came over the rail. Moving swiftly, she filed in behind them.

Ty's gaze snapped to her as she closed the door. A pain ghosted over him before he returned his attention to the man mumbling softly in his dining chair.

"Have you learned what caused this tragedy? How long they have been adrift?" Her voice was soft and low, unwilling to startle the pitiable remains of a man lolling on the verge of unconsciousness before her.

"Not as yet, but I know this man. His name is Randolf. We served together. Last I heard he was captaining a passenger ship." Ty knelt before his friend and held his head up. "Ran! Old man, open your bloody eyes. You're being rude to the lady!" Vanessa gasped. His shout seemed beyond inappropriate. She moved to pull him off the poor figure before she realized it had worked. The Man's head steadied and his eyes opened. For a moment he seemed to be completely lost, but finding Ty, he smiled broadly.

"Any and all for a pretty lady! Tibi! Good God man, is it good to see you!" He tried to stand, but his body no longer contained the strength. Falling back against the chair, he tugged Ty's massive frame down to him for a hug that left him screaming in pain. "How many?" His smile was gone, lost in the grimace. Heavy tears hung in the corners of his eyes but did not fall.

"We have not finished fishing them out of the other boat. Of yours, only three, aside from you, sir." Vanessa's voice was still soft and low. Randolf found her, standing before the door and blinked several times before he spoke.

"Bless my soul! Tibi allowing a woman on his precious *Siren*? And a beauty at that! Things have indeed gone awry." Vanessa could not contain the scowl that creased her brow. So much death and he was still trying to rib his old chum. Sensing her displeasure, Randolf cleared his throat and did his best to improve his posture.

"I beg your pardon, lass. This is no time for such talk. It's just that Tibi...I mean Tiberius has always avoided women, especially the pretty ones. Always said they were nothing more than a distraction meant to lead a man astray. I assure you, lass, I do not share his feelings." Vanessa gasped, her gaze

231

jumping to Ty and locking on. *Always avoided women.* He had been forced to be near her. Fear pulled at her stomach. Was his affection no more than a character weakness?

"Ran, hold your tongue. Lady Everly is concerned with the care of your passengers, not my aversion to females. What happened to your ship?" Ty could not meet her eyes. He strained under her gaze but did not venture to return it.

Randolf looked from Ty to her and back again, "I don't know, she looks quite interested..." Seeing the scowl darken every inch of Ty's angular face, he shifted and cleared his throat. "A fire broke out on board not four days from port. My *Lucy Ann* was taking a compliment of military supplies and passengers to New England. Bloody buggering arses didn't tell me their *supplies* were barrels of gunpowder! When we lost control of the fire we started evacuating the ship, but only two boats made it into the water before the flames reached the hold. I was on deck helping load the third boat when it blew. I awoke nearly a day later in one of the two surviving boats, fished from the drink by its passengers." A solemn sadness washed over him. Vanessa read it perfectly. He was reliving the moments before the end, the seconds after waking up and realizing all but a few had been lost. "We

232

have been out here for nearly a week now..." His voice faltered.

"That long without fresh water it's a wonder any of you survived!" Vanessa took a few steps closer to the beaten-down man. A captain without a ship was a sad sight indeed.

"We gave all we could spare to the other boat for the girl."

"Girl?" Ty had been listening, still struggling not to meet Vanessa's eyes.

"Oh Lord! The girl! Does she live? Is she..." His eyes shot up, frantically looking for an answer neither of them knew.

Vanessa needed no more information. Turning she ran from the cabin. Three bodies now lay on the deck for her assessment, but she bolted past them. Leaning over the rail, she looked down into the lifeboat alongside the hull. There were still well over a dozen forms in the craft, but all appeared to be full-size. "A child!" She called down to the young sailor struggling to fling one of the passengers over his shoulder. He stopped the second he had heard her and looked up in panic. "There is a child in this boat! Find her!" He immediately returned the form

233

to the floor of the boat and began examining each body in turn.

Reaching a covered form at the rear of the lifeboat, he froze, then turned and called back to her. "I have found her!" Vanessa watched, terrified, as he flung the blanket back to reveal a woman cradling the small figure of a very young girl. Neither body moved as he lifted the tiny form into his arms and turned for the ladder.

Vanessa's heart stopped and roared at the same time. Pain radiated out from it, begging in silent prayer for the poor child to have survived, but she knew it was likely in vain. Small children were usually the first to be lost in situations like these as their bodies did not carry the necessary stores to provide for them in times of trial.

Fighting to cling to hope, she met the crewman at the rail as soon as he crested the top, scooping the little one from his shoulders and carrying her to the shade. Laying her down gently, she took her in. The child was not nearly as burned and blistered as the other bodies they had retrieved, but her skin was pallid and sunken from lack of even basic provisions. As she was gingerly lowering her head, the girl, no more than four years old, coughed. It was a rough, labored sound and the sweetest she had ever heard.

"She lives! Mort! Bring the water!" Vanessa cradled the small body in her arms as she slowly funneled water into her tiny mouth. After a moment, she looked up to see another form being hauled over the rail in Ty's arms. The mother had been brought up next. Passing her task to Mort, she stood from the child and sprinted to tend to the woman. The second she placed a hand on her forehead her heart shattered. Cold, hard flesh met her fingertips.

Looking back at the child she felt tears stream down her cheeks. Drawing herself up a bit, she met Tibilt's eyes. He had come to carry her to the line of survivors. She shook her head slowly and he seemed to slump, knowing precisely her meaning. Motioning to Connor, he turned and moved to the rail to hang his head.

"Be kind to her," was all Vanessa could say as Connor met her gaze. His eyes pleaded for another truth, but there was no other to give. He lifted the corpse into his arms and, forcing himself to move, drifted sadly away. Turning slowly, she found Ty still standing beside her. She wanted to rush into his arms and from the sadness etched in his chiseled features, he wanted the same, but they hadn't the time. There were other bodies and the day had only just begun.

Looking back at the girl, Vanessa struggled with her fear. She had not been much past four when she had lost her mother and she did not wish to be party to another girl living what she had. The world was still moving around her. She swallowed down her grief and checked the others laid out before her.

The second boat had fared better than the first, but not by much. When the last of the passengers had been brought over the side, there were another eight survivors to care for and nearly twenty that needed to be cataloged and disposed of. In all, thirty seven small bags of personal effects lined the bow rail, no longer having an owner and awaiting their tragic delivery. The entire crew focused on the effort to aid the survivors, wanting to block out the dead floating around the *Siren;* leaves on the surface of a calm pond.

Well after noon, Ty emerged from his cabin after sharing the grim news with poor Randolf. She couldn't help but feel for him. He looked exhausted and utterly defeated. His ship was now carrying more than double its capacity with nowhere for his new passengers to sleep and likely not enough food to sustain them. As she tended to the burned and dehydrated newcomers, he made arrangements for their care and board for the remainder of their journey back to London.

His crew volunteered to give up the bunk room, choosing to sleep on deck. At first, Ty argued against the suggestion. The nights were growing bitterly cold and he felt concerned for their health under such conditions. They rallied and convinced him tossing cargo overboard this close to port would be an unnecessary waste. She could tell from the stubborn jut of his chin he was still very much against the idea, but he eventually caved to their demand.

Once it was decided the crew's quarters would be the passengers' quarters, the poor souls were helped down into the ship. All but the little girl. According to Randolf, her name was Nancy. Her father had sent her and her mother on ahead of him, expecting to follow in only a few months, but it would not come to pass. Being so young, and the other passengers being in such poor condition, it was decided the child would share Vanessa's stateroom and remain under her care until London was reached. While she was happy to care for the little girl, her heart ached. Ty could not come to her again as he had promised, not that he would have time to now.

The days after the event were crowded and demanding. They ran out of their food stores only two days later and Ty had to have his men fish each and every day to sustain their new meal count. The only bright side seemed to be that most of the men who survived were happy to pitch in and help. Ty now had the crew to run his vessel full sail night and day, making the time lost for fishing easily recouped in the dark.

Vanessa's days were no less hectic, though far less scenic. She could not venture farther than from her room to the bunk room, the deck becoming little more than a fading memory from better times. Between caring for little Nancy and the few survivors still barely clinging to life, her days were full of rushing back and forth. Ty had managed to steal a few moments here and there to hold her close to him and kiss her gently. Precious seconds to show her he still longed for her as she longed for him, but they never seemed to last. The sounds of approaching steps, or calls for assistance, broke each and every embrace far sooner than she wished.

Lying awake, she found herself crying softly into her pillow as Nancy lay beside her asleep. Fear consumed her. Fear that she would likely never know Ty. Not in the way she wanted. Her life would be filled with regret over the lost opportunity to know the thrill of a lover of her choosing. The bliss of belonging, completely, to the man she loved. The one man she now feared she would love for the rest of her life.

Chapter 15

It was well past eight before the knock on her door signaled dinner. The last few days had put more than a little strain on poor John and he had not handled it well. Running out of his stores and being forced to cook whatever fish they managed to catch was apparently beyond his patience. On only the second day after his pantry ran empty, he lost his composure in front of Ty. It had been a terrible thing to see and Vanessa had had a front row seat. John railed at the absurdity of it all. A ship meant for no more than twelve attempting to limp back to London carrying nearly thirty was not what he had signed on for.

At first, Vanessa had felt bad for him. He could not hope to keep up with all of the demands heaped upon him and still have the food taste as wonderful as it had before the tragedy. But to see him flushed and screaming at Ty not because he was overworked, but because he was not being thanked for each and every passable meal that left his galley sent her blood boiling. Ty had apparently had the same reaction. He demoralized poor John until the large man looked like little more than a wayward child cowering away into the corner. And what was more; Ty had done it with only a handful of words said barely above a whisper. After his beratement, John had taken it upon himself to remain in his galley permanently, at least until they reached port and he could find himself new employment. Their meals had arrived in the hands of the ragged-looking Mr. Mortimer since that day.

While all of his men were looking worse for wear, sleeping in the open cold was not ideal under the best circumstances; Mortimer was suffering beyond the others. His age and hard life compounded the ill effects of the cold to cause his entire body to curl in on itself in obvious pain. He could barely stand up straight without groaning, and his face had become so darkened by exhaustion Vanessa had on three occasions pulled him into her room and forced him to sit before the stove for a while.

Despite all her duties and all her patients, Mort was special to her. He had been the first on this ship to show her kindness and to see him deteriorate before her was more than she could stomach. Tonight was no different. He appeared tray in hand, looking sunken and weary at her door.

"Your dinner, ladies." He smiled weakly down at little Nancy. She smiled back broadly and tugged on

Vanessa's skirt. The child had not said a word since she had awakened. Most attributed it to the shipwreck and the trauma of seeing such destruction, but Vanessa knew her silence was for her mother. Even at only four, the girl understood her loss better than most ever would. "To your chair with you girl. I'll be right behind you."

Nancy jumped into motion, pulling the second dining chair, brought from Ty's cabin especially for her, up to the side of the desk and settling down into it. "Just leave hers tonight, Mort. I feel no desire to eat." A wanton sigh leaked from her as she watched the tired old man putting on a display of elegance for the young child. As the small plate clinked to the table, Mort's eyes darted to Essie's.

"Are you sure, m'lady? Are you well?" The deep concern in his voice made her smile in spite of her unhappiness.

Taking a step closer to him, she placed her hand on his forearm as a gesture of thanks. "I am as well as to be expected, as we all are. I just find no use in food this evening." Her smile faltered as an image of Ty, his eyes sad and heavy, staring at her from across the crowded deck, flashed through her troubled mind.

"Aye, lass. There seems to be a lot of that goin 'round. The Captain refused his dinner, too, not ten minutes ago. Funny thing that. He had the same sad look in his eyes." Essie sucked in a ragged breath as she and the old sailor stared at each other for a long moment in silence. He seemed to be waiting for her to say something, to question his meaning perhaps, but she could not bring herself to speak. Thoughts of Ty too depressed to eat clawed at her heart, breaking it anew.

"Well, then. If you have no more use for an old man, I suppose I had better get back up top. We will be in London tomorrow..."

"Tomorrow!" The shriek had flown from her before she could catch it.

"Aye, lass. We have made excellent time, what with running full sail at night. Captain thinks we'll make the Thames before noon. You'll be home in time for supper."

The room tilted. Essie's balance left her and she wilted like a flower, too long cut without water. Her body collapsed under its own weight and she sank hard to the floor. They would reach London tomorrow. She would see her father, be spirited home, forced to marry Stephen, and all of it

243

happened tomorrow. Nancy jumped from her chair to aid her, curling into her lap and wrapping around one limp arm. The child nuzzled her, whimpering the concerned plea she could not utter.

Vanessa went cold and still. No time. She had no time left. She had spent the last week trying to convince herself that perhaps living with the regret of missing her chance was better than having taken it and walking away, but in this moment all her efforts failed. Given the choice now she would gladly choose the pain, so long as spending the night in his arms was hers first. The soft, pleading, squeezing actions of little Nancy's fingers roused her from her thoughts. Looking at the child, and then to Mort, her eyes carried a silent plea.

As if he read her request perfectly, he bent at the waist and extended her a steady hand. Allowing him to help her up, she continued to beg him for help with her gaze. "Go to him, lass. You both deserve to be happy." A bright smile curved her soft lips, before her emerald eyes drifted down to little Nancy still clinging to her skirts. "I will care for the girl. Now, go."

Vanessa could not believe it. Not only had he heard her plea, but he had understood it. "How did you...how long have you known that...?"

"That my Captain and the lovely Lady Everly are madly in love with one another? Ah, lass, it does not take a great mind to know this. I have been around that man for seven years now. I know him, better than his own mum I'd wager. And you do not hide anything. Your eyes dance when he comes into view. Now, go to him, before you miss your chance at happiness." His slight smile faltered when she wrapped him in a tight hug. He had made her so happy. Grinning down at little Nancy one last time, she turned and ran from her room. She flew down the corridor toward the hatch, and reaching the surface, made a beeline for his cabin door.

Her heart flared into a panicked beat as she stood before the door wondering just what she should say, or if she should say anything at all. She clenched her fists over and over again, trying to steady her fingers before she knocked. The night was cold and windy and as she stood, staring at the salt-bleached wood, tendrils of ebony hair began to drift around her. Her hair had come loose and gone wild around her shoulders. A sweet smile curved her trembling lips. He loved her hair, especially when it was as wild and loose as it was now.

Bolstered by the blanket surrounding her, she knocked firmly on his door and waited. Two voices sounded on the other side. He was not alone. Her heart fell to her feet. Suddenly she fought the urge to turn and run. When his door swung open to reveal him, shirt partially unbuttoned and his face flushed, she nearly fainted. Shock and excitement flourished in his eyes as he took in her expression.

"Ah, speak of the devil, and he, or should I say she, shall appear! The lovely Lady Everly! How opportune your arrival is!" From behind Ty's massive, firm shoulders came the voice she had come to know as Randolf's. Since the wreck, he had gone out of his way to monopolize Ty's time and he alone had ruined most of the secret moments Ty had found to pull her close.

"Hold your tongue, Ran! Or I'll pull it from your jaw myself!" Ty snapped over his shoulder at his friend before returning to her. His gaze softened as he took a small step toward her. "Essie, I...what are you doing here?" She swallowed down her panic. He had been drinking. Randolf's work no doubt, and a familiar uncontrolled fire burned deep in his navy blue eyes. It lit over her whole body and turned her blood molten.

"I need...I wanted to talk to you if I might?" Nodding he moved aside and motioned for her to enter his cabin. As she brushed timidly by him, she heard him

246

suck in a deep breath and realized he was scenting her, like a predator with prey, and it only served to excite her more. She wanted to be hunted, captured, and devoured by him. Nothing would bring her more pleasure, but she could not reveal her desire as they were not alone. Taking several steps into the dimly lit room, she found Randolf, sprawled out in a dining chair and slumped against the table. A large, nearly empty, bottle of rum and two glass tumblers sat on the table before him. The dining chair opposite his was canted out and she knew Ty had been there when she had knocked.

"I think it's time you retired for the evening, old man." Ty's voice had gone deep and dangerous, a tone she had heard only once before.

"Not until I have seen this mess sorted out! You are a good friend, Tibi, and a bloody brilliant sailor, but when it comes to matters of the heart you..."

"Perhaps you misunderstood me, Ran. Allow me to be more direct. Get out. Lady Everly would like to speak to me and I am quite done speaking with you. Leave us." His eyes never left hers as he ordered his friend to leave, in no uncertain terms. The light in his deep indigo eyes flickered hotter with each passing second they stood staring at each other.

"All right, all right, boy. No need to snap. Just remember what I told you. You can fix this; you just have to forgive yourself." Ran stood from the table. Wobbling for a moment, he reached out and scooped one of the tumblers and the remaining rum into his hands before he pushed between them toward the door. As soon as he had passed through the portal, Ty pushed the door closed and scooped her into his arms. His body tensed and burned as he hauled her against it, burying his face into the nape of her neck and breathing in deeply.

"Essie, are you really here? Did you really come to me? God, Sweets, you smell so good. Do you still taste of caramels and cream?" Before she could even breathe he was at her mouth. He fed off of her lips as if he hadn't eaten in days and she reveled in the need that seemed to be leeching from him into her. As his tongue probed the corners of her mouth she moaned and bent against him, pressing her chest to his and feeling his thundering heartbeat. He was on fire.

"Ty..." She whispered his name into his mouth and he sucked it in on a ragged breath before swallowing it down. Still holding her tightly, he pressed his forehead to hers and inhaled her. His hands tangled in her hair and she could feel the shiver created by touching her, ripple through his body. "You've been drinking?" He nodded absently as his taunt arms

248

tightened. "And discussing me?" He chuckled softly as he nodded again. He began taking small steps backward, into his room, and she followed.

"I only had one. Ran insisted. It was enough to flush my face and muddle my mind a bit, but I am me. As for the discussion of you, it was more a discussion of our arrival in London tomorrow than of you, Sweets. Though you did enter into the conversation a few times." Her turn to nod. He had mentioned London and with the word in her ears a knot formed in her throat. The reason she had knocked on his door kicked her in the chest.

"Ty, I came here to ask...well, to tell you that I would rather live with the pain." He lifted his head in confusion. He had backed them far enough that the dining chair he had only moments ago occupied pressed against the back of his legs. Grunting slightly, he swung her up and into his arms before he sat down, pulling her closer to him in his lap.

"The pain? Sweets, what are you talking about?" He lightly pinched a tress of her raven hair between his fingers and rubbed it gently. Twining it around him, he used it to tug her face closer to his. Her mouth suddenly went bone dry and so she licked her lips. A simple, involuntary motion that had him grumbling deep inside his chest.

"Tomorrow my father will collect me and I will be taken away from here. Away from you. I would rather have you now and live the rest of my life with the pain of losing you than miss this chance to hold you and regret it for all my days. Will you?" His breathing had become hard and labored. Hot, rough pants tickled over her goose-pimpled flesh as she waited for his answer.

"Will I what, Sweets?" The finger twisted in her hair tugged her a bit closer and his lips brushed lightly over hers. She wanted his kiss, but he did not give it to her.

"Will you lie with me?" He went rock hard instantly. Tension pulled at him and his strong body turned to stone, every muscle seizing with the effort to hold himself still. She wasn't sure what he would do next, but his reaction was not within her realm of possibilities.

"No, Sweets." *No!* He was refusing her? When it was so obvious he wanted her, and perhaps even more than she wanted him? Indignation flared within her. It had taken every ounce of her courage to say the words, to ask him for his love, and he had said no. She wrenched herself free of his arms and turned for his door, bent on fleeing from him as soon as possible. She did not get more than a step before he was pulling her back. His grip on her wrist was surprisingly gentle as he spun her around and back to his chest.

"Release me, Ty! Let me go!" Tears streamed down her cheeks as she struggled to free herself from his strength.

Cradling her cheek in his warm, callused hand he kissed her softly. She wanted to turn away from the touch, but she just couldn't. She wanted his kiss.

"That's just it, Sweets. I can't let you go. I do not wish to ever let you go. I know I once offered you what little time we had, but I am afraid I did not really mean it." She fought the arm circling around her waist. He had lied to her! "Shh, Essie, calm yourself. Let me explain before you spurn me." The fingers on her cheek caressed her again and she stilled. Fury and desire swirled in her eyes as he sighed against her lips. She remained tense, ready to run and he seemed to understand just how dangerous she had become. "I had hoped after a week in my arms you would have been so taken with me that when I asked you to run away with me you would say yes."

She blinked at him in confusion. "Run away with you?" She could barely speak.

He pulled her closer. "Sail away with me. We could go, run away. I want you for my own, Essie. I don't want to give you back to your father. Not knowing Stephen Everly is your fate if I do. We could sail around the world. Be happy and free..." Her love for him surged in her breast. He didn't just want to hold her, he wanted *her*. He wanted all of her and for the rest of his life. She had never been so utterly happy and completely miserable before. As much as she wished they could run from reality, hide out on the ocean from her fate, she knew it would destroy him.

"That sounds wonderful, Ty." He seemed to relax in her arms and it ripped her heart anew. "But I can't let you do that." He staggered as if he had expected her to say anything else. His mouth hung open, shock dulling the passion in his eyes. "My father would have you labeled a pirate if I agreed to such madness." Her voice had gone soft and sweet as she tried to reason her way through this, but he would have none of it.

"Your father's reaction is the least of my concerns, Sweets. I only want to be with you. Damn the consequences." He kissed her now. His lips plundered hers as if the ferocity of his efforts and the desire behind them would be enough to convince her to give.

With more than a little effort, she managed to free her mouth from his. She needed to make him understand, though in truth she had almost lost her argument. His passion was compelling and she wanted too desperately to flee with him. But she couldn't. As angry as she was at her father, he was still her father and she loved him too much to insult him, and their family name, this way. In that one act, she would bring shame on him and his title; a shame from which he would likely never recover. Not only that, but the damage to Ty's sterling reputation and honor would be unforgivable.

"If not for him then for you. I will not be the source of your disgrace. The cause of your downfall. You are perfect. The most noble, honorable man I have ever known. You are brave and honest and kind and you do not deserve to become a fugitive. Not for me." He cradled her head as he sighed against her. She could feel the frustration building within him and it pained her, but she could not allow him to be destroyed.

"You are the only thing that matters to me anymore, Essie. The rest is just noise, meaningless opinions that cannot touch us. What do I care what the world thinks of me so long as I have you?" She nearly crumbled. It would be so easy. A quick unload at the docks and then a sudden departure. No one would realize she was missing for weeks. Perhaps her father would even think her lost at sea. Better he think her dead than know of her betrayal, but that thought faded. He was nothing if not meticulous. Surely he would have a man waiting for her at the dock. And even if he didn't, there would be witnesses to see the *Siren* make port. People would know the ship had made the voyage intact and her father would know what she had done.

"My feelings for you are no less intense! What I want and what I know to be right are at war, Ty! I cannot destroy you for my selfishness. I won't." He groaned deeply as he ground his teeth. He did not want to hear her logic, did not want to face the truth. Turning her around, he pushed her toward his bed. A shiver lit through her. His bed was where she wanted to be most in this world, but not until this matter was resolved.

"If I am not allowed to care about your future, perhaps I can raise concern for your crew? What is to become of them? They would also be declared pirates! Have you not thought of that? Some of them have families and loved ones they would be divided from if we were to run as you suggest." He huffed his begrudged agreement. He hadn't thought of his men apparently and her words finally seemed to hit home. He sank onto his mattress, dragging her down and into his lap. The defeated, tragic look on his face made her soul ache.

"Make love to me, Ty. If this night is all we have let us make the most of it." She brushed her mouth over his. Back and forth, she dragged her plump, moist lips over his cheek and down to trace his jawline. With each gentle, coaxing caress his arms around her tightened. When his hand cupped her breast and squeezed her sensitive flesh, she moaned full and husky against his shoulder. "I want to belong to you. I want your name carved so deeply into my soul that no matter what the future brings I will always and only ever see your face in my dreams. Feel your flesh beside me..."

"Then that is what I will do, Sweets. Tonight you belong to me. I only pray tomorrow never comes..." His voice trailed off as he took her mouth.

Chapter 16

For a long while she reveled in his kiss. His strong lips caressed her soft pink ones as his tongue probed her mouth and his teeth nipped and tugged at her. *Wondrous. Breathtaking. Perfect.* Words flooded her mind as her senses heightened to take in each and every sensation his touch created. His arms about her pulled ever tighter threatening to squeeze the very air from her body, and it was magnificent. As the intimacy of his kiss deepened, he ran his hands over her clothes but made no move to strip them from her.

What is he waiting for?

While his adoring mouth intoxicated her, she wanted so much more. They had started down this path before, with soft kisses and slow progression. It was tender and passionate, and easily ruined by the unpredictable nature of life at sea. Even as her head swam in thoughts of his salty-sweet tongue tangling with hers, and the knot slowly twisting in her hips, she groaned impatiently.

Deciding to make the first move, she kicked off her small shoes. The soft thuds on the wooden floor seemed to draw his attention away from her lips, if only for a time. He grinned at her as his hard body shifted around her. With a little effort and surprising skill, his boots, heavy and worn, battered to the ground beside hers before his lips returned to their plunder.

He explored her gently, and a new excitement vibrated through him. It was contagious and she arched her back teasingly into his roving hands. His turn to groan lightly into her mouth. Without letting their bond slip, she began slowly losing the buttons on her vest. His arms stretched around her, giving the room she required to complete her task. When the last button slipped free, she pulled back from him to slide the garment from her shoulders. As the darkly tanned leather rustled to the floor at their feet, his wicked grin widened. The simple dark green waistcoat he wore tugged free of his torso, slapping softly to the ground a second later.

He was matching her, article for article; just as they had exchanged stories and memories on so many occasions in the past. She giggled slightly as she began to fumble with the clasps of her blouse. Her fingers had lost all their former agility as she trembled with anticipation. His grin grew dark and ferocious as he watched her efforts. She could feel his breathing grow rapid and irregular when the front of her shirt began to gape, revealing her simple undergarment. Pulling at the fabric, she tried to wrench it free of her skirt waist, but it would not release. Huffing slightly, she leaned against him.

"I cannot free it on my own. Help me?" She looked up into his lust-filled face. For a moment he stared at her greedily, licking his lips as if eying a delicious meal, and then shook his head.

"No. I want you to remove it. Stand up." She blushed as her heart rate flourished. Sliding over his thighs, her bare feet found the cool rough boards and she lifted her body before him. His broad hands slid down her torso to her hips where they squeezed her firmly, pulling her between his knees. She was only inches from him, his hungry gaze even with her bosom. Sucking in a timid breath, she grasped the silky fabric and tugged it free of her waistband, letting it slip down around her ankles.

The last time she had shed her clothing, he had done it. She had lain still and timid as he had peeled the fabric from her with care and caution, but this time she was not shy, not scared. She had come too far to allow it. There was no doubt left within her and that confidence radiated like light around her. He seemed blinded by it, enthralled by her glow as he watched her.

Without warning he pulled her to him, burying his face into her chest and holding her so very tight. He did not make a sound as he held her close, breathing hot and ragged into her flesh. She wrapped him up, curving her slender arms about his shoulders as she pressed her lips to the top of his head. She wasn't sure what he needed from her, whether it was comfort or reassurance, or simply affection, but she would give it.

Curled over him like a shield, she rubbed her fingers lightly over his shirt sleeves, feeling the fabric slip over the scars she knew were just below. "Your turn, love."

"Aye. That it is." He chuckled against her as he pulled back enough to wrench the shirt from his body. He did not bother to unbutton it and she could hear the cloth give way as he tore it from himself. As he wadded the shirt unceremoniously into a ball, she marveled at the rippling muscles along his arms and shoulders. Her fingertips, shaky though not unsure, traced the sinewy contours of his physique. His flesh burned from the inside out as if all his insides were aflame. Or perhaps it was her own heat she felt as she explored him.

He leaned into her again, preening under her touch as she continued to stoke him, petting his broad shoulders as one would a beast. Indeed he reminded her of one, so much raw power controlled by sheer will alone. He arched into her hands, groaning and growling as she caressed him. The sounds rumbling between them caused the heat swirling and knotting in her to flair brighter. *She needed him.*

"What shall I remove next, love? I leave the choice to you." Only a soft whisper, the question slipped from her without her allowing it. The thought had come to ask and her voice had done so. She shivered at the thrill of losing control, at the sense of freedom this exchange brought her. Freedom was a stranger, an idea destined to be studied but not lived. And yet here she was, living her wild dreams, and it was glorious.

A quick, uneven intake of breath pulled her closer to him. She was still running her fingertips over his flesh when she felt the shiver that had rippled through her transfer into him. The whole of his massive frame undulated before his head lifted from her.

"It is a tough choice you have given me, my Lady. On the one hand, if I ask you to remove your camisole I shall be rewarded with your lovely breasts. A sight that I very much long to see...and touch, and taste.

On the other, I could demand your skirt, bringing the whole of you one step closer to completely bear, which I long to see even more. What to do, what to do..." His voice was full and husky as he held her gaze. She could feel her face flushing, but it was not embarrassment that caused her reddening cheeks. Perhaps it should have been. He was talking to her in a manner she should have found vulgar, but she did not. His words caused her hips to tighten and a tingle to flourish throughout her thighs. He was stoking her fire and he knew it. *That* made her blush.

"The skirt is my choice, Sweets. In exchange for my trousers, I presume?" He chuckled as she licked her lips eagerly.

"I suppose so. I can't very well demand your smalls while your trousers are still in place, now can I?" He growled rough and fierce as he stood suddenly before her. Without warning he hauled her against him and dove into her mouth. He kissed her harder and more fiercely than he ever had before. Her head swam. Nothing could have prepared her for this. For the urgency and open desire racing over him. A week ago his unbridled passion had frightened her, but now it was necessary, vital. When at last he was forced to release her lips to breathe, he panted against her.

"You tease me, Sweets? Are you sure that is wise? I am only barely able to restrain my wild need for you as it is. What will you do if I lose my grip and falter to the animal within me?" Pulled against him she could feel it, the raw power, the aggressive way he held her. His need for her was fierce and frantic and she craved to have it freed.

The piece-for-piece exchange that had excited her only seconds ago lost all meaning. She did not want to build her passion any further, she wanted to release it, to have his released in unison, and to swim in the ocean they would produce. Letting her eyes fall from his, she followed the line of his strong jaw down his neck to his shoulder. She watched for a second as his pulse pounded strong and quick before she found the edge of the scare she had once traced with her tongue. Smiling wickedly, she leaned in and ran her moistened, swollen lips over his collarbone to the start of the mark. Allowing her hot, wet tongue to slip between her teeth, she traced the groove over and down, following it across his peck muscle and toward his nipple.

Stopping just shy of its conclusion, she spoke, "I will revel in it as that is exactly what I want. Everything you are, wild and pure and free. I want you, Ty. That's all I want. What I need..."

"And on my life, I will give it to you. But first...I want that skirt off." He smiled at her shocked gasp. He had just scolded her for teasing and now he tormented her in return. She wanted to rail against his demand, to insist that they have done with this game and get on with it, but he had frozen her to the spot. He was smiling—truly, fully smiling—at her and she could not look away. It, *he*, was magnificent! She had never seen it's like. His eyes glimmered in the dim light as joy ignited deep inside him. The broad expression seemed to soften his angular features, making him appear happier and younger than he ever had. Even the moon-shaped scar she adored was accentuated by the magical occurrence. It curved tight around his eye, and glinted in the glow as if his very skin were shining for her.

Her breathing had stilled. Her heart, which had been frantically beating only seconds ago, had almost stopped and in that moment she could do nothing but stare at him.

"The skirt, Sweets. I cannot wait all night..." His voice trailed away as he grazed his warm, moist lips over her frozen cheek. She whimpered at the touch, still reeling from the sight of him. Bolstered by her love, burning brighter now than a bonfire, she purred at him. All the while his mouth trailed over her flesh, his teeth catching and releasing small nibbles along her jaw.

"If you want it off so badly, then remove it." A gruff, utterly manly sound radiated out from him as he gripped her rough spun brown skirt. In a single harsh tug, the buttons holding it to her popped free and the sheath slid to the floor at their feet. The thick linen garment pulled away from her bare legs and silky underpants. The small, thin barrier now left between them was more than he could resist. She felt his arms circling around her as she leaned her head farther back, giving his lips free reign of her neck. She knew what he was about to do as he had done it before. He was preparing to lift her; sweep her into his arms and from there into his bed. She wanted it terribly, but he had insisted on finishing the game, so she would, too.

"Don't you dare! You demanded my skirt, and now it is gone. What of your trousers?" Her voice was teasing and hot as it slid from her throat and the arms around her coiled closer, but he made no more of a move to lift her. "Very well, I shall see to it myself." He moaned huskily but released her. Taking a single step back, he straightened to his full height.

She was a tall woman by most standards at five foot seven, but he was well over six feet and somehow seemed even taller as he swayed before her. Off balance, the fire raced over his face. He stared at her, waiting. When she lifted her delicate hands to his waist, he reached out and caught her wrists.

For a moment they stood, still and quiet, as if daring the other to move. Essie had never been one for patience. Pushing against his resistance, she grasped the first button. As it slipped free in her greedy fingers he sighed. His whole body seemed to tense and curl over her, like a large oak. She moved in a bit closer but continued to set his buttons loose. In seconds, his pants slid to the floor.

His smalls, threadbare and pale white, hung loosely from his narrow waist. She groaned, her eyes following the muscled straps under his tanned flesh as they converged just below the rim into a small crop of brown hair. He shivered before her as her eyes scanned over him slowly. She reached as if to tug his last layer to the floor, wanting to see him in all his glory, but his hands, which had never released her wrists, tightened. She licked her lips as she sighed. Leaning against his chest, she whimpered, begging for permission, but she knew full well it was his turn.

"Sweets..." he lifted her arms high over her head before he released her. His fingers shook as he grasped the bottom of her camisole and slid it slowly up her body. Inch by inch the thin covering eased away. His breathing quickened and a low, tumbling, rocky sound accompanied its creeping climb. Her breathing on the other hand had all but stopped. She froze, her arms drifting down to his shoulders as he continued to remove her top. When at last her breasts slipped free of the soft material he tore the garment from her the rest of the way. Casting it aside, his mouth dove for her flesh. She chuckled seductively as he pulled her taunt peak into his mouth with all the fervency of a starving animal.

His teeth squeezed gently around her tender flesh and she squealed at the thrill of it. She could feel his lips pull into a smile as he panted across her moist, swollen tip and did it again. "Oh God, Ty...don't stop..."

"Never. On my life....never..." His words were no more than wisps of air over her satin skin. A summer breeze off the ocean born to tease and excite. With his focus consumed by her breasts, she took advantage and quickly sloughed his smalls to the floor. He did little more than flinch as the over-worn layer left him bare.

He had her bent backward, curled over the arms holding her firmly across the lower back so that he could suckle her freely. From this position, she could barely reach him. Barely, but just. Her fingers, unsure and desperate, brushed over him, lightly at first and then more firmly. His teeth nipped her before rising to her mouth. Not once did he resist her touch. She had expected him to pull back as he had on so many occasions, but she was wrong. Instead, he moved closer to her, leaning into her exploring fingers. His hands spanned over her back, pulling in and tensing, begging her to tighten her grip in return. Biting his lips lightly, she squeezed him in her hands.

"Jesus, Essie, don't stop..." His voice was rasped and strained. His eyes pinched shut in a look that teetered between agony and ecstasy. He pressed his forehead to her and trembled as she stroked him once more with her now confident hand.

"Never. On my life." Without warning he wrenched her hand free of his manhood. She gasped as his eyes stabbed into her. The self-control, the leash tied around his need, had snapped. Her last layer was gone on a breath and then she was in his arms. The next heartbeat she was beneath him and he was draining her mouth of all she had. She clung to him, in awe of his power and determined to enjoy every moment to come.

At first, she thought he would simply take her, but as the tip pressed against her he paused. His muscles rippled and shook with the effort to hold back. He panted over her, squinting and blinking down at her as if he were struggling to see her in the glare of his passion.

"Sweets...are you sure?" Even as lost to his needs as he was he still feared for her. The love in her heart surged up her throat. She wanted to tell him how she felt, how she cared for him as she would never care for another, but she swallowed it back. To utter the words would likely kill her.

Instead, she smiled sweetly and nodded, rising off the bed to kiss him softly. Understanding her perfectly, he began to push. As he crested her threshold the white blinding pain surged through her. She pressed her lips to his to stifle the cry that climbed her throat. She felt invaded, stretched to the breaking point, and yet it was wonderful. She felt full, complete, whole, for the first time in her life. The blissful pain radiated out from her hips and caused a sweat to break over her.

Once fully seated, Ty pulled away from her lips. The second the contact was lost a whimper escaped on a pant. "Essie?" The concern and pleasure in his tone only made the ache throb more intensely. The pain was waning, but the emptiness was returning. She needed more. His presence was not enough, something was missing. She wasn't sure what was next, but she knew she needed it. Unable to speak, she dug her fingernails into his hips and pulled him closer. Grunting he pulled back and then returned slowly. The movement. That was what she needed. Moaning, she pushed his hips this time, away and then pulled them back to her.

"Essie." No more hesitation, only pleasure. Taking her lead, he began to move. Slowly at first and then faster. His speed was matched by his strength. She lay blinded, enraptured. The pleasure was beyond her imaginings, outside her wildest dreams. He took pleasure in her pleasure and the more she demanded the more he gave. When at last it overwhelmed her, shattering her more completely than he had in her cabin over a week ago, he broke with her. His body tensed and shook as she clung to him. Perfection. Every moment had been bliss and as the waves slowly stilled she tightened her grip on his shoulders.

"Ty..." Her voice was little more than a squeak. Rough and strained between rapid, ragged gasps as she tried to catch her breath. "Ty..." He flopped against her, his weight holding her steady but not crushing her. He grasped her face in his hands, brushing away the sweat-moistened curls of jet black from her cheeks.

"Yes, Sweets?" Her throat tightened as the words charged up her throat. *I love you! I love you!* Over and over in her heart, they sounded. *Say them, tell him!* But how could she? His smile broadened as he held her in his dark eyes. Swallowing down the phrase pounding in her chest, she returned his grin.

"Can we...do that again?" A hearty chuckle was all that sounded as he took her mouth and fulfilled her request. Whatever she asked for, whatever she desired, he provided and she found her pleasure was far more demanding than even he understood.

Chapter 17

Essie ran her hand over his bare chest as she sighed. In the faint light of the single lantern, his cabin took on a dream-like haze as they lay, tangled and exhausted, in his single bed. Her eyes were heavy with wanted sleep, but she just couldn't let her mind drift away from the moment. She lay there, contentedly listening to his heart as it thudded soft and strong beneath her head. It seemed to echo in his chest, beating out a rhythm that made the wild part of her stir and want to dance. Turning her face into his flesh, she kissed his muscles lightly and smiled. *Home.* He was her home. The wondrous realization lanced through her like a white-hot blade. He couldn't be her home no matter how badly she wished it to be true. In only hours she would be pulled away from him, never again to feel his arms draped around her as they were now.

Her dark, regretful thoughts drew a sad groan from her. Maybe she should let him spirit her away, at least then she could call him home forever. Even as the warmth of promise flourished, doubt ate at her. All the possible horrid results of such a decision lined themselves in her mind, each, in turn, showing her the inevitable fruits of her choice. *No.* She could not just elope with him.

Her thoughts then skewed to her father. Perhaps she could sway his mind. She had never successfully turned him from a decision before, but that did not strictly preclude the possibility. And she wanted so terribly for it to happen this time. If she could only convince him she would find greater happiness with another he might release her from this ill-formed bond.

The conversation unfolded in her mind over and over again. Her heart-felt speech wrote and rewrote itself in her thoughts, but each time her father's stern face towered over her and asked one simple question to which she had no decent answer. *Who is this man that would bring you happiness?* She loved Ty with all her heart, but her father, an Earl by title and birth, would see only his station. A simple ship captain could not hope to wed the daughter of an Earl, no matter the emotions involved.

Tears of hopelessness peeked at the corners of her eyes and she turned once more into his strength. The heavy arms holding her shoulders tightened. He stirred beneath her.

"Ty, are you awake?" Her throat was rough and dry, residual effects from their fevered activities. Hearing her own rasped tones made her smile despite her melancholy thoughts. He had promised to introduce her to pleasure and he had kept his word, several times over.

"Mm-hmm." His arms constricted, pulling her head higher onto his shoulder. Tenderly, he leaned forward and kissed her before wrapping her up and resting his head back onto his pillow, contented to return to a well-earned sleep. She, on the other hand, had no intention of resting tonight. This was her final night of freedom. Propping her elbow against his headboard, she cradled her head and gazed down at him. The flickering lamp light danced across his chiseled features and made her smile. He was beautiful, art. Tracing her finger along the bridge of his nose, she laughed as he snapped quickly as if he meant to bite her. Happiness warmed her hips and she shifted them closer to his.

Without warning, Randolf's parting words from earlier echoed in her ears. *You just have to forgive yourself.* She had paid little attention to the phrase when it had been said, far too focused on her mission to be distracted, but now it rang in her mind. What did he have in his past he needed to be forgiven for?

"Ty...what was Randolf referring to?" He stiffened next to her.

"What? Ran? What are you talking about?" He didn't open his eyes but she could tell he was not happy with her question. The muscles along his jaw pulled tight and his arm around her loosened. It almost felt as if his flesh cooled beside her.

"As you were shuffling him out the door he said something about forgiveness. I don't know why exactly, but it popped into my head just now and I simply must know what he meant." He shifted again, putting air between them. The more he pulled away from the topic the more fiercely her desire to know became. Perhaps it was an unhappy memory he did not want to share, but all of his life, his story, was vital to her. The more she knew about him the closer she felt.

"He said you needed to forgive yourself. I wish to know to what he was referring." A heavy sigh racked his chest as he pulled his arm from under her and sat up on the side of the bed. He was running from her, fleeing her question. Reaching out her small hand, she caught him by the elbow, a feeble attempt to keep him close. He could have easily freed himself from her light touch, but he made no move to. His head slumped from his shoulders, the muscles tracing along his spine tensing and flexing with his breathing.

"Why would you want to know something as long over and unpleasant as that?" His voice was soft, a plea for her to drop the subject, but she would not.

"It is part of who you are and I long to know you, Ty. Especially the unpleasant memories. I want to know you like no one else does." She tried not to sound demanding, but it was no use. She had no time for tact.

"You already do, Essie." He glanced back at her over his shoulder and she gasped. There was more than resistance in his eyes. Even in the faint light, she could see the pain, the sadness, as if it were written in ink on his very flesh. Tears welled in her emerald eyes as she took in the look of pleading panic that settled into his face as stones dropped into still water.

"Oh God, Sweets, don't cry." He shook his head as he allowed a small portion of the tension in his back and shoulders to lessen. Slumping toward her, he let a slow, labored breath leave him before turning his body to the side so he could face her more easily but still maintain the little distance he had acquired by sitting up.

"This is not a pleasant story, Love. I fear that when you hear what I have done, that need to know me so well will have served you ill." He paused as if waiting for her to shrug and release him from the obligation, but she had no intention of any such relief. Clearing his throat gruffly, he dropped his eyes from her to the rough spun sheet barely draped across his bare hips.

"I was engaged once." Her gasp was light, but he stopped on the sound, flinching as if she had hurled blades in his direction. "I should not tell you this, Sweets. It matters not..."

"Of course, it matters." Her voice was not at all what he was apparently expecting. Soft and gentle, she caressed his ears as her fingers did his arm, leading him forward. "Go on. Please."

"I was...very young. Seventeen. Her father was a merchant who did a great deal of business with my father and as a result, she and I grew up together. One day play turned to romance. Not long after I asked her to be my bride." The melancholy tones of his voice, barely above a whisper, played against the seemingly happy memory.

"Sounds like the perfect love story, Ty. Please don't stop." She squeezed his arm as her body lifted farther off the mattress. Her hips ached with a sweet pain she had never felt before as she pulled along his side.

"At first it was. Her father accepted my proposal and a date was set. But as with most young couples in love, we could not stand the wait. Only two weeks from our wedding day she pretended to fall ill. You see, she and her family were to travel on a country visit for the remaining fortnight of our engagement and she could not bear to be separated from me. Or so she claimed. My father offered her a room in our home until she recovered well enough to join her kin, but she and I had other plans. We...consummated our love under my father's roof before our time."

\Again his voice fell into desolation and it was beyond Essie, and all her faculties, to see fault in the tale so far. His story was one of love and passion, not unlike the one she had experienced with him on this very journey. Suddenly her mouth went dry and her skin turned to cold stone. Ty, sensing the change in her, shifted his gaze from his sheet to her face. His vacant stare was replaced with apprehension.

"Ty...are you married?" The words choked her as they slipped past her lips, hard and bitter. His tale seemed perfect and in her mind, their marriage became an inevitable conclusion that could lead her to only one result. He was a married man and she had shared his bed. Terrible thoughts swirled in her mind. She linked his reluctance to approach her at first and his plea to elope with him together in her memory with sickening certainty.

"What? No! Sweets, I swear, I am no one's husband! I never have been..." The final sentence croaked out before his eyes dropped from her, swollen with tears he would never shed.

"But...the merchant's daughter?"

"Lucy. Her name was Lucy. Good Lord, her name feels strange to my tongue. I haven't said it out loud in twelve years..." Now she was confused.

"Ty, I don't understand. Surely her family, or yours, did not end your engagement because you were too in love to wait? Such a scandal would have led to anger, I am sure, but to split up young love is a travesty!" Her face flushed with indignation. Happiness and love were things she prized most in this world. And the ability to marry for both was a blessing tragically out of her reach. The thought that someone else had it within their grasp to have it stolen away out of pride was beyond infuriating.

"Oh, Sweets. I tell you I loved another woman only weeks before I was to wed her and you are outraged I am not married. I said once nothing you could do would shock me, and I am glad to admit I was wrong. With all that has happened between us, I expected this anger and indignation, but towards me. Outrage that I had kept this from you, not at my lack of a wife." A sad smile pulled at the corners of his firm mouth as he ran a calloused finger along her jawline. Heaving a sigh, he continued.

"It was not our families that punished us for our transgression, but the Divine, Himself." Turning to better face her, almost joining her once again on the bed, he leaned his head down to hers and kissed her lightly on the forehead. "God took her from me."

"God? Ty you can't mean the woman you loved died before your wedding?" Her tears were more insistent than his as one rolled fat and hot down her cheek. His thumb lifted to brush it away before he cradled her face in his palm.

"He took her the eve before the date. She, and her entire family. The row of townhomes in which they resided burned."

"Burned!" Horror turned her stomach. She could think of no more gruesome death.

"To ashes in mere minutes. Lucy was gone and I was left with the guilt that her death was my punishment. My penance for breaking God's law." Agony settled into his eyes as his gaze drifted far away from his cabin. His stare jumped into the past and relived that terrible moment.

Trying to bring him back, she asked, "Is that why you joined the Navy? To escape the pain?"

The question had the opposite of its desired effect. His face drooped even further and his body, almost beside her again on the mattress, returned to the cold side of the bed. She found herself once more staring at his slumped spine.

"No. At least, not right away. I lost myself after that, Sweets. The guilt was more than my broken heart could bear and I am ashamed to say that I sought comfort in vices."

"Vices?" Fear crept up her throat. She knew where men found comfort. Kingston was full of such places and she had seen a few of her homesick colleagues fall victim to their promises.

"With Lucy lost to me, I fell into a bottle. I abandoned my family, my responsibilities, my life. I wanted only to numb the pain, to drown out her voice in my head." He paused as if waiting for her to attack his cowardice, or rail at his weakness, but she did not say a word. She did not know him then, she did not know that kind of pain, though she feared she would soon enough.

When she did not stop him, he continued. "When the rum and whiskey were no longer enough I sought...other...comforts. He flinched as if he expected to be struck and she did indeed lay a hand on him, but not in anger. She brushed her fingers over his back as she did for Nancy when she would cry in the night. A small gesture to be sure, but it was all she could do to comfort the pain he still suffered.

"I do not deserve you. You should know that. Nor did I deserve her." His face was away from her but the unmistakable sound of tears choked his words. In a heartbeat she was at his back, pressing her warm flesh to his cold clammy skin. She leaned against him whispering comfort.

"You should hate me, Sweets. Despise what I have done. And yet you stay." When he turned into her she wrapped him up, holding him close to her heart.

281

For a long while he held her, allowed himself to be held by her. After several silent moments, his head turned from her breast and his breathing slowed.

"For six months I died a slow death. Wandering no farther than the distance from bed to bottle and back again. I might still be there today, or dead more likely, if I hadn't wandered down the wrong alley one night. I wound up at the docks, face to face with his Majesties newest marvels. But it was not the iron-clad steamships that I adored. It was the classic war ships. The larger sailing beauties with sails that could cover the moon if flung over it. They had one docked right in front of me. Older than her berth-mates, she was a frigate, the largest of her generation and she was beautiful. The blind stupor in which I found myself did not lessen my passion for the sea, only my sense of right from wrong. I climbed aboard that ship without permission. I could have been killed for such an offense, but, as it was Ran who found me stumbling around on deck barking orders to an imaginary crew, I suppose I should count myself among the luckiest men alive."

"Is that how you met?" She combed her fingers reassuringly through his hair. When his story turned from Lucy to the sea he had seemed to calm and she hoped to keep him on that trail until he returned to himself.

It worked. He chuckled into her shoulder. "Yes. He wasn't as old and forgiving then as he is now, but he took pity on me as I was in need of it. He told me I had two choices, sign up to be a Queen's man or be thrown overboard."

"That doesn't sound like pity, Ty!" His laugh warmed as his arms tightened.

"Ah, but it was, Sweets. He saved my life that night. Of that I am sure. He signed me up and took me below. I awoke, sober for the first time in half a year, three days later, and well out at sea. I made a vow that very morning. Two actually. The first was never to take another drink. It did foul things to me and I wanted to have nothing further to do with it."

"And I forced you to break it. Oh, Ty, I am so sorry! Had I known how important your sobriety was to you I never..." He stopped her apology with a kiss. She could tell he had meant it to be quick and comforting but as she leaned into it greedily he allowed it to become far more intimate, unwilling to disappoint her. Pulling free for a breath, she asked, "And the other?"

"Never to take another woman to bed. And not to put too fine a point on it, but technically you have been the downfall of both of those hard-set vows, Sweets." He tightened his grip on her when she instinctively tried to pull away. Guilt flushed her face. He had made a lover's vow to Lucy and she felt sick to her stomach that she had led him to break it. "Shh, Essie. You did nothing short of free my heart. Calm yourself, Love. I have no regrets." She stilled but could not return his kiss, not yet.

"Ty, you made a lover's vow to her. I had no right..." She was silenced by his finger pressed against her moistened lips.

"That vow fell hollow the day I met you, Sweets. I knew the moment you used that sharp tongue of yours on me in that tent I wanted you. A vow such as mine is not broken by action but by desire. And while I thought I loved Lucy in a fashion, I have come to know what love truly is." She froze. His eyes were burning her and she could see the words forming on his tongue. She could not bring herself to say them, to hear them from him would be a thousand times more grievous. Before he made his feelings plain, she quickly placed her fingers on his lips as he had done to her.

"Please don't say it, Ty. I cannot bear to hear it."

"You can't be serious? They are my words to use and I long to tell you how I feel. I have waited twelve years to learn what I now know. Do not stop me, Love." He kissed her fingers, pulling the tip of one into his mouth and dragging his tongue over it. Need throbbed fast in her thighs and a moan escaped her constricted throat.

"Please, Ty. Spare me that agony. To say it to you, as I so desperately desire, would be torture, to hear it from you would slay me. Is it not enough that I know?"

"No. It is not. You deserve the words, Essie, and I deserve to say them. To hear them from you in return." His jaw tightened in anger for a moment but as tears peeked in her eyes he sighed, letting the tension go with a breath. Sadness scrawled over his face as he pulled her to him.

"Forever, Sweets. Forever." She silenced him with a kiss as tears of joy and grief rolled down her face. Pulling her against him he rolled onto her, desperate to leave no doubt in her heart of his feelings.

Chapter 18

The sound of screeching seagulls and gruff orders barked in succession lulled her from sleep. Ty's voice, booming over all else, drifted into her broken dreams from what seemed like miles. Yawning, Vanessa reached out her arm to him but hit nothing. Cold sheets and the wooden sideboard were all that met her fingers. Forcing her heavy eyes open, she found his cabin bathed in a strange rainbow light.

Everywhere around her, the bright mid-morning sun streamed through the stained glass windows. She was alone in this kaleidoscope. He was not beside her. For a moment she felt betrayed but as she heard his voice again, booming instructions for this and that, she calmed. He was the captain and she knew she could not keep him from his duties forever.

The bird calls grew louder as they perched on the sill at her back. Seagulls could only mean one thing, port had been reached. A heavy wanton groan left her as she sat on the edge of the bed and looked to the ground for her clothes. She needed to pack, to relieve poor Mortimer from his care of Nancy, but most of all she needed to escape his world. Her night of freedom was past and the pain she had expected upon leaving him was already consuming her heart. How could she go now? She belonged to him just as he belonged to her. How was she to depart his ship when it was now her home? Tears once again filled her eyes. Nanny would be so disappointed in her if she were here to see this. She had taught her to be strong, to carry herself not just as a lady, but as a human being, proud and steadfast.

"No one worthy ever drowned in their own tears." Nanny's voice echoed her own as she said the words out loud. Finding her clothes draped carefully over the back of a chair only a few feet from her she girded herself. He had seen to her needs before he had left. Swallowing her grief, she dressed in silence surrounded by his scent. As she sat in the chair to slide her small shoes back onto her feet, she could hear the sounds of harbor bells and the smell of soot and filth began to overpower Ty's scent. London. There was no mistaking the reek of the docks and the stench of the Thames. She was out of time.

Ducking her head, she moved as quickly as she could from his cabin door to the hatch. The men were far too busy bringing the vessel into berth to notice her short jaunt. At least that was what she prayed as she dove down the stairs and into the darkness of the hold. The foul smell of the water was far stronger here and her stomach turned. She would not be eating breakfast this morning, not that she had an appetite.

Mortimer paced quietly in her cabin until she finally slid the door ajar.

"Ah, there you are. I didn't want to rush ya, but I think I am needed on deck, lass. The girl is still asleep and I have done my best to pack up your non-personals and such. I hope you don't mind." He smiled briefly before he took in her tragic expression. "M'lady, are you well? He didn't...hurt you...did he?" Mortimer reached for her shoulders. He was such a kind man and it occurred to Essie a bit too late that she was showing far too much of herself on her face. Taking in a heavy breath, she replaced her true grief with false contentment and answered him.

"Of course not. I am just sad to see port, that's all. Thank you for all that you have done." Kissing him lightly on the cheek, she hugged the old sailor close for a moment. "Now, go to your post. I am sure the *Siren* cannot do without you any longer." Her fake smile fooled the sweet man and with a bow, he left her.

Nancy's soft breaths, the sound of gulls, and the soft slaps of the waves closed in on her as she stood looking around her cabin. Mort had packed everything but the dresser it seemed, unwilling to gaze at her unmentionables. Fighting the tears that seemed relentless to fall, she grabbed her trunk and emptied the drawers haphazardly. She didn't want to pack up, hated to leave, but she had no choice. They had returned to London where her desires no longer mattered.

Behind her Nancy stirred and Vanessa pushed her own feelings aside to help the child ready for port. Ran had pledged his assistance in locating the poor girl's father once they made the official report of the sinking. Vanessa had wanted to see to it personally, but as Randolf was all too quick to point out, she had duties and responsibilities of her own that would not leave her with time. It had infuriated her to think Ty had told him of her engagement, but as they barely saw each other she thought only of holding him close when those few precious moments came around, not of ranting about him confiding his troubles to his oldest friend.

She had just finished brushing and braiding Nancy's hair when the door to her cabin slid ajar. Tibilt and his counterpart stood in the hallway waiting for her permission to enter.

"I suppose you are here for my things." Vanessa did not move, only nodded. The two hulking men stepped slowly into her space.

"Captain wants to get you seen to first, before all the cargo and such. He said it was important you be taken care of." Tibilt attempted a smile, the first she imagined of his life. It was crooked and strained, but honest. She moved aside and watched. Nancy wrapped herself around Vanessa's legs as the men stacked her belongings on her truck. With inordinate and unnecessary care, they hoisted the luggage between them and just like that, it was gone. The room felt bitterly cold and empty now without a touch her left behind. She tried to ignore the feeling that he was getting rid of her. He had all but confessed to loving her last night, but his departure before she woke and now this rush to disembark her stirred her fears.

Rubbing Nancy's shoulder bracingly, she put excess effort into smiling down at the child. "Come. I suppose it's time to go." Nancy, unaware of Vanessa's grieving heart, took her hand and tugged her eagerly down the hallway. "All right, all right! I'm coming!" Despite her sadness, she couldn't help but laugh lightly at the girl's excited happiness. As Nancy galloped up the stairs to the deck and into the brisk light of noon Essie followed. Cresting the hatch, her eyes snapped to the figures across the boards.

Ty and Ran were standing at the start of the gangplank ahead of her. Her heart leapt at the sight of him and despite her already frantic pace to keep up with Nancy, she quickened. He turned just as she cleared the opening. His face seemed to furrow, a look of duress spreading over him. She thought for a moment his conversation with Ran was to blame for his souring mood but as she moved toward him it became clear she was the cause. His eyes grew heavy and without warning he turned and hurried down the gangplank, disappearing beyond the rail. Ran followed his last glance to find her as she rushed toward the spot where Ty had been.

"Ah, Lady Everly, I see you are ready to depart." His overzealous smile met her before she reached the narrow wooden bridge, planning to follow after Ty with all the speed she could manage. His hands on her shoulders forced her to stop and meet his eyes. There was something there she didn't understand. Joy. He seemed happy. How could anyone who knew what had just happened feel happy? Her lover had just spurned her, left without so much as a goodbye, and yet Ran appeared jovial.

"He had business to see to, my lady. He asked me to say his farewells." She felt her mouth flop open. Disgust and hopelessness flared within her. Nancy at her hip made her hold her outrage at bay, but only just. Leaving her in her silent trauma, Ran bent at the knee to speak with the four-year-old hiding in her skirts. "Well little lass, are you ready to find your father? I think perhaps that will be my first order of business."

"I thought reporting the wreck was to be first." Her voice was cold and toneless. She had only barely heard him over the tattoo of her broken heart, but for Nancy, she would contain her grief.

"I have changed my mind. Family is most important. Wouldn't you agree?" There was a strange inflection to his voice that left her curious, but she had no time to inquire after it. As she tried to form the question a familiar face crested the gangplank just before her. Ty's figure, which disappeared some moments ago, was replaced with Casbolt, her father's emissary. The time had come.

"Ah, My Lady Vanessa. Your father is anxious to see you well."

"His absence would argue that, Casbolt. But it is good to see you at least." The harshness of her sentiment did not seem to faze him in the slightest.

Turning to Ran, he continued, "Am I to assume you are the captain of this vessel, sir?"

"You may assume it if you like, but it would be false." Ran's attempt at humor was ill-received by the ever stoic Casbolt. Clearing his throat, suddenly nervous in the face of her father's replacement, he turned toward the quarter deck and shouted for Mortimer. "Captain Clark had urgent matters to attend to. His first mate can assist you. And to you, my Lady," he turned back to her, "I wish you happiness." Vanessa could do nothing to hide the cringe that twisted her lovely olive face. "Do not lose hope, my dear. Everyone's fate can be changed."

Ty's words from Ran's lips. The pain in her chest lessened to curiosity. She wanted to ask him what he meant, what Ty had told him, what urgent errand was more important than saying his farewell in person, but Casbolt at her elbow meant she was lost for time. Nodding to the ever-cold butler, she bent down and hugged Nancy close to her. Standing slowly, she gave the child's hand to Ran, hugged Mortimer one last time, and then led the way down the gangplank. Better to end this torture quickly. To linger on the deck of the *Siren* would mean deepening the grief and she could stand no more at the moment.

"Your father had business to attend to in Devin, ma'am. I have been instructed to take you home. He will join you as soon as he is able." Casbolt relayed her father's commands as he aided her into the carriage before joining her. The compartment was dark, affording the chance for her fear and grief to show on her face.

"No, Casbolt. First I wish to visit my husband." She leaned her head back against the velvet cushion behind her. So much pain. All of her seemed to ache. Her body, her heart, and now her head.

"Of course ma'am." Standing as best he could in the small space he pulled the curtain away from the window and opened the glass. After instructing the driver of their deviation, Casbolt returned to his seat. Before he closed the curtain he took in her pained expression. "Do you feel well, my Lady? Are you in need of a doctor?" She smiled slightly at the concern in his voice. To think Casbolt worried for her was amusing. He seemed more affected by her presence than her absent father.

"The journey has left me weary, Casbolt. Nothing more. As soon as I pay my respects I think a long rest is in order. Thank you for your concern."

"Of course." And then the cabin fell quiet. The curtain was drawn and in almost pitch-black darkness the pair clattered down the roads and alleyways of London in poignant silence. Vanessa could not appreciate the stillness, though. Her mind raced. Had he told Ran something important? Was he trying to comfort her, or did he have some secret message to deliver she had not understood? Did it even matter? She was in her father's care again and though she intended to try as hard as she could to free herself from this horrendous situation, she knew in her heart nothing she could say would change her father's mind.

Images of Ty smiling at her as they shared his bed mingled with the look in his eyes just before he turned and fled from her. The juxtaposition of such joy and such grief did nothing to brighten her mood. When the carriage bumped to a halt outside the Everly family crypt her spirits sank further into gloom.

"Shall I accompany you, ma'am?" Casbolt had climbed from the vehicle to assist her out.

"No, thank you. This is something I must do alone." Nodding to him, she waited until he hoisted himself back inside before she made her way down into the earth. Most people would find a crypt a terrible place to visit when in the throes of hardship. The dank, death-filled tombs only add to their melancholy, but not Vanessa. She had always found such places to be sources of calm and serenity. Finding Alfred's casket, she brushed the thin layer of dust from his name.

"Oh, Alfred. I fear I have made a horrible mess of things. If only you were still here. You would know what to do. How to manage this situation. But then, without your death, I would not be in this predicament in the first place." Kneeling beside him, she continued. "You told me once to go out and find love and I have. In the most unlikely of places. His name is Tiberius. He is a ship captain, brave and strong and handsome. No doubt you would fancy him, too."

Through the tears that had started to fall, she laughed in her throat imagining Alfred meeting Ty and watching that little twinkle in his eye as he envied her. "I wish I could tell you I will be all right. That my life will be what you always wished for me to have, but I cannot. What you feared, the reason you agreed to marry me, has come to pass. Stephen is to replace you. How am I to live with him? Oh, help me, Alfred! I miss your advice. I miss you! I need your guidance..." Sniveling she kissed the nameplate and stood. "Goodbye, my dear Alfred. You may not have been my husband in every sense, but you were more of a friend than I shall ever deserve." Wiping her tears away, she left the tomb behind.

How she needed Alfred now. He would know what to do, what to say to help her out of this predicament. After all, he had been playing this secrets game all his life. She had no tact when it came to the clandestine. Vanessa was nothing if not transparent and she did not want to hide her feelings. Not these feelings. She resolved that if Ty no longer wanted her, and she could not turn her father from this madness, she would join poor Alfred before allowing Stephen to have her. The grave would surely welcome her as she was. She steadied herself as she entered the dim sunlight again. One way or another she would be free of this engagement. Stephen would *not* be her future.

Chapter 19

Her family's estate seemed unfamiliar and cold. Her childhood here had been filled with laughter and learning, but that was when Nanny had made it home. Her father had only spoken to her once in the nearly two weeks she had been back. He had seemed happy to see her at first. He had come home late from his business and found her in the library reclining in a chair, watching the flames dance in the hearth. Initially, he had rushed towards her and she wondered if he might actually have missed her, but he stopped short of contact and cleared his throat.

He asked how her time in the Caribbean had been and told her how truly sorry he was she had been forced to leave on such short notice, and with such sad tidings. The more he said to her the more distant he began to become. She had hoped to start their interactions out with a plea to release her from Stephen, but when he finally asked how her trip home had been she lost her nerve. She nodded and mumbled something vague and then he left her. She had not seen him in almost a year and he was apparently satisfied with less than ten minutes of conversation. Her broken heart fractured into shards. What little hope she had gathered washed away.

He kept to his study after their brief interaction, taking what few meals he ate at home in his private rooms. She was left alone in the great empty house to walk in silence and stew on the tragedy of her fate. No word from Ty. Perhaps she had been fooling herself to hope his rush from the *Siren* was to do with her. No. She was alone in all things. There had been moments, blinks in time, when she had walked past her father's door and saw him sitting in contemplation. Time to walk in and start the conversation she so desperately wanted to have, but she had passed by in quiet agony.

Another roll of thunder rattled the panes before her. Looking up from the relic in her hands, Vanessa gazed out over the gray afternoon and sighed. Rain. It had started the very afternoon she had been collected from the *Siren's Call* and had not stopped in the interim. The gloom did little to help her escape the quagmire of her sorrowful thoughts. The world wept for her since it seemed she could not. The tears had been ever-present, pinching and tingling in the bridge of her nose, but not a single one had fallen. She was too sad to cry. The droplets traveled down the glass, meeting strangers and picking up speed toward their ultimate demise, crashing into the band of lead between panes with such velocity they threw debris in all directions. New droplets formed from their remains and raced on, heading toward yet another shattering fate.

"Vanessa...daughter, might I speak with you?" Her father's voice, shy and soft, came from her door. She swallowed her shock before she turned, afraid the sight of her honest reaction to his visit might end it.

"Of course, father." She stood from her desk and motioned for him to join her on the couch in front of her fire. Choosing instead one of the wing-back chairs opposite her, he settled in and stared at her. The conversation he had promised hovered between them as if it would bite the first to approach it. Vanessa sat hopeful for a moment but as he let the minutes tick by without a word she began to lose faith. Images of him nodding and standing to leave with not another syllable passing between them flashed in her mind until she could no longer stand them. Deciding that while this was not the ideal moment for her plea, there might never be a better one, she made her move.

"Father, I...I have something I wish to ask of you." She lowered her eyes to her hands, clasping and unclasping in her lap. Why was it so hard to speak to the one man in the world who should always be on her side? Perhaps, she mused inwardly, because as yet he had never felt like that man.

"Of course. What is it, my dear?" There was a warmth to his voice. It felt foreign and strange, but she needed it and would not waste it.

"It's about my engagement to Stephen."

"Ah, yes. He will come tomorrow to speak with you concerning the arrangements. I have already made all of the necessary plans for the wedding. I am sorry I have been distracted these past weeks, but I had no idea how many considerations were required for an event such as this. Lady Everly took care of it for your union with Alfred, but I could not ask a woman who so recently lost her youngest son to aid in something as trivial as these nuptials. It is opportune that this is what you wish to discuss as it was my goal as well." He smiled at her, but she could not bring herself to return the expression.

Vanessa was lost as to which travesty to be offended by first. The way he seemed almost giddy at the prospect of tying her to a man nearly twice her age? Or the callous way he treated her marriage to Alfred? Or the idea that this wedding, that all weddings, were trivial things worth no more than the difficulty of navigating them?

"What? Plans? I do not understand." She swallowed the outrage in her throat. She could not afford to lose her composure before she had made her plea.

"I thought you knew. Perhaps I should have spoken with you sooner, but you seemed so exhausted from your journey that I did not wish to burden you. Your union with Stephen, what I hope will see you happily settled and able to start a family, is scheduled for just over a month from now." Her mouth fell open.

"A month!? But, father, Alfred has been dead for not three months. Is not the customary grieving period a year?" She stood from the sofa, no longer able to sit still. It was terrifying enough to know that Stephen was in her future, but her near future was not possible. She had thought to have months not days.

"We felt the grieving period unnecessary as you have spent the last year already separated from Alfred. I am surprised to see you so torn, my dear. It has come to be clear to me that Alfred did not hold so high a place in your heart as a husband ought." There was a chill to his words and she cringed. He knew. She had suspected as much from his letter, but now there was no doubt.

"You will marry Stephen and you will be happy." The last was more a command than a request. A sharp tug on her chain. An order was issued to a wayward pet, one she was bound by ownership to obey. Something inside her snapped.

Turning from the fire, she glared at the man who had betrayed her for a second time in the interest of her happiness. "I will not! Father I do not wish to marry Stephen! Please...do not force me."

"Of course you will! The plans are set. Now, calm yourself! What will Stephen think when he sees this wrath in you!"

"I can only hope that he feels doubt and changes his mind! Do I have no say in my future? I do not, will not, love him, father! How am I to have happiness, *if* that is truly your wish for me, without love?!" The last question seemed to stab him. He slumped and for a moment she thought perhaps she had reached him. She was mistaken. Standing quickly, his face had turned hard. She saw in him her rage, her own self-righteous indignation.

"If not with him, then with whom? Who would you prefer, Vanessa? There have never been suitors lined at my door begging for you, my dear. Even Alfred hesitated to take you! It would seem he never did. I have feared this day since you were born. It is my fault. My heritage has left you marred, cursed with a look that is unwelcome and unwanted. I am determined to see you wed and happy. So, if you have a nobleman that is willing to take you to wife tell me his name! I will have him here today and you married tomorrow! I will not allow you to spend your life alone! You are the last of my line and I would see you bear a son that I might pass my legacy!"

She could do nothing by stare at him. *His* legacy....how little he thought of *her* life, *her* happiness, *her* future. Of *her*. In his eyes, her own father's eyes, she was marred, unwanted, cursed. His words. His venom. He gave a heavy sigh and flopped, defeated, back to the chair he had left in anger. The pain and sadness on her face ate away at his strength.

"Vanessa, I am sorry, but this is the only way." He was about to leave. To stand and walk away from her and she could not stop him. 'What *noble* man wants you.' That's what he had said. *Noble*. Ty's name hung on her tongue, begging to be shouted, but she held it in. She was no longer sure he wanted her anymore, after all, it had been two weeks of silence from her beloved ship captain. What was more, even if he did love her as she loved him, her father would never allow it. Perhaps she could give Andrew's name. He had a title to please her father and she knew that he wanted her, but that cruelty would only delay the inevitable as she no more wished to marry him than Stephen. Though life with him would no doubt be better, it was not the life she wanted.

Seconds of silence stretched into minutes. *Say something!* Her mind raced, begging her not to miss this chance, to let this opportunity go without a fight. But she had no more fight left in her. Just as she had foreseen, her father stood and moved to the door. Looking over his shoulder one last time at his defeated child, he shook his head and then he was gone.

She crumbled to the floor the second his shadow disappeared from the hallway. Why had she lost her temper? Why could she not have approached this rationally and argued it logically with him as she did with all of her intellectual endeavors at university? She could be highly persuasive in those circumstances and it might have worked. But instead, she had become emotional and irrational, a spoiled child. She knew why. This was not about some tribe hundreds of years dead, or a monument that needed restoration from years of neglect. This was her *life*. Her attachment to it *was* irrational and emotional.

Another crash of thunder vibrated the marble beneath her knees. Standing, she ran to her door and down the hallway. The time had come. She would *not* marry Stephen! As she flew down the back stairs she saw the forest beyond the gardens illuminated by the lightning. *Yes. If I am to leave this world that is where I would have it done. My cave.* She bolted through the kitchens without so much as a nod to the cook, busy preparing something or other for their evening meal. Shouts followed her out the back door, warnings of cold and rain. No one seemed to notice her grab a small paring knife off of the counter as she passed. A coat was all they begged of her, but what use does a corpse have for a coat.

The rain was ice cold as it soaked through her dress. Her shoes were mired in the wet sod as she trudged toward the tree line and the blade in her hand growing heavy. The forest had changed, but not enough for her to forget the way. Under the trees the pounding droplets slowed, allowing the wind, rushing through their branches towards nowhere in particular to slice through her like waves of razors. It didn't matter. Not now. Not anymore.

Over fallen trunks and around large, unruly bushes she wound her way to the only place left on earth where she still felt welcome. No tears. She wanted to cry. To scream at the desperation and stupidity of it all, but instead, she measured her steps in cold concentration, certain that in a few moments, it would no longer matter. Leaning against a large oak she stopped to catch her breath. A light giggle left her. Perhaps she was only fixing a mistake. Maybe she had been meant to die in that fall so long ago and all the hardship and cruelty she had come to know as life, the broken promises and false hope, were God's way of telling her she had fouled up his plan. If that were true she would fix it.

Taking a deep breath, she pushed off and continued. There, just ahead of her would be the broken swing. Below it was the hole. Or, at least that is what should have been before her as she entered the small clearing. Instead, she found a structure built of beautiful stained glass and marble. A miniature vestibule, almost a shrine, stood over what had been the entrance to her cave. Her determination faded in the face of curiosity and the knife clenched tightly in her hand slipped free and buried to the hilt in the soaked ground.

Where had this structure come from? When had it been built? What purpose was it meant to serve? Surely her father had not done this. It was stunning. Even in the gloom of a stormy afternoon, it seemed to glow, radiating light and color in the gray surrounding it. Hope warmed her and suddenly she realized how terribly cold she was. Shaking and miserable, she ran for the structure. Moving around the outside she found an ornate set of wrought iron doors. Pushing against their weight she fell into the tiny, surprisingly warm, room, though it was less of a room and more of a stairwell. A tight path, lined with finely crafted handrails and gas lamps encircled the start of a spiral staircase made to match. The haunting glow of candlelight floated up from below, calling her down. She smiled, real and true, for the first time since the night she had spent with Ty as she descended down into her cave.

Light was everywhere. The floor, once covered in leaves, branches, and dust was clean and strewn with warm earthy rugs. Around the outside of the large dome were positioned lamp posts, each flickering the orangey light she had seen from the head of the stairs. In the center of the space was a grouping of comfortable chairs and a large table, covered in books and papers. The room looked to be well-used and deeply loved. Moving to the desk, careful not to drip all over the letters scattered upon it, she looked over the delicate hand and knew it to be her father's. This was his space. The place he came to think, to concentrate, to be happy.

The tears she had been unable to shed flooded her face. He had made her special cave his. Such care and thought, such depth of emotion had gone into turning the dark musty place she had spent so many days as a child into the bright warm room around her was staggering. Perhaps he did love her. In his own way, this was his attempt to be close to her. All thoughts of death disappeared. He might be stubborn but if he truly loved her like this she could not give up yet. She had a month to convince him she could find her own happiness, just as she had found this cave. It was messy and dangerous and had happened entirely by accident, but she had found love and he *would* understand. He had to.

Settling down in one of the chairs she allowed the tears to rush out. New conversations, refreshed efforts to move her father's heart, swirled in her head as she waited for the rain to stop. Somehow she knew it would. This storm would pass, she just needed a bit of patience. And she was right. After an hour of sniveling and silence, the sounds of birds crept in from above.

With new hope for the future, she climbed from her cave and strolled back to the house to find it in an uproar. All the servants were in a fit wondering where she had run off to and what had become of her. Even Casbolt seemed concerned as he helped her to her rooms and gave her over to her maid for a bath. Dinner was brought to her and bed soon followed. Tomorrow was a big day. She would confront Stephen for the first time and hopefully have another chance to impress upon her father her worth.

Chapter 20

"Your father wishes for you to join him for tea in the library, ma'am." Casbolt stood, arrow straight, in her doorway as she pulled the earring through her lobe. Looking her reflection over in the mirror one last time, she smiled. She had tried salt, now she would try sugar. Swathed in her favorite dress, she had taken great care with herself this morning. She looked as if she was about to be ushered to a ball, not afternoon tea with her father. Hoping that seeing her as a woman, strong and confident, would help her repeated attempt at freedom; she straightened her dark olive satin skirt front and nodded to Casbolt's reflection.

Brushing past the older man into the library, Vanessa caught sight of Lord Mansfield standing by the windows. Picking up her pace, she entered the room true and full, eager to confront him concerning what had become of her cave. It took her only a second to realize they were not alone. To her right, hidden initially from view by the floor-to-ceiling shelves laden with books, stood the frightening form of Stephen. He was larger and far more imposing than she remembered; time having softened him in her mind. Seeing him again, looming like a bear in front of the fire and eying her as if he meant to devour her on the spot, sent bile up her throat and terror down her spine.

"Father...I didn't realize you were not alone. I can return later." She turned to leave quickly, hoping to retreat before he could muster a reply, but Casbolt had closed the door behind her.

"Nonsense, my dear. It is our visitor who has requested your presence. Please, join us." Her father moved to her swiftly from his contemplative perch at the window and took her hand. "I thought it wise to have you present for this meeting, as it pertains to your future as well." His smile was an attempt to lessen her tension but it failed miserably. The muscles along her spine, already straining against the corset she had pulled tighter than usual, began to ache.

"Ah, Vanessa, you look lovely." His oily tones touched her like fingers and she suddenly regretted all of her preparations. She had wanted her father to see her as a woman, whole and complete, not Stephen. His eyes traveled over her with a sickening slowness, making her squirm. She could feel his gaze, almost hear his unseemly thoughts.

"Good afternoon, Lord Everly." Her tone, as cold and unaffected as she could manage given her circumstances, cooled his approach. "My father told me of your visit, but I must admit it slipped my mind. I apologize."

"You are but a woman, my dear Vanessa. Flippancy is a flaw wholly common to your gender. Do not fret on it. I will never hold it against you." His slimy smile beamed down at her and her stomach turned. *Only a woman.* Rage burned in her throat, coating the words she longed to say with venom that might just kill him if only she could unleash them. Before she could share her thoughts her father shared his.

"Ah, there now. How wonderful. I thought perhaps it would be reassuring to my daughter if she could hear from you that her happiness is your primary concern, Stephen. She is, I am afraid, still reeling from Alfred's sudden passing and the future is frightening to her." Vanessa's eyes locked onto her fathers. How could he do this? Did he really think listening to Stephen give false assurances would calm her need for freedom?

"Of course! I must first say had I been granted your hand when I had initially pledged for it you would already be fulfilled."

"My life with Alfred was entirely fulfilling, Lord Everly. I regret nothing that has come to pass for me." Her snark was unmistakable and she could see the tendons in his neck tighten in anger. Good. Perhaps if he lost his famous temper in front of her father she could finally be free of this. Winston's shocked gasp to her left told her otherwise. If she prodded her betrothed into his anger as obviously as this her father would likely side with Stephen. Deciding her venom needed to be more carefully measured, she shifted to the sofa, sitting as comfortably as her current attire would allow, and attempted a faint smile.

"Please, we *are* to be wed. Call me Stephen. And I doubt Alfred supplied what a woman such as you deserved." His jab at his brother was unwelcome. He knew what Alfred was, who he was, and what he fancied. He was so much more than that to her, but she maintained her composure. He waited a moment as if to see if she would lash out. When she did nothing, he continued, "Your happiness is my only concern Vanessa, I assure you. After we are wed, filling my home with children is my only priority. Your life will be full."

"With children, yes. You have made that clear, but what of the happiness?" She couldn't help it. Why her father and Stephen both seemed to think a woman could be led to joy with a baby baffled her.

"They will fill your life with purpose and give you the task of creating the future, would that not make you happy? Of course, it will." He did not even wait for her to answer. His arrogance was astounding. Vanessa could no longer remain seated. Anger and disgust swirled in her stomach, fighting for room her corset did not allow. She moved to the hearth to better face her opponent.

"My career makes me happy, Lord Everly." She relished his grimace as she continued to use his title. "Alfred understood what my passion was and he allowed me to pursue it."

"My brother allowed you to pursue a great many things that made little sense. And I highly doubt he understood even a portion of your passion, *Vanessa*." Revulsion flourished again. Her father's groan was lost to her ears. He was still behind her, but her thought to preserve her composure for his sake disappeared in the face of her indignation. "As to your *career*, I see no room for it in our life together. While I admire your efforts to better yourself, there will be no need for you to work once we are wed."

"So I am to leave the university?" She couldn't help the shock in her voice. Until this moment she had never even thought he would demand this of her.

Laughing cruelly, he replied, "Of course."

"Very well, once the relics from the Caribbean are cataloged and studied I will, of course, step down from my research position." She dropped her eyes from him, unwilling to let him see how crushed this news had left her.

"Nonsense. Surely they have no need for you to complete such a task. There are other men more than capable of seeing to the rubbish you brought back from the islands. I see no reason for you to go back at all." As he finished his decree he took another casual drink of the scotch he had been nursing since she had entered.

"*Rubbish*!?" Her face flushed hot and angry. Even Stephen seemed astounded by the flare in her, taking a measured step farther away from her flashing eyes. "That *rubbish* is my life!"

"Our home will be your life. And I expect it to be run to its fullest efficiency. It might take you some time to learn my habits and needs, but you are a smart girl. I have every confidence that you will please me."

"I thought the goal of this union was *my* happiness, Lord Everly." Tears burned behind her eyes. How could her father still stand silent behind her listening to this? How could he not intercede on her behalf?

"And a wife's happiness is born from her husband's. In making me happy you will find yours, thus this *is* about your happiness." She could tell from the deepening of his tone he was growing angry with her resistance. He had expected her to be excited, or at the very least receptive, to this union. Her hesitance did not fit into his little scheme and oh, how Stephen loved plans.

"My happiness has never been contingent on another's, Lord Everly. What if this plan of yours fails to provide me with what I desire?" This was a lie of course. Ty's joy was her own and pleasing him had brought her no end of joy, but Stephen need not know that.

Slamming his tumbler down on the small table to his left he took a terrifying step closer to her and reached for her arm. Hard fingers dug into her flesh. Pain radiated out from his grip, forcing her to groan under the pressure.

"You *will* be happy with me, Vanessa." His words were forced through gritted teeth. A command she was behooved to obey or there would be hell to pay. Alfred's warnings of his violence echoed in her ears as she struggled against the vice grip.

"Stephen, I think perhaps you should release my daughter!" Her father's voice broke in to end her torment. Immediately his hold on her vanished. Winston was at her side, his hand landing lightly on her shoulder as he pulled her a step away from the beast occupying the space once holding her fiancé.

Instantly, Stephen changed from the bear back into a man. "Of course, Winston. I merely wanted to reassure her our life will meet with her standards."

Lord Mansfield had been about to speak when the library door opened. All eyes turned to find Casbolt entering, carrying the tea tray. Moving to the table, he placed his burden gently down and addressed her father. "Your tea, Sir. Before you begin, there is a visitor who wishes to speak with you. He says it is in regard to Lady Vanessa Everly and that it is urgent. Shall I ask him to return at another time?"

Her father looked from her to Stephen before releasing a deep sigh. "No, Casbolt, show him in." Moving away from her, he walked toward the door to meet the stranger. Vanessa moved a few steps farther from Stephen, afraid he would reach for her again now that she had lost the protection of her father. A visitor with urgent news concerning her had not seemed to register in her flustered mind, not until the caller passed through the door.

"Ty!" His name flew from her lips as she took several desperate steps in his direction. *He was here! He had come!* Realizing she was entirely too eager to see him, she cleared her throat and stood straighter. "Uh...I mean, Captain Clark. It is delightful to see you again. I had thought our acquaintance to be over."

She couldn't help the telling blush sweeping over her face as she met his gaze. For a moment his eyes held hers, and then they dropped to travel the length of her. She could feel him there, brushing over her body. Biting her lip, she scanned him in return. He looked more elegant and well-groomed than usual. His hair was slicked back and oiled, making him appear far more imposing and stern than she had ever seen him. His uniform coat was pristine as always, but it was what he wore beneath it that had her fighting a giggle in her throat. Below the deep navy jacket, he bore a kilt. A tartan pattern of navy, red, and gold coursed around his thighs, ending just above his knees.

She wanted to ask him why on earth he was wearing a kilt before she remembered his brogue. She had only heard it twice when he was enraged or distressed, but it had been unmistakable. So, she thought fancifully, he has a Scottish heritage. Another of his secrets became hers and the need of him that she had been struggling to forget for the last two weeks began to pound hot and fresh in her heart. God, how she wanted to run to him. To fling herself into his arms and beg him to carry her away from this nightmare. But she couldn't. Her father stood between them and Stephen was only steps to her back. Neither would allow her to reach him. Of that she was sure.

"Yes, Lady Everly. Seeing you again pleases me as well." His smile was telling and she pulled her knees together in an effort to calm the heat flourishing within her. "Lord Mansfield, I have come in regards to the money left with my first mate meant as payment for the transport of your daughter." His eyes never left her as he spoke.

"Oh? Was the amount insufficient?" Her father took in the electric tether between them with interest before Stephen intruded on the moment.

"A bicker over money does not seem urgent, Captain. You interrupt our tea over something this trivial?" He was at her side, his hand coming to rest on her back when he finished. Instinctively, she took a step away from him out of his touch and heard the aggressive growl low in his chest. Stephen seemed to understand the nature of their acquaintance and he was not the kind to step aside and release his claim.

"There is no bicker, Lord Everly. While the amount is in error, I felt it urgent Lord Mansfield know the circumstances of its recalculation. His daughter's actions aboard the *Siren* should be his to know." The manner in which he spoke was so formal, reminiscent of how he had addressed her at the start of the voyage. The memories it recalled made her want to laugh, but she didn't dare.

"Is that so, Captain? Shall we adjourn to my study? You can regale me with the tales of Vanessa's actions in private." Her father motioned for Ty to lead them out of the library, but they both halted when Stephen spoke again.

"Pardon me, Winston, but I feel I should be privy to this discussion, as your daughter is soon to be my burden. Any character flaws or weaknesses of constitution she possesses should be known to me. Wouldn't you agree?" Vanessa saw Ty's jaw tighten in anger. He hated hearing Stephen's callous manners toward her even more than she did.

Before Winston could respond, she interjected her own demand. "Actually father, I feel perhaps this discussion should be known to all present. If I am to be accused of *weakness and character flaws* should I not be present and able to defend myself?"

"Don't be ridiculous, Vanessa..." Stephen's chuckled, condescending retort was interrupted before he could finish.

"I think that is a marvelous idea. There you are, Captain, your audience is gathered. Please start your tale." Vanessa smiled as Stephen huffed his derision. From behind her, she could hear his teeth grinding. His anger from this would not subside quickly and if she indeed had to marry him she would pay dearly for this moment. Another reason she could not marry him fell into the overfull coffers with the rest.

"This particular voyage was fraught with accidents, injuries, and storms the likes of which I have not encountered since leaving His Majesty's Service."

"Surely you are not implying Vanessa is responsible for the weather?" Stephen's rude interruption grated on Vanessa's nerves, but Ty took it in stride as if it were meaningless.

"Of course not. In fact, quite the opposite. Lord Mansfield, I can assure you that not only did your daughter not cause any hardships, but that without her knowledge, assistance, and courage the *Siren* would likely have never made port."

"How interesting! Please continue, Captain, and won't you please call me Winston." Her father's words were warming and she took yet another step closer to the man she loved.

"She saved the life of my second mate and stitched an injury I myself suffered with expertise I have come to understand is owed to her late husband. Beyond that, she aided in the rescue of twelve survivors, one a child, from a sunken passenger ship."

Seeing her face change, he added quickly, "Little Nancy is safe with her father. I thought it would please you to know she is speaking again and asks for you daily, or so I am told." His sly smile sent a tingle through her hips. She had indeed been about to ask after young Nancy. He knew her so well. So completely. If only she could reach for him...

"And, against my fervent command, she climbed into the rigging to help during a gale that would have claimed my vessel whole if she had not. Your daughter more than earned her keep aboard my ship. It is for these reasons that I, and my crew, cannot accept your payment. In truth, we feel we owe her far more." She wanted to cry. He spoke of her so highly but the words were not what made her so flustered. It was the tone in which he said them, the heavy, rasp his deep melodious voice carried with it as he discussed her.

"Well now. This is certainly a surprise. Is there no compensation I can offer for the transport of my daughter? After all, you have done me a great service, young man."

"Indeed there is, Lord Mansfield. Winston. I would ask for your daughter's freedom from this engagement." The room went deafeningly silent for a moment before Stephen's wrath split the air.

"That is *absurd*! How dare you walk in here and demand that *my* engagement be ended! You have no claim here, sir!" Stephen stepped in front of her to show his dominance but she was not about to be fought over like a toy in a nursery. Rushing from behind him, she moved to her father's side, away from the fuming form of Stephen the bear.

"On the contrary, I feel I do have a claim, Lord Mansfield, I am deeply, madly, and completely in love with your daughter. That is my claim." Vanessa gasped at the truth written in his indigo irises. His eyes had not once left hers for this entire exchange, save the moment when Stephen had stepped between them, and she read the emotion there with delighted urgency. Her heart was pounding beyond measure and her corset was now so tight she could not breathe. He loved her. He had said it, admitted it, proclaimed it!

"Ty..." It was all she could say and it was barely above a whisper. Her father glanced from him to her, studying the look they exchanged with interest.

"Would you ask instead I bind her to you, Captain?"

"Winston, you can't be serious?! You would have your daughter marry *him* over *me*? I am a Baron! And what is he? Nothing more than a merchant ship captain. A man one step from piracy! He is no one! You would be dooming your bloodline to obscurity and poverty!"

Stephen hunched from his shoulders and teetered on the verge of violence. This was clearly not how he had seen his afternoon tea panning out. His breathing had become audible, ragged, and labored. Vanessa would have laughed at the sight were it not terrifying to behold. Alfred had once called him a monster and he was playing the part beautifully.

"Lord Everly, you appear to be terribly misinformed. Allow me to ease your distress. I am not merely a 'merchant captain one step from piracy' as you so eloquently described. My name is Tiberius Marcus Clark, Marquis of Albany, son of his honorable Lord Marcus Reginald Clark, Duke of Albany, Earl of March. I hope my pedigree is to your liking. And as to your question, Winston, my answer is no. I do not wish you to bind your daughter to me. I wish for you to give her the freedom to choose her fate."

Everyone but Ty seemed to stagger. Stephen lurched to his side, turning to the settee behind him for support while her father seemed in awe of the man before him. Vanessa reeled from his revelation. She now knew him in his entirety. He was a nobleman, a Scottish lord, a ship captain, the man who loved her, and, more importantly, the man who respected her.

"I see no reason to argue. She made it clear she wished the same yesterday and seeing as she has found love on her own, I feel perhaps I have grossly underestimated her all these years." Her father stepped aside as if to allow them to draw closer.

"You can't be serious! What of my claim? Have I not proven my intentions?!" Stephen rushed forward, grasping Vanessa's wrist and wrenching her away from her father and her love. "She is mine! I have waited four years for this betrothal!"

"Stephen, release my daughter at once! I had intended to end this engagement even before Lord Clark came to call. I have listened to your intentions and have cringed at each expression. You do not want Vanessa. You want a mindless woman who will be content popping out your children and waiting on your every need. I know my daughter well enough to see how futile and torturous her life would become in your care. She is bright and ambitious and she deserves better than the life you are offering! I think perhaps it is best you leave, Stephen. I will explain to your mother why our family association is to end. Immediately."

Stephen's grip on her tightened. Tugging her closer to him, he moved as if he would fling her over his shoulder and make off with her. Her father and Ty both lurched to free her, aggression tightening their forms into battle-ready weapons, but there was no need. In a whirl of green satin, Vanessa rounded on the hulk beside her, landing a hard, echoing slap to his right cheek. His flesh instantly pinked and his eye began to swell. Releasing her at once to cradle the aching side of his face, he blinked at her in disbelief.

"You stuck me?! You ungrateful harlot!" In a flash, Ty was between them. One arm snaked backward around her waist pulling her close along his back while the other stretched out before him to press against Stephen's raging chest.

"It is time for you to leave, Stephen. I will not hesitate to show you out myself. And if you value your face, I suggest you refrain from insulting the woman I love." Vanessa pressed her body against his, sucking in his scent for the first time in so long. It made her lightheaded and giddy. Part of her had begun to fear this was all a dream concocted by her mind to ease her anxiety, but it was real. *He was real.*

Stephen was a large man, but he appeared dwarfed by the strength of Ty's frame. While the elder Everly brother was big by most standards, Ty was clearly stronger. Years of toiling on a ship had turned his body into a lean mass of muscle. Still, Stephen, ever the demanding child, reared again, attempting to remove Ty's massive frame from his path.

Vanessa heard the crashing blow from where she stood cradled in his arms. Ty's grip on her had remained tender and constant as he, in one solid and shattering blow, turned Stephen's left cheek into a quagmire of cracked bone and bruised flesh. He crumpled to the ground before them. Crimson flowed from his nose and a small cut along his oddly twisted cheekbone. For a moment he remained, head down on all fours and struggling to gather his fractured thoughts.

"Casbolt! Casbolt! Fetch Master Everly's driver! He is leaving this estate, post haste!" Her father's voice echoed in the hall behind her. He had witnessed the events and was as eager to see the wounded bear returned to his own as she. Within moments Casbolt and an imposing-looking footman entered the library.

"Winston...I only wanted..." Stephen's grabbled and pained words were cut short by her father's unforgiving tone.

"Save your breath, Stephen. I have no use or care for you or your words. You have disgraced my home and my family. You will leave now and never return. Are we clear? I think perhaps it would benefit you to leave London. I feel that your actions here will make society life in the city quite difficult for you from now on." Looking at the two men, he continued, "Well, out with him." Lord Mansfield directing every move with his cold aristocratic precision, hoisted the broken baron between them and made for the entry and the front door.

When Ty's protective arm slid from around her, she felt compelled to move. Even though she wanted nothing more than to stay squeezed against him, her father's presence behind her forced her to take a step away from his warmth. Ty turned to face her and then looked at her father.

"Vanessa?" Winston's voice, shaken and somber, was at her ear. She spun to find him reaching for her hands, sadness, and fear still etched in the lines on his face.

"Father." She smiled at him and he seemed to calm.

"Can you ever forgive me? I should have trusted you. Listened to you. I was just so afraid you would never know joy that I tried to force it upon you. All I have ever wanted is to see you fulfilled." Tears peeked in the corners of his eyes as they darted to Ty. She felt him take a few steps away; giving Winston the privacy he sought with his glance.

"Your mother was the most important person in my life until the day you were born. But I confess, I had no idea how to care for you, and when she passed I lost myself to doubt. I turned my efforts from loving you to protecting you and in so doing I have neglected you." He sighed roughly before continuing. "Your smile is hers, have I ever told you that?" She laughed as a tear rolled down her face. "I love you, Vanessa. Your freedom is yours."

She wrapped her arms tightly around his neck. For a split second, he seemed stunned, and then his arms encircled her, returning her hug. "Thank you, Father." A whisper into his coat collar was all she could manage through her tears, but it was enough.

"I think I had better see our unwelcome guest out, don't you? And I have a rather unpleasant message to send to his mother and my associates. No Everly shall see a shilling of Mansfield money again." He kissed her gently on her forehead before nodding to Ty and turning to leave. Vanessa watched him disappear through the open door before facing her companion. For a long while they simply stared at each other, as if neither could believe the moment had come when they were alone and free.

In an instant, Ty dropped to one knee and extended out a hand to her. "Vanessa Mansfield Everly, would you do me the hon..." She rushed into his arms, falling into his lap and silencing him with a kiss. He held her tight, returning her passion, the kiss becoming all there was in the world.

"I love you, Ty. I love you so much!" She had pulled away from his lips just long enough to make her declaration and having delivered her message took them again.

"Will...you...marry...me..." Between fervent kisses, he managed a word here and there and she redoubled her efforts with each syllable.

"Yes...yes...yes..." She too answered between takings and his grip on her increased. He stood, lifting her into the air and then lowering her feet to the ground, never letting her mouth slip from his.

Pulling her face from his just far enough to rest his forehead against hers, he took several deep breaths, eyes closed and fingers trembling against her cheeks. He was entirely out of breath and she loved every minute of it. "I love you, Sweets." She smiled as she arched her neck and kissed him lightly.

"I know." He laughed hotly as his hands tightened around her face. His fingers brushed over her satin skin as he inhaled her again. "Even though you seemed to enjoy making me doubt you. Why did you not talk to me that day? Why did you just leave? Why am I only now learning of your heritage?" She didn't really care but if she could not kiss him, could not taste his taffy tongue, she would hear his musical voice.

"If I couldn't steal you I knew I had to earn you. I had to ask your father for your hand. For that, I would need my titles restored before I could approach him. So, I left that morning for my father's house. I didn't say goodbye, Sweets, because I couldn't. I will never say goodbye to you. I can't. It would kill me." He kissed her with urgency as if the time spent away from her lips had been painful. After a moment they returned to breathing each other in.

"Restored?" She was puzzled and he understood perfectly.

"I told you I abandoned my family after Lucy's death. I left my titles behind when I signed into the Navy. My father was far more forgiving than I had feared. I am his eldest son and he welcomed me back with open arms. But my titles have come with a price." There was a sadness to his voice she hated. Only one thing could hurt him this way.

"The *Siren's Call*?" She leaned back to look into his eyes and saw the truth of it.

"She will never sail a trade run again, Sweets." Her heart broke for him.

"Oh, Ty, I cannot ask you to give up the sea for me. It is your passion!" He ground her hips against his and he pulled her closer still.

"You are my passion, Essie. Nothing is above you in my heart. And I said she shall never sail another trade run. I said nothing of giving up the sea." A wicked grin pulled his lips into a thin line as he backed her toward the settee.

"Ty, I don't understand..." She could feel his thighs pressing against her, feel the fire burning within him. When her back met the sofa, she groaned and arched into his hard heat.

"My father has holdings and interests all over the world, Sweets. He has charged me with seeing to all of his investments. The *Siren* will still sail the seas but as a diplomatic vessel. She is being converted to her new purpose as we speak. She will carry us all over the world. That is what I promised you, is it not? Of course, we will not set sail until after the

Caribbean artifacts are cared for. I know how important your work is to you."

She could barely believe her ears. Yesterday at this moment she had been prepared to end her life for fear of the misery it promised and now her future seemed too good to be true. The man she loved loved her in return. She was free of her chains and could marry whom she wished, and she was going to sail the world and see all the wonders she had only read about in books.

Unable to restrain her passions, she dove into his mouth, an action he greedily allowed. When her hands traveled below his waist, he caught up her wrists and laughed against her lips. "Easy, Sweets. Patience."

"Patience? I have waited two weeks to hold you again. Is that not patience enough for now? Besides, I am curious..." She leaned in for another kiss but he pulled his mouth just out of her reach.

"Curious about what?" He was teasing her and she was in the mood to be teased.

"As to whether you wear your kilt in true Scottish fashion." He pounced on her. His kiss was almost painful, reaching deep into her as if trying to lick her very core.

"Good Lord, Sweets. You are going to make this hard...aren't you?" He panted against her.

"Oh, I do hope so." She snickered as she again tried to reach for him.

"Stop, Sweets. Please." He sounded pained as he tugged her hands once more away from him.

"Why? I love you. You love me. We are to be married. Why should I stop wanting to feel you?" She redoubled her efforts and for a moment it seemed he would give in but his resistance returned. She groaned as he freed her fingers from his hips.

"You have no idea how badly I want...but we can't. Not until after the wedding." He clenched his jaw as she stopped fighting him. "I am not taking any chances this time. Not with you." He leaned his head against hers. She could feel him tense as if he expected her to rail at his decree.

"Then the sooner the better. My father has already made all manner of arrangements for a wedding in just under a month. I think perhaps I can wait that long." He lifted her off the ground to kiss her this time.

"That should work. The modifications for the *Siren* should be finished by then."

"I thought I would be able to finish the Caribbean collection before we set sail. Are you going to leave me here alone?"

"Never, Sweets. I have a home here in London where we shall live while you work, but I intend for our first night to be on the Siren. That is where I fell in love with you. That is where I will make you my wife." She wrapped her arms tighter around his neck and hugged him. *Perfect*. Her life was to be perfect.

"Ahem. I take this to mean there is indeed a wedding in your future?" Her father's voice sheepish and faint traveled across the stillness. Laughing she pulled back slightly to look into Ty's night sky eyes once more.

"Yes. And soon. It would be a shame for all of your hard work to go to waste." Ty's smile, full and bright was the last thing she saw before she closed her eyes and kissed him again. Winston's embarrassed cough did not concern her. She was finally, truly, freely happy.

www.ingramcontent.com/pod-product-compliance
Lightning Source LLC
Chambersburg PA
CBHW030016180626
46810CB00001B/71